Highland Angels

Fated Hearts Book 3

By
Ceci Giltenan

.

Duncurra LLC
www.duncurra.com

ISBN-10: 1-942623-23-2
ISBN-13: 978-1-942623-23-6

Cover Art by Earthly Charms

Produced in the USA

Praise for Ceci Giltenan

"Few authors touch hearts so deeply."
- *Sue-Ellen Welfonder, USA Today Bestselling Author*

"Fine historical romance writing at its best."
- *Suzan Tisdale, Bestselling Author of Scottish Romance*

"Ceci Giltenan continues to leave me spellbound weaving her trail of exceptional books that are absolutely magnificent the ones that stay with you long after you have read it."
- *Barbara, Tartan Book Reviews*

"Ceci Giltenan tells beautiful stories with strong characters and an intriguing storylines"
- *Lily Baldwin, Bestselling Author of Scottish Romance*

Other Books by Ceci Giltenan

The Fated Heart Series

(Available as digital, paperback and audio books)

Highland Revenge, Book 1

Highland Echoes, Book 2

The Duncurra Series

(Available as digital, paperback and audio books)

Highland Solution, Book 1

Highland Courage, Book 2

Highland Intrigue Book 3

The Pocket Watch Chronicles

The Pocket Watch

The Midwife
(Coming March 2016)

Dedication

To Eamon, the circle of your arms is my universe.
My heart beats with yours.
Our souls are entwined.

.

Pronunciation Guide

Curacridhe	CURrahCREE (the MacLeod stronghold)
Eoin	OHwen
Fiona	feeOHna
Isla	EYE luh
Loch Islich	EYE litch
Loch Uarach	you AHR ahk
Mairi	MAHree
Naomh-dùn	NAYV DOON (the MacKay stronghold)
Tasgall	TASS gull

Glossary

Bairn	(BAIRn) A baby
Canonical hours	The medieval day was ordered by these times, rather than clock times Vigil, Matins, Lauds, Prime, Terce, Sext, None, Vespers, Compline
compline	(COMP lin) Night prayer, after sunset, before bedtime
eejit	A slang term meaning idiot
lauds	(LAWDS) Sunrise
matins	Just before sunrise
none	(rhymes with bone) Literally the ninth hour, about 3 in the afternoon
prime	After the first hour of daylight, about 6 in the morning
quoits	An ancient game similar to horseshoes except a quoit is a closed ring.
sext	Literally the sixth hour, noon
sweetling	An endearment
terce	Literally the third hour of daylight, about nine in the morning
wheesht	Shh, hush
vespers	Evening prayer, sunset
vigil	The night office, the period from compline to matins (just before dawn)

"Angels whisper to our hearts. When we fail to hear them, they take pleasure in using the least likely people to magnify their voices."

~ Susan Cusack

Chapter One

Anna MacKay knelt with the child at the loch's edge, looking up at the MacLeod warriors who surrounded her. Numb with cold from the icy loch water soaking her woolen léine, she was painfully aware she had made a terrible mistake.

After fighting with her brother at the midday meal, she had been angry and just wanted solitude. Eoin never allowed her to ride alone, but as long as she was on foot and didn't go too far, her brother believed she was safe.

She had walked westward out of the village surrounding the MacKay stronghold, Naomh-dùn, then turned north once she reached the top of the bluff rising out of the east side of Loch Islich. She should not have gone that direction because it took her very close to the disputed MacLeod border. Her brother would be furious when he found out, but she had wanted him to be as angry as she was. It would serve him right. She also wanted to be alone, and no one would follow her onto the windy bluff on this bitter cold day. She hadn't intended to actually enter the disputed land by the strait where Loch Islich and Loch Uarach joined together, but that was before she saw the wee lad.

Lost in her thoughts, she had walked along the bluff until it began to slope more gently toward the northern tip of Loch Islich and the strait. Aware that she had come much farther than she intended, she started to turn toward home when the bright colors of his plaid caught her eye. He seemed to be alone, walking on the thick ice covering the strait. He wielded a wooden sword as he pretended to do battle with an invisible enemy. She was momentarily amused by his antics but became worried as he moved off of the thick ice covering the strait and farther onto the deep loch where the ice thinned dangerously. Anna had yelled at him to go back, but he hadn't seemed to hear. There was nothing else to do; she lifted her skirt and ran headlong towards him, down the slope to the loch's edge, straight into the disputed territory. Trying to get his attention, she waved her free hand and continued to shout.

She was too late. As he lunged forward, thrusting his sword into his invisible prey, the ice gave way. He plunged into the loch, screaming and flailing, just as she reached the shore. She ran out onto the solid ice as far as she dared. Knowing she would need something dry to wrap him in, she pulled off her mantle and plaid, hurling them backwards. She threw herself onto the ice on her stomach, distributing her weight over as wide an area as possible before she slid to the broken edge. Her body weight pushed the sheet of ice under the surface of the water. It soaked her, but it didn't completely give way. She was able to stretch far enough to grab the back of his tunic just as he slipped under the surface. Staying as flat as she could, she pushed backward, dragging him with her onto the ice, the edges breaking away as she moved.

Finally reaching ice thick enough to hold their weight, she scooped him up, grabbed her dry clothes and carried him to the nearest shore, the east bank of the loch, MacKay territory. She whispered a prayer of thanks. The child was unconscious and blue with cold, but still breathing. Vaguely aware of the sound of horses approaching, she quickly pulled off his wet clothes, wrapping him in her dry plaid and mantle. She rubbed his limbs gently through the cloth, trying to warm him. His eyes blinked open and his little body began to shiver violently.

She smiled at him. "Ye'll be all right now, little one." Looking up, she saw the source of the pounding hooves. Men on horseback thundered down the western side of the strait. In an instant a tall, broad-shouldered warrior with golden hair and angry crystal blue eyes was off his horse and had crossed the strait. Several of the others were not far behind him. The angry warrior pulled the child from her arms. These were clearly MacLeods, the clan with whom the MacKays had feuded for years. This was exactly why she wasn't supposed to walk northward. In a moment of terror-filled realization, it became abundantly clear—she was staring trouble squarely in the face.

~ * ~

While hunting, Andrew MacLeod, the eldest son of Laird MacLeod, heard the child's screams coming from the direction of the loch and immediately turned with his men toward the sound. The screaming stopped after a moment, and his panic rose tenfold. When they broke though the tree line near the strait at foot of Loch Uarach, a lass knelt on the other shore. She was stripping wet clothes off of a small child. Filled with dread, he rode hard towards them before jumping from his horse and crossing the frozen strait on foot. It couldn't be Davy; they were several miles from where the lad should be.

Reaching them, his heart nearly stopped before anger supplanted his fear. The pallid shivering child, now wrapped in what appeared to be the lass's plaid and mantle *was* his six-year-old son David, but the lass holding him was not Nessa, the maid charged with David's care. One look at her fiery red hair and the terror in her green eyes told him she was one of the lying MacKays. In his panic he could not fathom how this MacKay wench had abducted David or how they had fallen into the loch, but he was not going to take the time now to sort it out. He wrenched his child from her arms, taking her plaid and mantle with him. He crossed the strait, shouting orders to the other men. "Cormag, Finlay, ride with me. Graham, bring her and see to the rest!" He mounted his horse, holding his half-frozen son to his chest. Wrapping his own plaid around David too, he leaned low over the horse's neck, riding flat out for Curacridhe.

As he rode, he tried to figure out what could have

happened. David had begged for weeks to let him go hunting with the men. Andrew had finally given in. It wasn't a real hunt, strictly speaking. It was really more of an outing for David. Nessa, the young maid who minded David, rode with them while they hunted small game in the morning. After securing a brace of rabbits, they built a fire in a sheltered clearing. Nessa and several men-at-arms stayed with David by the fire while Andrew and the other men left to hunt for larger game. How could a MacKay, a woman no less, have taken his well-guarded son in broad daylight, and what was she doing with him on the MacKay side of the loch?

~ * ~

On her knees, wearing only a wet léine, Anna was frozen and confused. As the MacLeod warrior rode away, the man he called Graham looked down at her. She read pity in his eyes for a moment before they turned hard and angry. Clearly the MacLeod warrior who had taken the child from her was furious, but she didn't understand why. How could they be angry with her? After all, she had pulled the child from the loch. *But they are angry. Run.*

Graham roughly pulled her to her feet but, taking him by surprise, she twisted out of his grip, running towards the bluff. He easily caught her. "Nay lass, the only place ye're going is Curacridhe." He too had blond hair and blue eyes. Although he was shorter and had a slimmer build than the other warrior, he still had no trouble subduing her as she struggled against him. He lifted her and carried her effortlessly across the strait to his horse. "Things will go better for ye if ye cooperate and aren't responsible for injuring any more MacLeods today. So, how many men are with ye?"

"M-m-men?" *What was he talking about?* In her confusion she stopped struggling.

He frowned at her, giving her a shake. "Aye, men, lass. How many men attacked so ye could abduct the lad?"

She heard the question but her frozen brain refused to process his words. Why did he think someone abducted the child? Trembling with cold, she could only stare blankly at him.

Graham growled. "Fine, have it yer way. Ye're bringing on yer own suffering. Rory, ride with me. The rest of ye, go back to the clearing where we left David and Nessa. Be cautious. We have no way of knowing what happened there."

One thought crystalized in Anna's mind. *Dear God, I can't let them take me.* As he lifted her onto his horse, she started fighting again for all she was worth, hammering him with her frozen fists and trying to twist away.

He grabbed hold of her, pinning her arms to her sides and practically crushing the breath from her. "Stop it! Ye'll behave and ride without fighting me or, by God, I'll bind ye and throw ye over the horse face down."

Petrified by the threat and realizing the futility of her efforts, she ceased struggling. He put her on the horse's back, mounting behind her. She began shivering uncontrollably. Perhaps he took pity on her because he pulled her close against him and wrapped his plaid around her before kicking his horse into a canter.

"The back of yer dress is dry." He sounded confused. "Ye didn't fall in with the lad?"

She shook her head.

"He fell in while ye were crossing the ice with him? By God's teeth lass, how could ye be so careless? A dead hostage has no value."

"Hostage? I don't understand. I wasn't crossing the ice with him."

"I'll warrant that MacKays are not overly bright, but this stupid act ye are putting on will only bring ye misery."

"I don't understand what ye think happened."

"Ye don't?" His mocking tone only served to confuse her more. "Then why don't ye tell me what did happen."

"Clearly ye won't believe me."

"Tell me anyway."

Anna remained silent. She decided that the less she

said the better. She was so cold she could barely form words anyway, but her captor didn't accept her silence. He gave her another shake, "Answer me, lass!"

She had never been so cold or so afraid. "I—I was on the bluff and I saw h-h-him walking toward the thinner ice. I tr-tried to get him to turn back but he didn't hear me. He f-f-fell in before I reached him. I slid on my stomach until I could g-grab hold of him and pull him out. I removed his wet clothes and wr-wrapped him in my plaid and mantle to try and warm him. Th-th-that is when ye arrived."

"Do ye expect me to believe ye were on the bluff alone, this far from Naomh-dùn? And that Davy wandered away by himself? MacKays *are* stupid."

~ * ~

His son squirmed in Andrew's arms, snuggling against him. Then Davy's voice, penetrated the layers covering him. "I like riding with ye, Da, but I'm cold."

"I know, Davy, we'll be home soon."

"Why did we leave the fire? It was warm." His son clearly didn't remember what had happened.

That was a blessing at least, if he witnessed the ambush he wouldn't remember the horror.

"Hunting was fun but I wish ye hadn't left me with Nessa. I'm big enough to go with ye. I would have liked that."

At that moment Andrew too wished with all of his heart that he hadn't left the child, but he had believed his son was well-guarded. How could this have happened? "Rest now, lad, we'll be home soon."

David was quiet again for a while but then he grumbled, "I don't like staying with Nessa. She's no fun. She just likes talking to the men and won't play with me. I like dragon hunting," he added sleepily. "That's how I got cold. I went dragon hunting on the loch. The dragon must have broken the ice."

The lad looked as if he were trying to figure out what happened but clearly had no memory of it. Seeing his son's furrowed brow, he said, "That must have been it."

Davy closed his eyes for a few moments. Andrew thought he slept until he spoke again. "Where is the angel, Da?"

"Wheesht, Davy, everything is going to be all right."

"But where is the angel?"

"There is no angel, lad. Rest now, we're almost home."

"But where is the angel, the angel that pulled me out? She was pretty, only I didn't see her wings. I wish I had seen her wings. Did ye see her wings?"

"There was no angel. Wheesht."

David became more agitated. "Nay, Da, why would ye say that? There *was* an angel. Don't ye remember? I got lost hunting a dragon on the ice and it broke. The angel pulled me out."

Andrew wanted to soothe his son's agitation. "Don't worry lad, the angel is fine."

David calmed. "Did ye see her wings, Da?"

"Nay, I didn't see her wings. Rest now, lad."

"I wish I had seen her wings. I wonder if they would be red like her hair." With that Davy snuggled close to his father again and closed his eyes.

When they arrived at Curacridhe, Andrew immediately sent for Isla, the MacLeod healer, then handed his son to Cormag just long enough to dismount. He rushed into the warmth of the great hall with his small bundle in his arms. He had barely reached his own chamber when Isla arrived and quickly checked David over.

"Andrew, God must have great plans for Davy. When I heard he'd fallen through the ice so far away on Loch Islich, I feared the worst."

"It isn't that far, Isla, riding fast it took much less than an hour."

"That may be, but wet and freezing that would have been too long for a wee lad in this bitter weather. I expected to find his hands and feet cold and waxy." She rewrapped him in a warm blanket and moved close to the fire with him on her lap, gently warming him.

"Will he be all right?"

"Aye, Andrew, I think he will be. I need to warm him up to know for sure. It will help to get some hot liquids in him now, but drying him right away was his salvation. He might still take a fever but at least his limbs aren't frozen. Frankly, I am surprised Nessa knew to strip the wet clothes off. That's probably what saved his life."

There was a knock at the door before Andrew could correct Isla. He opened it to a serving maid who said, "Graham and Rory have just arrived with a woman. Graham asked me to fetch ye."

To Isla he said, "I have to see to this. I'll be right back up." He stroked Davy's head once before leaving the room.

When Andrew reached the great hall, their father was listening to Graham explain what had happened. Laird Dougal MacLeod glared at the bedraggled young woman who, still in wet clothes, stood before him shivering uncontrollably. *Well woman was a bit of a stretch*, he thought as he looked down at her. She appeared to be little more than a child herself.

Dougal's ice blue eyes shot daggers as he roared at her. "By God, wench, I'll beat ye to death with my own hands if that lad dies."

~ * ~

Tall and powerfully built, Laird MacLeod resembled an angry Norse god with long grey hair and a flowing beard that still held hints of gold. He terrified Anna and she couldn't understand why they didn't believe her. *Nay, that's not true.* The MacLeods hated the MacKays and the MacKays hated them back. They would naturally believe the worst about each other. At this moment she was fairly sure no MacLeod would have pulled a MacKay from an icy loch so they must assume the reverse was true as well. Even worse, they assumed she had abducted the child, allowing him to fall through the ice, and only saving him because of the ransom he would fetch. Piecing it together, she learned that the lad she saved was the laird's grandson, David.

The only blessing she could discern was they didn't know her identity yet. Perhaps there was a chance she could escape without her brother finding out what she had done. He was the only person on earth who could possibly be angrier with her over this than Laird MacLeod appeared to be.

The old laird looked up when the warrior who had taken the child from her entered the hall. His voice thick with concern he asked, "Andrew, son, how is the lad?"

So that formidable warrior was Andrew MacLeod.

"Isla thinks he'll be all right."

"MacKay won't get away with this, son." He turned to Anna again. "Wench, what's yer name?"

"Eve," Anna lied.

"Who's yer father?"

"My father's dead."

"Well praise God. The only good MacKay is a dead one."

Anna trembled and fought back tears at the thought of her dear father.

"So, Eve, are ye the village whore?"

Tears did slip down her cheeks at that. "Nay, Laird. I am a seamstress," she whispered. It wasn't a complete lie. She was skilled at needlework.

"How many MacKay scum were with ye, Eve, *the seamstress*?"

"No one was with me," she answered barely above a whisper.

"Why protect them? Yer clansmen have abandoned ye, but curs will do that, won't they? If ye're their whore, ye must not be a very good one."

"No one was with me, Laird. I didn't take the child."

"Lying bitch," Dougal spat and backhanded her with enough force to knock her to the floor. "Rory, toss her in a cell until we find out what happened. Then I'll decide whether she dies quickly or just prays to die."

Before she could wipe the blood from her lips, Rory jerked her up roughly. Glancing around in a panic, her eyes locked with Andrew MacLeod's for a moment and the venom she saw there sent another wave of fear and despair coursing through her. She could no longer hold the tears back. *Dear God, please let me freeze to death soon so I never have to see these men again.*

The devil must have heard her thoughts because he said, "Give her something dry to wear."

"What?" asked Dougal. "Why?"

"Isla said the only reason Davy will survive this is because this filthy MacKay stripped off his wet clothes and wrapped him in her dry plaid and mantle."

"Ye can't ransom a dead child, Andrew. It was in her own best interest to keep him alive."

"Still, she did it. Give her something dry."

His father gave a curt nod and with that Andrew left the hall.

Rory dragged Anna through another door. Taking a torch from the wall, he forced her down a flight of steep stone steps. At the bottom they entered a long dark hallway. She stumbled alongside him to the end of it until they reached another set of stairs, these even more steep and narrow than the first. When they reached the bottom, he pushed her through another door into a dark, cramped hall off of which were several small, dank cells with doors made of rusting iron bars. He shoved her roughly into one, slamming the door and locking her in. She had barely taken in the damp stone floor and the cell's only furnishing, a wooden bed without a mattress standing against the back wall, before he left. Taking the torch with him, he left her in utter darkness.

Frightened and colder than she had ever been in her life, she made her way to the bed and sat on it, drawing her knees to her chest, trying to conserve what little body heat she had. Dear God, what had she done? She should have just turned and gone home instead of venturing onto the ice. Nay, she never could have left the child to die, regardless of whether he was a MacLeod or not. *I should never have walked the bluff in the first place.* Nay, the child would have died then too. She could only believe that God had led her to where she needed to be, or at least to where the child needed her to be, but at what price?

Rory returned shortly with a coarse woolen léine and a thin blanket. He tossed them into the cell before leaving again. With cold, numb fingers, Anna struggled to untie the laces of her garment, peeling off the damp heavy wool. The dress he brought her was much too large but it was warm and dry. She slipped it on, wrapping the thin plaid around her shoulders and over her head before curling up on the wooden bed. Still freezing, but overcome with exhaustion and despair, she fell asleep.

~ * ~

Andrew tried to shake the disturbing image of the trembling MacKay lass with terror-filled eyes out of his mind as he returned to his son's side.

Isla still held David on her lap near the fire, but he was awake and drinking the soup that she patiently spooned into him.

"Da, I told Isla about the angel who saved me."

"And I have been telling David that it wasn't an angel, it was Nessa."

"Well it wasn't Nessa," said Andrew. "We don't know what happened to her." He shook his head slightly at her questioning look.

David frowned. "I told ye Nessa didn't save me, Isla. But, Da, nothing happened to her."

"Son, drink yer soup. Ye need it to warm ye up."

David acquiesced and finished the bowl. He curled up in Isla's lap again and began to doze off. When she thought he was asleep she asked, "What happened?"

"It isn't clear. We think the MacKays attacked and abducted David, but we won't know for sure until we find the men I left to guard him—or their bodies."

Isla made the sign of the cross. "God protect them. But if Nessa didn't dry Davy, whose plaid and mantle was he wrapped in?"

"They belong to a MacKay lass who we found him with. We think she didn't act alone. There had to have been others. She might have lured him away while they attacked. Davy doesn't seem to remember the attack, and for that I'm thankful. Apparently, while fleeing with him, she let him fall through the ice. Da is keeping her in the dungeon until we find out for certain exactly how she was involved."

"Is she the one that stripped his wet clothes from him?"

"Aye."

"Well, at least she did that much. But poor Nessa, I hope she's all right. She doesn't deserve to be ravaged by a horde of MacKays."

"Nessa's all right. She was talking by the fire when I left," said David.

"Oh, lad, I thought ye were asleep. I didn't mean to wake ye," said Isla.

Andrew was puzzled by his son's statement. "What do ye mean 'Nessa was talking by the fire'? Was that when the MacKays took ye?"

"No one took me, Da. I already told ye, I went dragon hunting. Nessa didn't want to play so I went by myself."

"Ye went into the woods alone? The lass wasn't with ye?"

"Nessa was busy talking. I didn't mean to go far but I got lost."

"I meant the MacKay lass. Didn't she lead ye away?"

"Nay. I was alone until I fell through the ice and the angel with red hair came and saved me."

"David, there was no angel, just the MacKay lass who stole ye."

"No one stole me, and I saw the angel." He frowned. "She ran down off the bluff waving at me before I fell through the ice. Then she slid on her tummy and pulled me out of the water. I wonder why she didn't fly. That would have been something to see. Anyway, I'm not sure exactly what happened next, but all of a sudden ye were there and ye took me from her before I could see her wings."

David seemed so sure of his story. His confidence disturbed Andrew.

"Maybe he dreamt it?" Isla suggested.

"He must have."

"I didn't dream it, Da! Why won't ye believe me? Ye saw her too."

"All right, son, let's not talk about the angel anymore. Come here. I'll tuck ye under the covers and stay with ye till ye fall asleep. Ye need to rest now."

He helped his son into the bed and sat with him until the lad was sleeping deeply. It chilled his heart to realize how close he had come today to losing his child, the last precious link to his wife. He wanted those responsible to pay. When David was sleeping soundly, Andrew rose to leave. "I'll come back later. Send for me if ye need me, Isla."

The things David had said confused Andrew. He believed the MacKays had to be behind this, but the lad's story never varied. When Andrew reached the great hall he joined his father and brother at the refectory table, sitting down wearily. "Is there any news?"

"Not yet. Only Rory returned with me," said Graham. "I sent the rest of the men to try to find out what happened. As soon as I arrived back here I sent another contingent out as well. I couldn't get the lass to give me a clue about how many of them there were."

"Did she tell ye anything?" Andrew asked.

"She wanted me to believe she saw Davy from the bluff. According to her, he was alone on the ice. She tried to get him to turn back but he fell in before she reached him."

"She said she came from the bluff?" Andrew asked in disbelief.

"Aye."

"Lies," said their father.

"I would have thought so, but Davy said the same thing. What else did she say?"

"Something about sliding on her stomach to pull him out and taking his wet clothes off."

Andrew swore, scrubbing his face with his hands. "It can't be."

"I believe he fell in and she was panicked enough about losing her hostage to get him out and try to warm him up. But I don't believe she wasn't involved with kidnapping him. She's just lying to protect herself," said Graham.

"Graham, Davy has talked about the 'angel' who saved him every waking moment since we found them."

"It was just his imagination, son," said their father reasonably. "There are no MacKay saints. How does he explain them stealing him in the first place?"

"That's just it, Da, he says no one stole him, he wandered away. He tells the same story she told ye. The 'angel' as he calls her, ran down off the bluff and pulled him from the water."

"Why would an innocent MacKay lass, and I use the term 'innocent' loosely, be on the bluff alone, that far from Naomh-dùn on a bitter cold day like today?" Dougal asked. "If she was there, she was probably up to no good. Nay, son, the MacKays are behind this."

At that moment, the men who had stayed with Nessa and David, along with the additional men Graham sent to find them, entered the great hall with a tearful Nessa in tow.

Nessa rushed forward saying, "Laird, please forgive me. I was playing with little Davy and lost him. We looked everywhere. I never imagined he could walk all the way down to the loch. Please, Laird, I am so sorry."

"What?" roared Dougal.

"Donald, explain," demanded Andrew.

Donald, the captain of the MacLeod guard could barely keep the irritation out of his voice. "I rode back from the loch expecting to find those left behind slaughtered. When we reached the clearing, we found everyone searching for Davy. There had not been an attack. It appears that Nessa simply hadn't watched him properly and he wandered off. Everyone thought he was with someone else. I don't know what that damned MacKay lass was doing at that end of the loch but it's probably a good thing she was there. Everything seems to suggest she was alone. We found no signs of anyone else."

Dougal put his head in his hands and Andrew trembled with suppressed fury. He strode toward the stairs leading to the dungeon as he ordered, "Make a room ready."

Donald asked, "Andrew, is David all right? Where are ye going?"

"Davy's fine," Graham answered. "It appears the '*damned MacKay lass*' saved his life, and I suspect Andrew is going to release her from the dungeon."

When Andrew reached the cell, he found the lass huddled in a ball, wrapped in the thin plaid she had been given. "Come, angel, let me get ye out of here." He lifted her from the wooden bed. She was blue with cold and her breathing was shallow. He prayed fervently that it wasn't too late.

He carried her to the empty chamber the servants were preparing and tucked her into the bed. Isla arrived shortly, clucked her tongue and started working to warm her. Andrew couldn't bring himself to leave until he knew the lass would be all right. But, in spite of all Isla did, later that evening the little MacKay began to tremble violently as she succumbed to a fever.

Andrew still stayed with her, unable to do anything but unwilling to leave. Her fever raged through the night and into the next day as he sat helplessly by.

~ * ~

Anna became vaguely aware that she was in a soft bed. Clearly she was no longer in the dungeon. Everything hurt and, no longer cold, she was so hot she knew she must surely be surrounded by fire. *I must have died and gone to hell*, she thought. She forced her eyes open, sending a piercing pain through her head. She closed them again, smiling grimly. If she was in hell she thought, at least one of those MacLeod devils was here too. With that she slipped back into oblivion.

Chapter 2

"Where in the hell can she be?" demanded Eoin MacKay.

Marcas, the captain of his guard stood before him. "I don't know, Laird, we've been searching for her since we discovered her missing this morning."

Eoin blamed himself that it had taken so long for anyone to realize she was gone. He had argued with her the previous afternoon and thought she was in her room pouting. At the time, he had been angry enough with her to ignore her pique, so he left her there to stew.

"Eoin, ye shouldn't have threatened her," said one of his younger brothers.

"Dammit, Aidan, do ye not think I feel guilty enough? She needed a taste of reality."

His other brother's brow furrowed. "Perhaps threatening to marry her to Laird Morrison's heir was a larger bite of reality than our little sister could stomach. Ye know she wants to stay here—or at least close. Sending her to the islands would break her heart."

"Are ye going to turn on me too, Tasgall? God's teeth, she surely didn't believe I'd agree to that betrothal."

"I believed ye," said his wife quietly.

"Fiona, love, I want her married, but I wouldn't marry her to a Morrison or send her that far away. I just wanted her to start taking this seriously. She's almost twenty." He turned back to Marcas. "Did ye find anyone else who saw her leave yesterday?"

"Like I told ye, several villagers said she walked up the bluff, but no one saw her after that. We have searched to the south end of the loch and found no sign of her."

"Did ye search to the north end?" asked Fiona

hesitantly.

"No. She knows better than to go that direction. Surely she wouldn't venture so close to MacLeod territory," said Marcas.

"Oh, God's breath I hope not," swore Eoin.

"It would explain why no one saw her after she climbed the bluff. No one would expect her to go that direction. She just might have done it to goad ye," reasoned Aidan.

Eoin shook his head. "Nay, she can be rash, but she wouldn't be that foolhardy." In truth, he wasn't all that confident. At the looks of doubt on the other faces Eoin swore loudly. "Let's go, Marcas!"

"Laird, it's getting late. I don't think it's wise for ye, or any member of the family," he looked pointedly at Tasgall and Aidan, "to venture that close to MacLeod land after dark. It could be a trap to capture ye for ransom."

"Marcas, if they've set a trap, they have my sister to ransom."

Marcas' brow furrowed. "Laird, ye don't know that. They haven't sent a ransom demand."

Marcas was right. If Anna was dead, they couldn't ransom her.

At the look of stunned disbelief on Fiona's face Eoin said, "My love, Marcas is not suggesting anything is amiss, we simply don't know."

Marcas nodded. "Aye, my lady, and therefore, I think it wiser not to take a risk until we investigate."

Eoin waved him away. "I can't argue with that. Take at least a score of men with ye and if ye run into trouble, show no mercy."

~ * ~

When they returned, the news was bleak. "Laird, it looks as if she might have fallen through the ice."

Fiona buried her head against her husband's chest and started weeping. Stunned, Eoin asked, "Are ye certain?"

"We can't be certain of anything. We followed the

bluff to the head of the loch and something clearly has broken through the ice there recently. But there were also signs that horses had been on the opposite shore. There is no way of knowing what happened or even when it happened."

"Maybe the MacLeods do have her," Fiona said hopefully. "I hate to think of her as a captive. I know how frightening that can be." She gave Eoin a pointed look. "Still it is a good sight better than drowning in a frozen loch. Besides, I've met the MacLeods; they aren't as bad as ye think. If they have her, I can't believe they would hurt her."

Eoin, Aidan and Tasgall looked shocked by her faith. Eoin said, "Ye were a MacNicol. There is no enmity between the MacNicols and the MacLeods, although I don't understand why, because they'll rob ye blind if ye let them. But the MacKays and the MacLeods have a long-standing feud. They will not treat her well."

"The MacKays and the MacNicols were in the midst of a long-standing feud when ye kidnapped me, but ye didn't harm me."

"That was different."

"How?"

"I'm not a MacLeod."

Fiona rolled her eyes at him.

"Besides we don't even know if they have her. We can only wait and see if they make a demand." He never imagined he would pray to receive a ransom request from Dougal MacLeod.

~ * ~

Late in the afternoon on the third day after she was captured, the lass's fever still raged. Andrew stood by the hearth watching as Isla bathed her face and arms with cool water. He remembered a similar night several years ago when he sat by his wife's bed watching helplessly as death claimed her. He believed he was to blame then as well. Joan had just delivered their second son, but the bairn came too early and never drew a breath. Joan had lost so much blood during the ordeal it was as if she simply faded away.

Dougal stepped quietly into the room, nodded a greeting to his son and asked Isla, "Will she live?"

"I don't know, Laird. She grows weaker. I can't seem to get her fever to break."

"Sweet mother of God," he swore and sank into one of the chairs in the room. "She saved my grandson's life and I called her a whore, struck her and threw her in my dungeon."

"Da, this isn't yer fault. I saw her on the shore stripping Davy out of his wet clothes, wrapping him in her dry ones and still believed she was trying to hurt him. None of us could believe that a MacKay would do that for a MacLeod."

Isla frowned, "With all due respect, Laird, Andrew, stop it. I don't need ye licking yer wounds while I am trying to keep the waif alive. This didn't happen only because of the errors in judgment each of ye made. It happened because of the decades of hate both clans bred. Now this lass, who risked her own life to save our Davy, is paying the price for that hate."

Andrew glanced at his father and saw the shame he felt mirrored on Dougal's face. With a disgusted huff, Isla turned back to tend her charge.

After a moment, Dougal asked, "How is Davy today?"

Andrew shrugged. "He's fine. He didn't get so much as a sniffle and apparently talks incessantly about his angel. I dismissed Nessa and sent her back to her parent's croft. I can't lay eyes on her without my blood boiling. Cora will care for him for the time being." Andrew sat brooding for a few minutes. Finally he asked, "Have ye sent a message to Laird MacKay?"

"To tell him what? 'I have a MacKay seamstress named Eve. I'll send ye a ransom demand if she lives?' He isn't likely to pay a ransom for a fatherless seamstress anyway. Nothing good can come from telling him now."

They continued to sit in vigil as Isla worked, but by

evening when the lass's fever still burned, Isla asked them to fetch Father Ninian.

"Isla, is there nothing ye can do?" Laird MacLeod asked.

"Laird, she's only a wee thing to begin with. I'm doing everything I can, but she was half frozen and now she's very weak. Would ye deny her Extreme Unction?"

"Nay, of course not. I prayed it wouldn't be necessary."

Andrew rose to leave. "I'll go, Da."

"Nay, son, stay here. I'll fetch him."

Isla continued to gently bathe the lass's face and arms, still trying to bring her fever down.

~ * ~

Anna became vaguely aware of the people who stood around her praying. Someone intoned "*Adjútorium nostrum in nómine Dómini,*" Our help is in the Name of the Lord.

Then the others in the room murmured the response, "*Qui fecit caelum et terram,*" Who made Heaven and Earth.

I must not be in hell yet. The prayers continued. She wanted to join them but she was very tired. She heard the Latin words asking for the protection of angels, "Hear us, holy Lord, almighty Father, eternal God: and be pleased to send Thy holy angel from Heaven to guard, cherish, protect, visit and defend all that dwell in this house. Through Christ our Lord."

Yes, God, I think I need an angel. She whispered, "Amen," before slipping away again.

The murmuring continued, drawing her back. The prayers were familiar but in her groggy state, it took her a few moments to realize what they were. *Oh how sad, someone's dying. I should pray too.* It was just so terribly hard for her to concentrate.

Then from somewhere very close to her, a gentle voice said, "Eve, daughter, are ye awake?"

Is he talking to me? She blinked several times and tried to focus.

An elderly priest smiled kindly at her and said in Latin, "Receive, sister, the Viaticum of the Body of our Lord Jesus Christ; and may He keep you from the malignant foe, and bring you to life everlasting. Amen." He placed a tiny piece of the Blessed Sacrament in her mouth.

She whispered "Amen," and struggled to swallow it. Her foggy brain cleared enough for her to understand what was happening. The prayers of the Last Rites were being said for her. *But why did he call me Eve?* It occurred to her that she should probably pay attention, but the people sounded so far away. She could no longer hear them properly, so she would rest instead.

She was on the bluff again. Thank God, she could go home. If she got home soon Eoin wouldn't know she had left. She walked and walked and yet she didn't seem to get closer. The sun was hot and she was growing tired but she kept walking. She saw Fiona on the bluff ahead of her and waved. Fiona called to her "Go back, pet, he needs ye."

"Nay, he doesn't Fiona. The lad's fine now. I'm hot and I'm tired. I want to go home."

Fiona drew closer; at least she thought it was Fiona. "Not yet. Go back, he needs ye."

Anna was getting angry now. "Nay, he doesn't, Fiona. I don't want to go back. I'm sorry I made Eoin mad, but I want to come home."

The woman drew closer. It wasn't Fiona after all. She was just as beautiful but taller and her hair was a lighter brown. "I'm sorry," Anna told the stranger. "I thought ye were someone else. I need to go home now."

"Walk with me for a bit first." The woman took her by the elbow, walking away from Naomh-dùn.

"But my home is the other way. I don't belong here."

"Of course ye do. Don't leave just yet. He needs ye."

"He doesn't. I already saved him." As if in direct response to what she had just said, she heard the lad screaming.

Nay, it couldn't be. She had already pulled him from

the loch and she needed to go home. She heard his terrified cries again. She couldn't let him drown. Just like the first time, she picked up her skirt and ran towards him. She ran as fast as she could, but she was so hot and tired. How could he have fallen through the ice again? It was much too hot for there to be ice on the loch. The water would feel good now, if only she could find it.

~ * ~

The next time Anna woke she was still terribly hot only now she was drenched in sweat. She pushed at the covers; why were they so heavy? She thought she would suffocate if she didn't get out from under them. The old woman was at her side immediately. Her hands felt blessedly cool on Anna's face. "Saints be praised, her fever is breaking."

Soon there were other women there too. They bathed the perspiration from her and changed the linens. The old woman put a cup to her lips, "Drink some for me, pet." Anna tried—the cool water tasted good—but it hurt to swallow and she was so tired.

~ * ~

Anna opened her eyes to late morning sun filling the room. She didn't suffer the stabbing headache she had before and she no longer felt the flames of hell licking at her. However, everything still hurt. She felt too weak to lift her hand from the bed. The strong but gentle older woman she had seen before touched her face and smiled. "I think ye've fought off the fever, lass. My name is Isla, I've been taking care of ye. For a while I was worried we'd lose ye. We even called Father Ninian, but thanks be to God, the fever seems to be gone. Now we need to make ye stronger. If I hold ye up, can ye take a few sips of broth for me?"

Anna closed her eyes and turned her head away. She was in hell after all. She was still at Curacridhe in the hands of the MacLeods who planned to kill her, or worse, for something she didn't do.

"Nay lass, don't slip away from me."

The woman slid her arm under Anna's shoulders, lifting her into a semi sitting position before putting a cup to her lips.

"Here, ye must drink this."

"Please leave me be," Anna whispered.

"I can't do that, Eve. Be a good lass now and drink this."

Who is Eve? Then she remembered the lie she'd told to the MacLeod. She had never been in such a desperate situation. Even if the MacLeod didn't kill her, she would only have to face her brother and at the moment she wasn't sure which would be worse. Again she turned her head away.

The woman holding her gave her a little shake and said in a firmer voice, "Nay, lass. Ye must drink this. Don't make me force it down ye." She put the cup to Anna's lips again and tipped it into her mouth. Having no other option, Anna swallowed.

"That's not so hard now, is it?" The woman's voice was gentle again. "Have a bit more."

Anna didn't have the energy to fight so she swallowed the warm liquid a little at a time. When the woman was satisfied that she had had enough, she lowered Anna back onto the pillows. The tears welled in her eyes and she couldn't keep them from spilling down her cheeks.

"Oh, little lamb," the old woman crooned as she brushed the tears away. "Don't cry. Ye'll be all right."

Anna clenched her eyes shut and turned her head away from the woman's touch. She wanted to tell Isla that she knew very well she wouldn't be "all right" but she just didn't have the strength.

~ * ~

The lass's fever had raged for over three days before breaking but even then, things didn't get much better. Two days later, after the evening meal, Andrew and Dougal spoke with an anxious Isla outside of Eve's room. "After the fever broke, I was optimistic that she would recover, but she fights me at every turn. I try to get her to take some broth every time she wakes but I have to force her to drink it. And then when I've managed to get some into her, the lamb turns her head and cries. It tears at my heart to see her so frail and frightened, but nothing I say seems to console her."

"I suppose that's understandable after the way we treated her," admitted Laird MacLeod. "Is there anything else ye can do?"

"I just need to keep trying. She's not getting any worse and in truth she may be marginally stronger."

"Isla, ye can't keep this up around the clock. Ye look ready to drop under the strain yerself," observed Dougal.

"I won't leave her, Laird. She saved Davy and she isn't nearly out of the woods."

"But ye need to rest, Isla," said Andrew. "We can have a pallet put in there for ye and have others sit with her while ye sleep."

"Nay. I don't want just anyone with her. It takes a firm hand to get her to drink every time she wakes. Otherwise she just closes her eyes and turns her head."

"Then I'll sit with her tonight," offered Andrew.

Exhausted, Isla conceded and Andrew watched over his son's "angel" while Isla lay sleeping on her pallet.

As he watched the lass sleeping he thought again of his wife. Joan was a Sinclair and their fathers arranged their marriage to put an end to a feud the Sinclairs had started years ago. Nevertheless, it was a good marriage and Andrew grew to love her. She was tall and slender with dark chestnut hair, rosy cheeks and blue eyes that sparkled when she laughed. David was her miniature in every way, so much so that it hurt to look at him.

Davy's angel, lying motionless in the bed, did not remotely resemble his Joan. She was a wisp of a lass and her red hair glinted like copper in the firelight. A smattering of freckles stood out in relief on her unnaturally pale skin, and the only thing he had ever seen reflected in her green eyes was abject terror.

Almost as if she heard his thoughts, her eyes fluttered

open and he saw her fear yet again.

"I'm still in hell," she whispered and turned her head away, closing her eyes.

"Nay, ye're in Curacridhe."

"Same thing."

"Not even close." He chuckled. "Now, lass, Isla wants ye to drink this broth and she's asleep at the moment, so I'll help ye."

Andrew started to slide his arm under her shoulders but she feebly tried to pull away from him. "Don't touch me!"

He arched a brow at her. "Bossy bit of goods, aren't ye to be such a wee thing? I can help ye up or ye can sit up on yer own, but either way, ye'll drink this broth."

"Why are ye doing this?" She blinked as if she was holding back tears.

"I want ye to get better."

"So yer father can kill me? Has he decided whether it will be fast or slow yet?" Even though her question was bold, several tears slipped down her cheeks.

Andrew shook his head. He had forgotten that threat and now it made his heart ache. He brushed away her tears. "No one's going to kill ye, Eve."

"But the only good MacKay is a dead Mackay." She bitterly echoed more of his father's harsh words.

"We made a terrible mistake, lass, and I am sorry. I know no one abducted my son and that ye risked yer own life to save his. Please, let me help ye now."

"Even if the MacLeod won't kill me, the MacKay might," she muttered. "Just leave me be."

Andrew frowned, "Nay, lass, I won't let the MacKay kill ye either. Now, ye need to drink this." He lifted her to a sitting position before putting the cup to her lips. She had no choice but to swallow the broth that he tipped into her mouth.

~ * ~

Anna was tired of having no control over even the smallest detail of her life and she was particularly tired of bending to the will of these MacLeods. She realized the only way out of this was to get her strength back so that she could return to Naomh-dùn and face her angry brother. She stopped fighting Isla and did what the old healer told her to do, which was mostly eat and sleep.

Anna had never slept so much in her life. She completely lost track of the days, but as she began to feel stronger, her thoughts turned to what she needed to do to get away. As long as they thought she was just an unimportant MacKay clanswoman, maybe they would simply let her leave. She didn't even know how long she had been gone.

While Isla helped bathe her one day Anna asked, "How long have I been here? What day is it?"

"Ye have been here over a sennight lass. 'Tis the third Friday of Lent, the last day of February."

"I didn't realize it'd been so long." What must her family think happened to her?

"Ye had a fever for well over three days and then ye slept the biggest part of four more."

"I want to go home now."

"Aye lass, I'm sure ye do, but ye've been gravely ill. Ye need to rest here a few more days."

"I can rest at home."

Isla leveled a stare at her. "Eve, ye aren't leaving this room, much less this keep, until I am sure ye're well enough." At Anna's crushed expression Isla added, "Everything will be all right, lamb. Ye'll be right as nails soon."

Now that Anna was on her way to recovery, Isla left her for short periods, but more often than not, some other MacLeod stayed with her. The laird and both of his sons visited frequently. Anna knew she was a coward, but she feigned sleep anytime they appeared. She hated the MacLeods and, if she was truly honest with herself, she feared them.

However, one visitor that Anna enjoyed was Mairi, the laird's youngest child. A blond-haired, blue-eyed, charming lass of four and ten, Mairi was cheerful and entertaining. On her very first visit, she rushed into the room, kissed Anna on both cheeks and declared her lifelong gratitude for saving Davy. Anna had trouble hating this MacLeod.

As it turned out there was another MacLeod she also had trouble hating. Late in the afternoon, the same day on which she had met Mairi, the rosy-cheeked, dark-haired little lad she'd pulled from the loch, tiptoed into her room.

Awestruck, his eyes were as big as saucers. "Ye're the angel. Ye saved me."

"Ye must be David," Anna said gently.

"Aye. Can I see yer wings?"

"Ye can come here and sit with me, lad, but I'm sorry, I don't have wings."

He climbed up on the bed beside her. "But ye're my angel."

"I'm not an angel, sweetling."

"But ye must be, ye came from nowhere and saved me."

"Well not exactly, I saw ye from the bluff." He looked disappointed so she added, "I think sometimes God makes sure people are where they need to be to help, when angels can't be there."

"So God put ye there instead of an angel?"

"Something like that."

"And ye saved me?"

"I pulled ye out of the loch, aye."

He leaned forward and put his arms around her, laying his head on her chest. She returned the embrace and stroked his hair. David whispered, "I was scared and so cold."

"I was too."

"I wasn't scared anymore when I saw ye."

"I'm glad. I don't like feeling scared either."

"I'm sorry ye got sick."

"I'll be all right, sweetling."

"Can I stay here with ye for a while?"

"If ye wish."

David snuggled against her and closed his eyes. His breathing grew deep and regular as he fell asleep in her arms. While holding him she realized that regardless of the price she now paid for her actions, this little life was worth it. She smiled wryly to herself, thinking her family would probably be appalled if they knew she was cuddling Laird MacLeod's grandson while the lad napped.

~ * ~

Several hours later, when everyone was in a panic because they couldn't locate David yet again, Andrew found his son held securely in his angel's arms, both of them sound asleep.

Eve woke as Andrew lifted the sleeping child away from her.

"I hope he didn't bother ye," he said softly.

"Nay, he's sweet."

David rubbed his eyes, rousing from his nap. "She isn't exactly an angel, Da."

Andrew grinned. "Nay?"

"Nay. She doesn't have wings, but maybe God put her there instead of an angel."

"I'm sure that's true, Davy."

"Still, that's kind of like an angel."

"Aye, that's a lot like an angel." He held her gaze for a moment before she looked away. "We should let yer angel rest now, son."

Chapter 3

It was impossible to avoid Laird MacLeod forever. By Anna's tenth day at the MacLeod stronghold, Isla began to get her out of bed for longer periods. That afternoon, while Anna sat in a chair by the hearth, the laird came to see her.

"Eve, I am so glad ye're awake and feeling better."

Afraid, Anna looked at her white knuckles as she clenched her hands in her lap. "Thank ye, Laird."

Dougal sighed. "Yer fear scalds me, lass, but I know I deserve it. I'm sorry for the way we treated ye when ye arrived."

"I understand, Laird." She still avoided looking at him.

"Is there anything I can get ye?"

"Nay, Laird. Thank ye."

"There's nothing ye need?"

There certainly was something she needed. She looked up at him, "I need to go home."

"Ah, little dove, that is the one thing I cannot grant ye. Ye can't go home yet. I need to know that ye're well and that ye'll be safe there."

"Of course I'll be safe there, it's my home."

"Eve, ye've been living with yer clan's enemy for well over a sennight. Ye'll be here for a bit longer, at least until ye're fully recovered. With our clans feuding I must know there'll be no repercussions against ye before I let ye return."

"There won't be," she insisted.

"Ye said yer father was dead. Are ye married?"

"Nay, Laird."

"To whom do ye belong then? Another family

member? Laird MacKay?"

"I have brothers." *Of course one of them is Laird MacKay*, but Laird MacLeod didn't need to know that. "Please, Laird, let me go home."

"Not now. We'll discuss it later, when ye're well."

Frustrated, Anna looked down at her hands again. She didn't want to discuss it later; she wanted to go home now, but she remained silent. Showing Laird MacLeod disrespect would get her nowhere.

"I know ye don't understand, Eve, but for now ye're under my care and I have to do what I think is best for ye."

Anna didn't understand. How could Laird MacLeod possibly know what was best for her? What was best for her was to get away from the MacLeods before they found out who she really was.

The next day it was Graham she was unable to avoid.

"Hello, Eve, ye're looking well."

"Then tell yer father to let me go home."

Graham laughed, "Oh, lass, no one tells my father what to do."

She clenched her jaw and looked away. Graham sobered a bit. "Eve, I'm glad ye're feeling better, but ye aren't strong enough to travel yet."

Andrew walked in just then and added, "Certainly not. Give it some time. Let us take care of ye. We owe ye that."

"Ye owe me nothing. Just let me go."

"When Isla is satisfied that ye've completely recovered, we will send a message to Laird MacKay to see how ye'll be received. I'm sorry, lass, but he may not welcome ye back."

"He will welcome me back. I have to go. Please."

Andrew looked puzzled. "Why are ye so sure, angel? Ye said to me that he might kill ye."

"Well I exaggerated. He won't. He'll be angry but he won't hurt me."

"If ye're sure he'll be angry, how can ye be certain

ye'll be safe?" asked Graham.

"Because..." *he's my brother.* No, she still didn't think it was wise to reveal her identity. It was one thing to have a simple seamstress from an enemy clan as a captive and something entirely different to have the laird's sister. "Because, I just know. He's a good man. He won't harm me."

"I'm sorry, angel. Ye aren't well enough to travel anyway. Once we know more about what ye might face, we'll decide what's best."

She frowned. There it was again. They'll decide what is best. *They* will. What right did they have to decide what was best for her? *Hold yer tongue Anna*, she cautioned herself. Anna the laird's beloved sister might challenge Laird MacKay's authority and live to tell about it, but she suspected that Eve the lowly MacKay seamstress could get herself in a world of trouble in the midst of the MacLeods.

~ * ~

After the evening meal, Laird MacLeod and his sons retired to his solar to discuss clan business. Andrew raised the subject of their MacKay guest.

"Da, have ye decided what to do about Eve?"

"I was hoping she could be convinced to stay on her own. She would have a safe home here forever."

"But she wants to go home, Da."

"I know she does, Graham, but she doesn't understand what could happen, what her clan might think, how they might treat her."

Andrew nodded. "I agree. Graham, what would ye think if a MacLeod lass were captured by the MacKays and held for weeks?"

Graham sighed. "I would think they had used her and grown tired of her."

"Aye. Even if we knew she had been held against her will and welcomed her back, her life would change. Many in the clan would never look at her in the same way."

Graham still seemed unwilling to accept it. "But,

Andrew, she's a MacKay. What kind of life can she have here?"

"She saved my son's life. The MacLeods will respect her. They already do."

"I know they respect *her*, but will she ever respect us? Hell will she ever even tolerate us? Whenever possible, she feigns sleep when one of us enters the room. She risked her life to save Davy and we instantly repaid her with abuse and neglect. It was exactly what a MacKay would expect from a MacLeod."

"And what would likely have happened to a MacLeod lass if the situation were reversed, son?" Dougal asked. "I will regret the way we treated her forever but, if she had helped abduct Davy, I would not have thought twice about it."

"But that's my point. Our clan will respect her only because of her selfless act. The enmity between the clans still exists. At the risk of oversimplifying things, ye are asking a lass to live among us when she loves our mortal enemies, and her hatred of us is even more justified now."

"So my choice is either force her to stay where I can keep her safe but she will be miserable, or let her go home to God knows what?" He paused for a moment. "She can adjust to life with us. I'm inclined to keep her safe."

"As am I," agreed Andrew.

"Da, ye have to at least send a message to the MacKay and see what his response will be. Ye know she is not going to just stop asking to go home. It is practically the first thing out of her mouth every time someone enters her chamber. Perhaps if she learns she'll be going home to misery, *she'll* make the decision to stay."

"It would crush her if her clan rejected her," said Andrew. "Ye heard her defend the MacKay. She firmly believes she'll be welcomed home. Maybe it's kinder to spare her that disappointment."

"She'll resent us forever if we do. The truth may hurt, but we can deal with that if it happens," said Graham.

Dougal sighed. "Fine, Graham, I suspect ye are right. I'll send a messenger to Laird Sutherland tomorrow and ask him to contact the MacKay on our behalf. I'll make sure Laird Sutherland knows the MacKay's reaction to this news is more important than whatever message he sends back."

~ * ~

Eoin read the missive from Laird MacLeod, delivered by the Sutherland messenger. Although relieved at last to learn that his sister lived, his brow furrowed and he said nothing. He dared not give anything away in front of the messenger.

"Is everything all right, Laird?" the messenger asked.

"Nay. One of my clanswomen is being held by the MacLeods."

"Will there be a reply, Laird?"

"Aye, but I need to speak with her kinsmen before I compose it. Please, rest and refresh yerself, I'll return soon." Eoin left the hall, sending servants with instructions to bring his brothers and Marcas to his solar.

While he waited, he considered the contents of the message. It indicated that a seamstress named Eve had wandered into MacLeod territory. This would normally not be tolerated, but she had helped a MacLeod child who was injured. For that reason, after giving the matter some thought for a time, Laird MacLeod would consider returning Eve to her family. However, one of his guardsmen had taken an interest in her, and if her family didn't want her back, he would see her married as a token of his gratitude.

Like hell.

There was no MacKay seamstress named Eve and Eoin knew full well that the lass they held was Anna, but it appeared his little sister had prudently kept that secret. His relief was profound. Still he didn't want to let it show to the messenger. It looked as if he could secure Anna's release simply by asking for it, but he doubted it would be possible if the MacLeod knew who he actually held. If he showed too much enthusiasm it might lead Dougal MacLeod to suspect

Anna's true identity. Eoin didn't even want Fiona to know until after the messenger had left, for fear she would not be able to contain her reaction in front of him. When his captain and brothers arrived in his solar he filled them in.

"She lied to Laird MacLeod? Well done, little sister," said Tasgall.

"Are we sure it's her?" asked Aidan.

"Aye, it's Anna," he said confidently a huge grin splitting his face. "She identified her brother as 'Sorely'. I don't know whether to laugh or be insulted."

The other men laughed heartily at this news because Sorely was the name of Anna's gelding.

"Do ye believe that the MacLeod is just going to let her go?" asked Marcas.

"I don't know. The whole story sounds odd to me. She 'wandered' into their territory but because she helped a child, MacLeod will let her go?"

"She didn't wander in," said Aidan bitterly. "I'll warrant the bastards saw her alone on the bluff and helped themselves."

Clearly, that thought worried them all.

"Why the story of the child then?" asked Tasgall.

"I don't know," said Eoin honestly. "I'm not sure it matters."

"How are ye going to respond?" asked Aidan.

"I am going to tell him the truth, that her brother does not wish for her to marry a MacLeod guardsman. I will suggest a meeting at our border under white flags, five days from now. He can return her to us then."

"Aren't ye worried he might ambush us? Maybe ye should suggest he escort her to Sutherland and we can get her there," suggested Tasgall.

"Nay. I agree it's a risk but Laird Sutherland knows Anna and he has a son in training with the MacLeods. While we aren't feuding with the Sutherlands, neither are we on particularly good terms."

"Well, stealing Bram's betrothed didn't exactly

endear ye to his father," said Marcas.

"Aye but that tension eased a bit when Bram married his beloved. Still, I can't trust Laird Sutherland not to reveal her identity to Dougal MacLeod. That would put her in much more danger than she's already in. Can ye imagine what might happen if the MacLeod finds out that she's been lying to him?"

"But a direct meeting, Eoin?" asked Marcas. "Even under white flags, I don't trust the MacLeods not to attack. Perhaps ye could suggest he escort her to Laird MacNicol instead. Ye could send a message telling Alec what's happened; he won't reveal Anna's identity. The MacLeods have no formal ties with the MacNicols."

"No they don't and they are on good terms. But given that Fiona is Laird MacNicol's sister, MacLeod is not likely to go along with that."

"He may be more likely to agree to it than a direct meeting. It poses less risk to everyone."

"Ye're probably right. However, it'll take more time to arrange and I hate to leave her at the mercy of the MacLeods any longer than necessary. If he refuses a direct meeting, we'll suggest Laird MacNicol as an intermediary. In the meantime we can send word to Alec and begin making arrangements, should it become necessary." Eoin smiled and added, "I'll also send her a little message from Sorely, letting her know her family is overjoyed to learn that she's safe."

~ * ~

"He wants a direct meeting under white flags?" asked Andrew incredulously when his father revealed the contents of the message from Laird MacKay. "Does he honestly think we'll agree to that? It's not as if our hostage is of any value to him. She's only a seamstress."

His father shook his head, dumbfounded. "Aye, we would be daft to agree to that."

"Is there any indication of how she'll be received?" asked Graham.

"Not much. The messenger said Laird MacKay was

reserved and didn't seem overly concerned by the news. Still, the MacKay did include a message from her brother Sorely in the response."

"What was it?" asked Andrew.

Dougal read from the missive, "Sorely has been saddled with grief since her disappearance. Her family is overjoyed to learn that she's safe."

"Well, at least it seems as if her family will welcome her back," said Graham.

Andrew didn't see this as wholly positive. "I don't think that matters, Graham. Her family is not the whole clan and we know nothing of the MacKay's reaction."

"We'll have another chance to learn more," said Dougal. "I'm not going to agree to a direct meeting. I'll send another message indicating that I might consider escorting her to Laird Sutherland. We'll see what his reaction to that is."

"Do ye plan tell her about the message?" asked Graham.

"I have no intention of telling her that I won't let her go home yet. Ye and Andrew can handle that."

Andrew arched an eyebrow. "If I didn't know better, Da, I'd say ye were afraid of a wee MacKay lass."

"*She* is afraid of *me*. She won't look me in the eye except when she asks to leave."

"Ye're the laird of her clan's enemy, and she's just a seamstress, I wouldn't expect her to look ye in the eye," said Graham rationally.

"Aye, I am the laird who backhanded her and called her a whore. Lads, do yer father this kindness."

Andrew rose from his chair. "None of us treated her well, Da, but I'll tell her."

When he arrived at Eve's chamber he found Mairi and David enthusiastically playing a guessing game with her. Cora, the old widow who had been Mairi's nursemaid and who had agreed to care for David now, watched on. Eve laughed at their antics and Andrew couldn't help but notice how lovely the copper-haired angel was when she smiled, her eyes sparkling with laughter. Sadly, that beautiful smile was fleeting. As soon as she was aware of his presence, she became quiet and guarded.

He sighed knowing she wouldn't like what she was about to hear. David spotted him next and bounced joyfully where he knelt on the bed beside Eve. "Da! Come play with us!"

"I can't play now, Davy."

"But it'll be fun, Da."

"I'm sure it would be, but it is getting late. Ye need to go to bed and I need to talk with Eve."

Eve looked down, her hands folded in her lap.

"Da, just for a minute? Ye never play with me."

Cora gently lifted David off of the bed. "David, yer father said 'nay' and he's right. It's time to get ready for bed. Say good night now before we go."

David hugged Eve vigorously. "Good night, Eve."

She kissed his head. "Sleep well, David."

He looked up at his father. "Good night, Da."

Andrew ruffled his dark hair "Good night, son. Sleep well." The lad nodded but hung his head sadly as Cora led him from the room.

"Good night, Mairi," Andrew said pointedly when she showed no sign of leaving.

"Ye aren't my Da, Andrew, ye can't boss me around. Maybe Eve doesn't want me to leave."

"Mairi, don't push me."

Ignoring him, Mairi turned towards their visitor. "Eve, do ye want me to go?"

"Sweetling, that isn't important. Ye should do as yer brother asks."

Mairi sighed dramatically. "All right, but I'm going to talk to Da about this, Andrew."

"Of course ye will, Mairi, but ye should know—he'll take my side."

She stuck out her tongue at him and left the room.

Andrew just shook his head as he watched her leave then turned back to Eve. "Thank ye."

The lass shrugged and said, "I have brothers."

"Aye, ye do, and that is what I need to talk with ye about. Will ye sit with me by the fire?" He offered her his hand.

She sat for a moment staring at the hand he held toward her but made no move to take it.

"Eve, I'm not in the habit of being ignored."

With a sigh she took his hand, letting him lead her to a chair by the hearth. He sat in the opposite chair. She opened her mouth to say something and he put up his hand. "I know ye want to go home, please don't ask again."

She frowned looking into the fire for a moment. "Then what did ye come to tell me?"

"We sent a message to Laird MacKay and have received a response."

She brightened immediately, "What did it say?"

"Yer brother, Sorely, asked that we tell ye he has been saddled with grief since ye disappeared and yer family is overjoyed to learn that ye are safe."

Amusement flashed in her eyes before she bit her lower lip, looking away again. He thought her reaction was odd, but after a moment she turned back to him, full of confidence. "I told ye I would be welcomed home."

The sparkle in her eyes cheered him. "I'm glad they want ye to come home, angel, but we still aren't sure how ye'll be received by the laird or the rest of the clan. Apparently Laird MacKay was very reticent when he read the message concerning ye."

She seemed amused. "That doesn't surprise me, but I'm sure it won't be a problem. Ye're unnecessarily worried."

"Nevertheless, we will not release ye to him until we are sure."

Instantly all hint of her merriment disappeared. "How do ye intend to assure yerselves? Did Laird MacKay not suggest a way for me to come home?"

"Aye, he did, but it isn't acceptable."

Clearly frustrated she demanded, "Why not?"

"Because he suggested a face to face meeting at our border and that's too risky. It leaves us vulnerable to an ambush."

"They *won't* ambush ye. Please, just let—"

He put up his hand to stop the predictable request again. "Angel, ye're nothing if not persistent. We've sent a message suggesting Laird Sutherland act as an intermediary and, based on Laird MacKay's reaction, we will decide what to do then."

"What gives ye the right to decide?" she demanded.

"Eve, ye're being insolent and I've had enough. Ye're in our care and I know ye would prefer not to be, but that can't be helped now. I owe ye more than I can ever repay and whether ye like it or not, I will not allow ye to risk yer safety. I will protect ye until I am certain that someone else will do it adequately."

Tears filled her eyes. "The only protection I need is from the MacLeods."

"I have told ye before, ye are in no danger here."

She looked away, angrily swiping the tears from her face.

He sighed in exasperation. "Please try to understand, angel, this is for the best."

Chapter 4

Once again Aidan, Tasgall and Marcas sat with Eoin in his solar discussing the newest message from Laird MacLeod.

"As we expected, he suggested Sutherland serve as an intermediary."

"Do we risk agreeing?" asked Aidan.

"Nay. He hasn't actually committed to sending her to Sutherland. He has only said he would 'consider' it and has offered no specific plan.

"What game is he playing? If he thinks he has a seamstress, someone of no importance, why is he being so cautious?" asked Marcas.

"I don't know, and I worry that he will wonder the same thing about our reaction, but I don't completely trust Sutherland. Alec MacNicol has agreed to be our intermediary and I am going to ask that MacLeod send 'Eve' there before the feast of St. Zacharias. The MacNicols will escort her here after that."

"Maybe Fiona's Uncle Bhaltair will bring her the rest of the way. He is particularly fond of her after all. Perhaps he'll stay for a nice long visit," teased Tasgall.

"If it means getting Anna back, I won't complain" said Eoin.

~ * ~

Disbelievingly Graham asked, "MacNicol? He wants ye to spend a whole day taking a seamstress to Laird MacNicol? What does he have against Sutherland?"

"Well, Eanraig arrived on his doorstep with an army a couple of years ago, after Eoin married Bram's betrothed.

Some men might hold a grudge over that," said Andrew, dryly.

"But they reached an accord, there was no battle and if anyone has a right to hold a grudge it would Bram, but he certainly doesn't. Nay, Sutherland is more of a neutral party than MacNicol. MacNicol is Eoin's brother by marriage for the love of God."

Dougal paced in front of his hearth. "Something's wrong. Perhaps he's intentionally being obstinate. Maybe he's trying to goad me into keeping her."

"Aye, perhaps," agreed Andrew. "I'm certain Laird MacKay is more aware of the problems she will face with his clan than her family is. He may mean to spare their feelings by ensuring that she doesn't come back. Was the messenger able to provide any more information?"

"Not really. Laird MacKay continues to be reticent, revealing nothing, and this time there was no message for the lass."

Andrew was convinced that sending her back was not the right course, but he couldn't tell what his father was thinking. "What are ye going to do?"

"Nothing for now. I am going to think about it for a few days. At this point the only thing I would be willing to do is take her to Sutherland and if MacKay doesn't agree, she won't be returned."

Graham shook his head. "That will break her heart, Da."

"I know, but she will just have to adjust. Perhaps it would be best if she started getting used to life here. Give her something to do."

Graham looked astonished. "Ye can't be serious. Ye want to put her to work? Da, a bit more than a sennight ago, Father Ninian was giving her the Last Rites."

"Nothing strenuous. God's teeth, lad, she's a seamstress. See that she has some mending to do or something."

Andrew chuckled. "She is not very happy with the

MacLeods at the moment. I fear she would sew sleeves shut or work some other mischief if given the opportunity."

"Lads, help me out here."

Graham shrugged. "She likes Mairi, perhaps she would make a new dress for her."

"There ye are, ye can keep Eve busy and make Mairi happy at the same time. I also think Eve should take her meals with us in the great hall beginning tomorrow."

This time it was Andrew's turn to be shocked. "Now that's an interesting idea, Da. What exactly are ye proposing?"

"Just what I said, I want her to dine in the great hall."

"At yer table?"

"Aye, I suppose so."

"Da, ye know full well she is terrified of ye."

"Well if we want her to be accepted by the clan, they need to understand her status. I can't very well have her sit at the trestles with everyone else. As I said, she will have to adjust. She must learn she has nothing to fear from me."

"Aye, I can see how forcing her to dine with ye will help her there."

"Don't mock me, Andrew, just see it done," commanded Dougal irritably.

Andrew and Graham exchanged amused glances but didn't argue further.

~ * ~

"I don't want to dine in the great hall. I don't belong there."

"I'm not giving ye the option, angel, and ye do belong there. Ye will join us for the evening meal tomorrow," said Andrew.

"Do ye normally ask yer prisoners to dine with ye?"

"Ye're not a prisoner, Eve, ye're a guest."

"Guests are free to leave. So if I'm a guest, I will thank ye for yer hospitality and bid ye farewell."

"Eve, don't start this. Please do as ye're asked and join us for the evening meal with no argument."

"And what if I refuse?"

"Then Davy will be extremely disappointed. I understand he is very excited that his angel is going to sit with him at supper." By the look of defeat on her face, Andrew instantly knew he had wielded the proper weapon.

She sighed. "I don't want to upset him."

"I thought not, so ye will join us?"

"Aye. I suppose I can manage one meal surrounded by MacLeods."

Andrew decided this would not be the best time to tell her she would join them for all meals going forward.

~ * ~

The next evening, dressed in a soft cream-colored wool léine that belonged to Mairi, but with her own plaid around her shoulders, Andrew escorted her to the great hall. All eyes followed them as he led her to the table where the family dined. She avoided making eye contact as much as possible, but it pleased Andrew to see the MacLeods accept her presence without question. Everyone knew what she had done, and warm smiles followed her, even if she didn't see them. Andrew thought it best to seat her well away from his father. He took a seat near the end of the table, placing Eve between himself and Davy, across from Mairi.

The evening meal went well and although Eve was subdued, David and Mairi kept her distracted. Andrew glanced around to see how the clan seemed to be responding to the little MacKay at the head table. Again, he was generally pleased. However, he noted that one young man, Boyd Sutherland, kept staring at her and whispering to his comrades.

Andrew wasn't the only one who noticed the lad's odd behavior. Near the end of the meal Dougal called the young man to him. Boyd conferred quietly with the laird for a few moments. Andrew knew there was a problem when he saw his father's expression turn grim.

When the meal was over and the family stood to leave, Dougal looked down the table at them. In a surprisingly gentle voice his father asked, "Eve lass, would ye join me in my solar for a bit? I have a few things to discuss with ye. Andrew, Graham would ye come as well?" He stared pointedly at Andrew.

Andrew nodded, taking her elbow. "Aye, Da."

Eve looked worried and balked but Andrew put his other hand on the small of her back, urging her forward. They followed his father out of the hall and up the stairs to the solar.

Dougal entered and lit several candles, then gestured to one of the chairs near the fire. "Lass, please come and sit down." He used the same gentle tone he had in the hall.

Eve stiffened, eying him as if he were a wild beast poised to attack. Andrew urged her towards the chair, but again she balked and pushed back.

If anyone else had openly defied an order, Dougal would have roared, but he looked at her intently and said, "Anna, I know who ye are. Please sit down."

Stunned, her head snapped up and she looked terrified. She stumbled backwards trying to get away and Andrew steadied her. "Calm down, angel, ye're safe."

"Nay. Nay, let me go." She tried to twist away from him.

"Wheesht, no one is going to hurt ye."

"Da, what's going on? Did ye call her Anna?" asked Graham.

"Aye, I did. Anna, calm yerself," Dougal commanded firmly. "Andrew is right, ye are safe here and no one will hurt ye."

"Are ye Anna MacKay?" asked Graham, stunned.

"Aye, I'm Anna MacKay. I lied. What did ye expect? I'm one of the lying MacKays after all."

"Anna, please…," Dougal tried to calm her.

"I was a-afraid when Graham brought me here," her voice caught. "I-I thought maybe, once ye knew I hadn't tried to hurt Davy, if ye thought I was nobody ye would just let me go." She looked at Dougal and couldn't hold the tears back

"Ye said t-terrible things to me. Ye h-hit me. Ye've been worried about my b-brother and my clan hurting me. N-no one can hurt me as ye have."

Dougal walked toward her. She shied away but he put his arms around her and gently pulled her close, as a father would a frightened child. Anna trembled and sobbed against his chest "I know we hurt ye, lass, and by all that's holy, I'm sorry. I understand how scared ye must have been and that ye're still scared. Please don't cry."

"Boyd Sutherland recognized her?" Andrew asked his father.

He nodded. "Aye. He met her at the celebration of Bram's wedding a few years ago." Anna continued to weep in his arms. He stroked her hair. "Wheesht lass, ye're safe. Everything will be all right."

"That's why Laird MacKay didn't want ye taking her to Sutherland. He knew Laird Sutherland would recognize her," said Graham as the implications became clear.

"I suspect."

Anna began to regain her composure and stepped back, away from Laird MacLeod, wiping the tears from her face. Dougal kept his hands on her shoulders. "Please sit down now." He gently guided her to a chair.

Laird MacLeod sat again and motioned for his sons to sit as well. Graham did, but Andrew moved to stand by the hearth, close to Anna's chair.

Anna sat and while she seemed embarrassed by her outburst, she finally looked Laird MacLeod in the eye. "Will ye let me go home *now*?"

"Anna, there are a few things to sort out before any decisions are made."

"That's not an answer," she whispered and biting her lower lip looked away.

Andrew suppressed a smile. He finally understood the source of her boldness. She was not a lowly seamstress who didn't know her place. She was a noblewoman with an impudent streak, not unlike his sister's.

"Lass, why were ye so far from home and unaccompanied the day ye saved David? Is yer brother always so careless with ye?"

She stiffened angrily. "My brother is not careless with me."

"Then why were ye alone?"

"Eoin and I had an argument and I was angry. If I had ridden out that day, I would have had an escort but I don't need one if I am walking close to home."

"But ye weren't close to home," said Andrew.

"I didn't intend to walk that far. I was preoccupied. I wasn't supposed to walk northward on the bluff anyway. I just wanted some time alone. That's why I said that Eoin would be angry."

Dougal frowned at her. "I would certainly be angry if ye were mine. But maybe God did lead ye there so that ye could save Davy. What had ye argued about?"

Anna frowned and looked away, eventually answering, "My betrothal."

"Are ye betrothed then?"

"I wasn't when I left."

"What is that supposed to mean?"

"It means that my brother was considering a betrothal but hadn't agreed to it yet. That is what we argued about."

"Who was he considering?"

"Fearchar Morrison," she said miserably.

"Fearchar Morrison is an idiot," said Graham.

Anna's expression suggested that she agreed with him, but she said, "I thought the MacLeods were allies of the Morrisons?"

"We are," said Andrew, "another of Laird Morrison's sons trains here, but that doesn't stop Fearchar from being an idiot."

"Fearchar will be chief someday but I'm surprised yer brother was even considering it. The MacKays and the Morrisons have never been particularly cozy, and the Isle of Lewis is so remote." said Dougal.

"Well, I admit I'm no great prize, but I'm not without skills. I do know how to run a household."

"Anna, that's not what I meant, lass."

"I know what ye meant," she snapped. "As ye said, the Morrisons and MacKays have never been cozy but he's an ally of yers. If I marry Laird Morrison's heir, the power shifts and the MacKays would have the tighter bond. In a conflict, if it came to choosing sides, the Morrisons might stand with the MacKays. Not that it does either of us much good with them on God-forsaken Lewis."

"Anna, stop it. I am concerned about ye, not whomever the MacKays choose to ally themselves with. It's clear ye wouldn't be happy that far away."

"Ye needn't concern yerself about me any longer. I have brothers for that. Let me go back to them."

Ignoring her Dougal asked, "Has Eoin considered anyone else?"

Anna flushed angrily. "Pardon me, but I don't see how my betrothal is any of yer business."

Andrew cringed. No MacLeod in their right mind would speak to Dougal like that.

Dougal however, smiled. "Ah let me guess, little dove, ye haven't agreed with any of his choices so far and he hasn't wanted to force ye into a match ye didn't want." Still glaring, Anna didn't answer him, but her silence was affirmation enough. "That at least tells me that he loves ye. He's probably ready to wring yer neck about now, but he loves ye. He might even have been baiting ye about Morrison in the first place. Andrew has a way of setting Mairi off regularly."

"And she, him," said Graham.

Andrew couldn't argue. It was true.

"Will ye demand a ransom now?" asked Anna tentatively.

"I'm not sure what I am going to do with ye, but it's clear yer brother and I need to speak face to face. I will send him a message tomorrow telling him that we have discovered who ye are, that ye are an honored guest here and we'll arrange a meeting. Cheer up, little dove. Ye'll see yer brother soon." Then as an afterthought Dougal asked, "By the way, ye told us yer brother's name was 'Sorley' and clearly it wasn't. Who is Sorley?"

It warmed Andrew's heart to see her smile as she answered, "My gelding."

Andrew and Graham chuckled at that but their father laughed until tears ran down his weathered cheeks. Dougal finally managed to say "I'm sure yer brother was less than flattered by that, but it serves him right for threatening to send ye off to Lewis!"

"And it explains why Sorley was *saddled* with grief," Andrew commented, remembering how delighted she'd been by the message.

"If it is any consolation to ye, I will not return ye to yer brother if he plans to marry ye to Fearchar."

She smiled weakly. "If he plans to marry me to Fearchar, I'll stay."

Dougal laughed again before calling for his squire. "Colin, lad, would ye escort our guest to her chamber please? Anna, ye need to rest and we have some other business to discuss. Sleep well, little dove."

"Thank ye, Laird. Good night," she said quietly before leaving with Colin. Her polite, meek veneer was back in place.

Dougal turned to his sons, shaking his head, "Kentigern MacKay should have settled her betrothal years ago."

Andrew snorted and Graham said, "Oh, like ye've settled Mairi's?" They were both fully aware their father had not yet arranged a betrothal for her. Dougal glared at them.

"I will never forgive ye if ye leave me to sort out a betrothal for Mairi," warned Andrew.

"If I didn't know better, son, I'd say ye were afraid of a wee MacLeod lass," replied Dougal, echoing Andrew's taunt from several days ago.

"Mairi's defiance would try the patience of a saint, and ye let her get away with it too often."

"I'll remind ye of this, Andrew, when ye have a wee daughter of yer own who wraps ye 'round her finger."

"Ye know I have no intention of ever marrying again. Joan was…well I have an heir and that's enough. Ye can warn Graham about the perils of daughters."

"I know ye didn't want to marry again, but I am going to ask Eoin MacKay to consider a betrothal between ye and Anna."

Nothing his father could have said would have shocked him more. "Ye're not serious, Da."

"Oh but I am."

"Nay. Marry her to Graham if ye feel the need.

"That isn't possible, brother. Ye know I was betrothed to Isobel Ross years ago."

"I am not marrying again," declared Andrew.

"And ye have the nerve to call yer sister defiant? Ye'll marry if I say ye will, Andrew, and make no mistake."

"Eoin MacKay will never agree to it and Eve—er—Anna only wants to go home," said Graham.

"Eoin will have no choice in the matter and neither will Anna," said Dougal confidently.

Andrew was not ready to drop this. "Why would ye do this? I don't want to be married, she surely doesn't want to marry me and Eoin won't want his sister married to a MacLeod."

His father looked at him intently. "Anna MacKay saved Davy's life, not simply by being there and rescuing him from the loch, but by acting quickly to warm him and risking her own life in the process. When I thought she was a simple seamstress, the only way I could repay a fraction of our debt was to ensure she was safe and had as easy a life as possible."

"How has that changed? I agree she shouldn't have to marry Fearchar Morrison, but that doesn't mean she should become *my* wife."

"This has nothing to do with who she does or doesn't wish to marry. The most valuable thing I can give Davy's angel is peace between our clans. The night ye brought Anna here, when she fell ill, Isla said it wasn't only our errors in judgment that had caused it but the decades of hate that both clans bred. She was right, lads. What happens if we allow it to continue? Maybe in twenty-five years Davy faces Anna's son in battle and slays him. How have we repaid her selflessness then? The best thing I can do for her children and yers is to end this feud once and for all."

"Then end it. Why must we marry to do that?"

"Ye know only a powerful tie between the clans will be enough to end this hostility permanently. Ye're my heir and she is Laird MacKay's sister. There is no tighter bond than a marriage between ye. Frankly, it's a match I had already tried to make once. I offered Kentigern a betrothal between the two of ye over ten years ago, long before I ever considered Joan Sinclair. MacKay would have no part of it."

This news stunned Andrew. "Then why do ye think her brother will agree now?"

"Because I have something with which to bargain that I didn't have before—the lass herself. The only ransom I will accept is a signed betrothal."

Graham was equally astounded. "Ye would keep her here as a prisoner if her brother doesn't agree?"

"Aye, I would. I think the stakes warrant it. However, he'll agree."

"Don't ye think forcing him into this will anger him sufficiently to cause hard feelings?" asked Andrew silently thinking that 'hard feelings' was a gross understatement.

"Aye it probably would, but I am prepared to offer something precious in return, which will also solve a problem ye were worried about."

"What's that?"

"Laird MacKay has two unmarried brothers. I'm going to offer a betrothal between one of them and Mairi."

Astonished, both Andrew and Graham stared at him,

unable to speak.

Finally Andrew shook his head. "I don't know, Da. Mairi might single-handedly make the MacKays hate us more than they already do."

Chapter 5

"Are ye really the MacKay's sister?" asked Colin as he walked her to her chamber.

"It didn't take long for that news to spread."

"So ye are?"

"Aye. I'm Anna MacKay."

"But ye saved Davy."

Anna wanted to say right about now she fervently wished she had run the other direction, but she couldn't. It wasn't true. "Aye."

"But ye are the MacKay's sister."

"Colin, that's been established," she said irritably.

"Well, I just mean, well everyone thought it was an amazing thing when they heard how a MacKay saved Davy. No one expected that, but now it turns out ye are the MacKay's own sister. That's just hard to believe."

"Colin, we are not monsters," she snapped. "We are people, just like the MacLeods. We laugh and we cry and we show compassion and we make mistakes!"

"I didn't mean to upset ye," he said solemnly.

She softened, "I know. I'm sorry for snapping at ye. I'm tired, I'm alone among people who don't like me simply because of my name."

"But we do like ye. Ye saved—"

"I know, I saved Davy. But I'm still a MacKay and I don't belong here. I want to…" Nay there was no point saying it. "Never mind."

"Is there anything I can do?"

"Can ye get me out of this keep?" He shook his head sadly. "Then nay, Colin, thank ye, there's nothing ye can do. Good night."

She entered her chamber, shut the door and leaned against it for a moment. This would change everything. She had hoped, out of gratitude, the MacLeods would let her go as soon as Eoin convinced them Eve the Seamstress would not suffer for her actions. Clearly, that was unlikely now. She knew the MacLeod's could demand a steep ransom because of who she was, regardless of the fact that she saved Davy. She needed to escape now more than ever.

Maybe she could just walk out. She had been so ill, they surely wouldn't expect it. She could slip out in the night and simply walk home. It would be a long cold trek but she knew she could do it. She remembered riding under a portcullis when Graham brought her here. No doubt it would be closed and guarded at night, but there might be another way out. She crossed to the window to see what options she might have.

The curtain wall surrounding the keep was wide. Sentries were posted on the top every hundred paces or so. Perhaps if she could hide in the shadows and watch, she could make it up the stairs to the top of the wall without being seen. But she worried the wall was too high for her to drop down the other side without risking serious injury. If she knew what was on the other side of the wall, perhaps she could pick the best place to try. Tomorrow she would try to go outside and try to see more.

~ * ~

The next morning the sun was bright but the wind was blustery and cold. She was already up, dressed and sitting on the window seat looking out when a young maid knocked and came in. "Good morning my lady, I'm Jesse."

"Hello Jesse, please just call me Anna."

"Isla is my grandmother and she said I was to help ye and make sure ye didn't overdo."

Anna closed her eyes for a moment. "Thank ye Jesse, but it really isn't necessary."

"But Gran said ye needed help and Laird MacLeod wanted ye to have a maid."

"I don't need a maid."

Jesse looked crestfallen, "But Gran worries so about ye, and I wanted to help."

A MacLeod maid was about the last thing on earth she needed, but Anna didn't want to disappoint the girl. She seemed to have her heart set on helping her grandmother. "I suppose ye could bring me something for breakfast, unless yer priest hasn't said Mass yet, in which case I would like to go to Mass."

"Father Ninian says Mass a bit later on Sundays. I will check with Laird MacLeod to make sure it's all right."

"Never mind—" but she was out the door before Anna could stop her.

A few minutes later, there was another knock at her door and Andrew entered with her mantle over his arm. "Jesse said ye were feeling up to attending Mass. I would be happy to escort ye."

"I'm sorry she bothered ye. It isn't necessary. I've changed my mind."

He held her mantle for her. "Anna, don't be silly. Put on yer mantle and let me take ye to Mass."

There was no avoiding it now. Anna turned and let him put the mantle around her shoulders. She had hoped to get outside the keep without one of the MacLeod men at her elbow, but it couldn't be helped. He walked with her downstairs and across the courtyard to the chapel. She had hoped maybe they didn't have a chapel within the walls and would walk to the village. Still, it was better than nothing, so she tried to take in as much as she could of the layout of the keep and the curtain wall.

With her mind occupied by plans of escape, she barely listened until one of the readings caught her attention. *Omnia possum in Eo qui me confortat, I can do all things in Him who strengthens me.* She wrestled with St. Paul's words. She wanted to believe it was a sign. A message telling her she could do anything, even escape, with the help of God. But a little voice inside her said, *it isn't license to do whatever ye wish, it just promises God's help to cope with where ye find yerself.*

After much thought, she decided she needed to quiet that little voice. She did not want to cope with living among the MacLeods. She wanted to escape.

When they left the chapel after Mass she tried to get Andrew to walk with her outside the walls. "It is a beautiful day, could we walk a bit?"

"It is a blustery cold day and ye haven't broken yer fast. If it warms up a bit later perhaps ye can take a short walk then."

It would do no good to argue with him now. Perhaps if she were compliant, he would let her go for a walk later. It was the only way she had a hope of seeing more of the grounds so she could learn enough to make a plan.

~ * ~

The day did not warm up but she unsuccessfully tried to get Andrew to take her for a walk anyway. When that failed, she tried Graham, who also refused. In desperation, she tried Mairi who pouted and said, "Andrew told me that if ye asked me to take ye outside I was to say no. I'd take ye anyway, but Da said if I did he wouldn't let me see ye at all. But, Anna, while I hate to admit it, they're probably right. It is much too cold and windy today."

The day had been frustrating and by evening she just wanted to be alone. When Jesse arrived to help her get ready for the evening meal she sent her away.

"It isn't necessary. I'm tired and I don't intend to eat in the great hall again."

"Are ye well? Shall I fetch Gran?"

"Jesse, I'm fine. I just don't want to go down to supper."

"But my lady—"

"Please call me Anna."

"Anna, Laird MacLeod expects ye to be at the table."

"Jesse, please just let me be."

The maid left quietly and while Anna felt guilty for

snapping at her, she was glad to be alone. She sat at the window seat, looking out over the courtyard. There was another knock and the door opened before she could answer. She spun her head around saying "Jesse please—" only it wasn't Jesse, it was Andrew.

"I've come to take ye down for supper."

"I'm not going."

"That's what Jesse said, but it isn't acceptable."

She gaped at him. "It isn't acceptable? To whom?"

"To my father. To me."

"Well, I'm sorry it *isn't acceptable* to ye and Laird MacLeod but I'm tired."

"Ye weren't too tired to try to get Graham and Mairi to take ye out for a walk today after I told ye nay."

"Well I'm tired now," she snapped.

"Then I suppose ye won't be wanting to take a walk outside tomorrow either?"

"That's blackmail!"

He simply arched an eyebrow at her.

"Oh all right, I'll go down to supper," she said in frustration.

She remained quiet throughout the meal. It was easy enough with Mairi and David chattering away. Still she couldn't help feeling out of place. *I don't belong here.*

~ * ~

The Sutherland messenger arrived at Naomh-dùn with the third message from Laird MacLeod during the evening meal. After reading it Eoin put his head in his hands.

"What's happened?" asked Aidan anxiously.

There was no longer any need to dissemble in the presence of the messenger so Eoin said, "They know who she is."

"How?" asked Tasgall.

"Boyd Sutherland recognized her." Eoin glared at the Sutherland messenger before adding, "Damn him."

"What ransom does Laird MacLeod ask? We'll pay it." Fiona, who held their wee son on her lap, kissed the lad and hugged him tighter.

Eoin knew this whole ordeal had been extremely upsetting to her. She understood what it meant to be held for ransom. Unfortunately, he couldn't put his wife's fears to rest. "He hasn't asked for a ransom yet. Now *he* wants a face to face meeting."

"When and where?" asked Marcas

"By the strait between the lochs, at sext, on the Feast of St. Joseph."

"That's eight days from now. Why so long?" asked Tasgall.

"I don't know, but he says it is not negotiable. He also says he will have Anna there and any attempt at ambush will get her killed."

Fiona looked horror struck.

"What assurance do we have that he won't ambush us?" asked Marcas.

"None. In fact he demands that both Tasgall and Aidan attend as well."

"Does he think ye're daft? If he's planning an ambush, all three of ye could be killed."

"I agree, but that too is not negotiable. He says that if we all aren't there, there will be no discussion and he won't ever return Anna."

Fiona gasped. "Nay, poor Anna. Eoin, what will ye do?

"The only thing I can do; meet the bastard at the strait in nine days with Aidan and Tasgall."

"And yer full garrison?" asked Marcas.

"I can't do that either. I doubt that it is, but this could be a scheme to leave Naomh-dùn vulnerable. I must leave it sufficiently well-guarded too."

~ * ~

Monday dawned fair and bright. Anna felt sure she would be able to get a better look at the outside of the keep and the curtain wall today. However, once again it didn't happen. Laird MacLeod, Andrew and Graham had gone out with a hunting party. Donald was left in charge and he allowed her to go for a short walk in the courtyard, with Mairi and under his watchful eye, but she wasn't able to see anything more than she had the previous morning. There was nothing for it. She would have to leave tonight and figure out how to get past any obstacles as she came to them. *I can do all things in Him who strengthens me.* Again, she hushed the voice that warned against this.

She spent the day helping Mairi make a new dress, which of course thrilled Mairi.

"I love having ye here, Anna! I've never had a sister. I mean, I do have a sister, but she is much older, older than Andrew even. She was married and gone before my mother got sick and died and I barely remember my mother."

"I'm sorry Mairi. I don't remember my mother at all. She died when I was born."

"My mother wasn't Da's first wife. He was married to Arabella first. She was Ena's, Andrew's and Graham's mother. I'm only their half-sister."

"I have a different mother than my oldest brother too, but just like yer brothers love ye, my brothers love me very much and I love them."

"Aye, I do love my brothers *most of the time*, but I still would like a sister here. I wish ye didn't have to leave soon."

"Please don't wish that for me, Mairi. I miss my home and family so very much."

Mairi frowned and after a moment said, "I'm sure Da will let ye go home soon, but maybe ye can come back and visit?"

Good Lord, come back? Nay, as soon as she was back on MacKay land, she would never leave. "I don't think so, pet." At Mairi's look of disappointment she added, "But we'll see."

~ * ~

Talking about her family during the afternoon with Mairi reminded her of just how much she missed them. She knew she had to escape and get home before the MacLeod thought of some other reason to keep her. When Andrew knocked on her door that evening to take her to the evening meal, once again she declined. She wanted to rest for a while so she could make the long walk home.

"Anna, I refuse to have this argument with ye every day. Ye will join us in the hall for meals. *All* meals."

"Why are ye forcing me to do this? I don't want to take my meals in the midst of the MacLeods, especially now they know who I really am. Would ye look forward to dining at my brother's table?"

"I would if I were an honored guest."

"I'm not an honored guest. I am a prisoner!"

"Dammit Anna, ye're not a prisoner. And don't tell me that ye'll thank me for my hospitality and bid me farewell. Can't ye just put yer hatred aside and think of this as home for a while?"

"Put *my* hatred aside?" She looked at him askance. "The MacLeods hate me every bit as much. Can't ye just leave me be?"

"The MacLeods do not hate ye, for the love of God, ye saved my son! This argument is over, Anna. We are going downstairs now."

"The argument is over because ye say it's over? Nay, Andrew. I'm not going to eat among my enemies. Ye can't make me."

He arched an eyebrow at her, picked her up and put her over his shoulder.

Hammering on his back with her fists she demanded, "What are ye doing?"

"Proving ye wrong. I *can* make ye."

"Put me down!" she yelled, kicking her feet.

He barked "Stop it," and popped her lightly on the backside. "If ye are going to act like a bairn, I'll treat ye like one. Now ye have a choice to make. I can put ye down, and ye can walk to the great hall with me for supper, or I can carry ye down kicking and screaming like a petulant child.

Which will it be?"

Defeated, she sighed heavily and said, "Put me down."

She went downstairs with him but once again, she kept her eyes down, refusing to look any of the MacLeods in the eye. Just as he had done the last two evenings, Andrew sat her between himself and Davy, across from Mairi, who chattered happily throughout the meal about her new dress and Anna's skill with a needle. Anna pointedly ignored Andrew and only spoke to anyone when asked a direct question. Even then her answers were short. It was rude and she knew it but she didn't care. She seethed with anger at Andrew and by extension all of the MacLeods. Although she knew she should eat so she would have energy for the journey, she had very little appetite. To her chagrin Andrew noticed.

"Ye need to eat, angel."

"I'm not hungry."

"Ye have been ill and have not regained yer strength yet. Ye need to eat."

"Perhaps my appetite would be better if I were not sitting in the midst of the MacLeods," she hissed.

"We've had this discussion and it's over. Eat!"

She took a sip of ale from her goblet and ignored him.

"Anna! I said ye must eat something!" he snapped.

"And I said I have eaten all that I want!" she snapped back.

Beyond frustrated Andrew threatened, "Shall I bind ye to that chair and force ye to eat?"

"So I *am* a prisoner?"

"No Anna! Ye're not, but I am worried about yer health and ye must eat."

"If that's yer concern, perhaps ye should just let me go—"

"Don't dare say it. By all that's holy, Anna MacKay, ye would try the patience of a saint."

"Well I guess I had better watch myself, because I

doubt that ye or any other MacLeod could be accused of sainthood," she said scathingly. Suddenly she realized that Mairi and David had grown quiet and were watching the argument with wide-eyed horror.

Andrew, quick to exploit the situation, said, "Davy, I am trying to convince Anna that she needs to eat a bit more so she can get better soon, but I'm having trouble. She doesn't want to be here in the great hall with us. Perhaps ye can try. Yer angel needs to eat."

"Anna, don't ye like us?" David asked sadly.

Anna glared at Andrew for a moment and was rewarded with his smug smile. She turned to David and said "Of course I like *ye,* Davy. I'm just not very hungry."

"Well Da says ye need to eat, so here try some rabbit; it's my favorite," he said pushing a dish of braised rabbit towards her.

Not wanting to hurt him she took a piece and nibbled on it.

"Do ye like it," he asked with an expectant smile.

"Aye, Davy, it is very tasty."

"Good," said Andrew, adding, "Now Davy ye make sure she eats it all," with an I-won-again smile on his face.

Anna ate the rabbit Davy had given her, remained quiet until the meal was over, and then fled to her chamber. The day had been long and frustrating, and sparring with Andrew over supper exhausted her.

She sat in her darkened room, looking out the window, waiting for the stillness of night to envelop the keep. She dozed briefly but before long awoke to the patter of rain on the window. *God, are ye conspiring against me too*? Attempting to escape in the cold rain would have her soaked and frozen within minutes. She knew better than to do something that foolish. She would have to wait another day. Dejectedly she crawled into bed and went to sleep.

Chapter 6

The following day, the Sutherland messenger arrived at Curacridhe with Laird MacKay's response.

"Well lads, he has accepted my request for a meeting."

"Did ye doubt it?" Andrew asked.

"Nay, but I'd be mad as hell if I were him. We should increase patrols near our border."

"Why did ye set the meeting so far out? He's got nothing to do for a week but stew," observed Graham.

"Anna is still weak. I want to make sure she is completely recovered before the meeting."

Andrew snorted, "If her temper is any measure of her health, she is well on the road to recovery."

His father scowled at them both. "Need I remind ye, she nearly died? Just over a fortnight ago she received Last Rites. The weather has been blustery and if she took a chill, I would never forgive myself. Furthermore, if Eoin sees her from a distance looking anything but hearty, trouble could start before I have the chance to talk to him. Considering all of this, it is not unreasonable to wait another week. But the fact is, it won't hurt Eoin to stew a bit either. Lads, going into a meeting like this, it is imperative that ye control as much as possible so ye maintain the upper hand. Anything ye do to make yer opponent bend to yer will gives ye an advantage. If Eoin had suggested an earlier date I probably would have agreed. But he didn't. It tells me he is desperate and didn't want to take a risk that I'd pull out altogether. He'll do whatever it takes to see to his sister's wellbeing. And that is exactly where we want him."

Ignoring him Graham asked, "Are ye going to tell

her, Da?"

"About the pending meeting? Aye. But I have no intention of telling her about the betrothal…or that she won't be going home."

"I should hope not," agreed Andrew.

"I understand about the betrothal, but Da, it will break her heart if she can't go home. Can ye not let her go for a while? Get Eoin to sign the betrothals and agree to bring her back for the wedding?"

"Are ye jesting, Graham?" asked Andrew. "If the situation were reversed, would ye honor a betrothal like that for Mairi, or once we had her back, would ye seek to crush MacKay?"

"I see yer point." Graham sighed. "But when she finds out, she won't see it. No more than she'll understand the reason for it all in the first place."

Dougal smiled confidently. "When she sees this is the only way to achieve a lasting peace for her children, she'll understand."

Graham shook his head. "We can hope, but I wouldn't count on it."

~ * ~

The evening meal was nearly ready and Andrew stood by the hearth, steeling himself to battle once again with his soon-to-be-betrothed. He must have looked grim because when Graham approached he said, "What has ye so troubled, or should I ask?"

"A wee, stubborn, sharp-tongued MacKay lass. Why is everything with her a battle?"

"It is all bluster, Andrew. She's afraid."

"God's teeth, what is she afraid of?"

"Da. Ye. Me. All of us."

"I know her first few hours here were bad, but since then she has been treated with care. No one is unkind to her. She has no reason to be afraid anymore."

"I know ye believe that and it seems perfectly logical. Ye and Da are always logical but because of that ye miss a few things."

"What have I missed? She has no reason to fear us. I have told her that over and over."

"She isn't afraid of being mistreated. Andrew, we are MacLeods, her clan's worst enemy, we won't let her return home and I suspect she fears that we never will. Not an ungrounded fear as ye are well aware. She is like a cornered animal, terrified, growling, and trying to appear formidable, yet all the while searching desperately for an escape. If ye think it's bad now, wait until she learns that we aren't letting her go home." Graham shook his head as if imagining the eventuality. "What do ye think Ena would do if the MacKay held her, even if he were kind to her?"

"Make his life a living hell," Andrew said dryly, but he couldn't keep from grinning.

Graham laughed. "That she would. Truthfully, I suspect she would be much worse than Anna and Mairi combined."

"Ye're probably right in that." Andrew sighed in frustration, "After Joan died, I never planned to wed again and now I am forced to marry a wee fire-spitting devil who hates me. I just wish we could end this feud some other way. She deserves a husband who can love her."

"She might *think* she hates ye now, but give her time; she has a gentle heart. Ye've seen her with Davy."

"True, Davy loves her. At least she'll have that, and Davy will have her."

"And why do ye think ye can't love her? Ye care for her already."

"Aye, I care for her. I owe her everything. Losing Davy would have...dear God, I can't even think about it. But Graham, I *loved* Joan with all my heart. Part of me died with her. I can't love anyone like that again. I don't even want to."

Graham's expression suddenly turned hard, "Ye're right, Andrew. Ye owe Anna everything and she deserves a husband who can love her. I don't care if ye *want* to or not. Try. Or, for the love of God, hide the fact that ye don't."

Andrew was both taken aback and angered by Graham's words. "Brother, ye have no idea what it feels like to love someone as I did and then to lose them. Pardon me if I don't take advice from ye on this subject. Please excuse me. I have to go fetch our unwilling guest for supper."

He turned and strode toward the tower stairs. How could he forget Joan and try to love the angry, scared, lass upstairs simply because she saved Davy? He would marry her if he had to in order to bring peace between their clans. He would care for her and protect her, but love her? He couldn't do that.

When he reached her door, he tried to quiet his anger before knocking. She was difficult enough to deal with when he was calm. Taking a deep breath, he knocked on the door and listened for a response. As he expected, there was none. He opened the door and saw her sitting sideways on the window seat, hugging her knees to her chest and staring out the window. "May I come in?"

"Well, there's a first, ye normally just walk in uninvited."

"Anna, may I come in?" he asked again, his frustration clearly reflected in his voice.

"Aye. I don't suppose I could stop ye anyway."

She stared at him warily from the window seat and he just watched her for a moment. God's breath, she really was a beautiful woman. Her hair shimmered in the firelight like a dark copper veil around her shoulders. The color had returned to her cheeks and her eyes were a lovely green and gold, even though they glittered with anger. "Why are ye so determined to stay angry with me?" he asked.

"Because ye are so determined to keep me here."

"Anna, I'm sorry ye're unhappy, but can I ask ye something?" She shrugged her shoulders and, taking it as assent, he went on. "Knowing everything ye know now, if ye could change what ye did that day and be safely tucked away at Naomh-dùn right now, would ye?"

She looked surprised for a moment, but immediately

answered, "And let Davy drown in the loch? Nay, of course not."

"Do ye believe what ye told him, that sometimes God makes sure people are in the right place to help when angels can't be?"

"Aye. I suppose I do."

"Then is it possible ye're still meant to be here?"

"Why would God punish me like that?" She said plaintively.

Andrew laughed, "Maybe he is punishing us?" She frowned, but he went on "Or maybe, he put ye here to learn the MacLeods are not the source of all evil, and for us to learn the same is true for the MacKays."

She looked away, but didn't say anything.

Andrew went on, "I've already told ye the MacLeods respect ye for what ye did for Davy."

"But that is the *only* reason. The fact is, I'm still a MacKay and ye hate the rest of us. Do ye know what it feels like to be surrounded by people who would as soon k—kill my family as look at them?" Her voice caught. In that instant he knew Graham had been right—at least about her being afraid and feeling cornered.

"Anna, what ye did allowed us to put our hatred of one MacKay aside and to see ye as the compassionate, courageous lass ye are. Don't ye think it's possible our attitude towards other MacKays might change as we learn more about ye?"

"I don't know. I suppose it's possible."

"Is it also possible yer attitude about us might change as ye get to know us too? How can that be a bad thing for either clan? That's why I want ye to take yer meals with us in the great hall."

She didn't answer immediately, but turned her head to look out the window into the darkness.

"Anna, will ye please join us for the evening meal?"

"I'd rather not."

"But will ye?"

Still not meeting his eyes, she asked, "If I say no, w-will ye carry me down over yer shoulder?"

"Nay, angel, if ye aren't willing to join us, I'll have yer meal sent up."

He saw her body relax and he thought he had lost, but after a moment she nodded, "I'll join ye."

He smiled broadly, offering her his hand. When she took it he said, "Anna MacKay, ye're a brave lass."

~ * ~

During the meal, Andrew paid closer attention to Anna than he ever had before. Aye, she was frightened. She remained tense and never made eye contact with anyone except David and Mairi. No wonder she had fought so hard to avoid dining in the great hall. She firmly believed she was surrounded by enemies.

When his father spoke to her near the end of the meal, it was in the unusually gentle voice he had used towards her in the past. Andrew realized it was the same voice he used when trying to calm a spooked horse. "Anna, I have some good news for ye."

Anna looked up. "Really?"

"We will be meeting yer brother at the strait in a week's time, on the feast of St. Joseph."

"So I am going home?" The hopefulness in her tone caused Andrew's heart to ache.

"Yer brother and I have some things to discuss.

"But, I'll be able to go home."

"I'm sure we will come to an agreement."

Anna smiled. It was something he had seen far too little of and it lit her face. "Thank ye, Laird."

"Anna's leaving?" asked David, his brow furrowed.

Anna turned to him, caressing his cheek "Not for a while yet. I'll be here another sennight."

"But ye'll come back for a visit?"

Anna looked as if she didn't know how to answer.

Andrew stepped in. "Davy, let's not worry about that now. Ye still have quite a lot of time to spend with yer angel."

David didn't look convinced but he answered, "All right, Da."

Chapter 7

The laird's news thrilled Anna. She was going home in a week. The strain that she had felt from her first moments at Curacridhe finally lifted. She spent as much time as possible with David. She loved him and she knew he would miss her. She avoided answering his questions about when she would return for a visit. She had no intention of ever returning. Still, she knew Davy wouldn't be able to understand that. Every time he raised the subject, she redirected his attention. After she was gone, she believed he would eventually stop asking.

Anna would miss Mairi as well, however it was much more difficult to divert Mairi's attention when she discussed her plans for Anna to return. Anna didn't want to hurt either of them, but once she was on MacKay land again, she would agree to marry whomever Eoin wished, as long as her betrothed agreed to live at Naomh-dùn.

The week flew by. The evening before the feast of St. Joseph, the skies turned leaden as clouds thickened and the wind began to whip. A storm was brewing. As darkness fell, Anna stood looking out the window of her chamber. She was worried. What if it was pouring rain in the morning? Would they take her to her brother anyway? The MacLeods were terribly over-protective and she feared they wouldn't. They might worry that she would catch a chill. She didn't think she could bear it if they didn't let her go home tomorrow.

There was a knock at her door and she called, "Enter," without turning to see who it was.

"I've come to escort ye downstairs for the evening meal," said Andrew.

She glanced over her shoulder at him. Her anxiety

must have shown in her expression.

Andrew frowned. "Anna, what has ye bothered?"

"Nothing."

He arched a brow at her and smiled. "Ye don't lie well—for a MacKay that is," he teased.

She gave him a small smile but turned to look out the window again.

His voice took on a more serious tone. "Anna, please tell me what's upsetting ye." He placed a hand on her shoulder and turned her to face him.

There was really no avoiding it and she would rather know the answer than continue to worry. She sighed. "The weather seems to be turning. It looks as if a heavy rain is coming."

"Aye it does. Why does that have ye concerned?"

"I was just wondering..." she hated how small and vulnerable her voice sounded. "I was just wondering whether, if it is still raining tomorrow...well, will ye still take me to my brother?"

"Anna, the arrangements are made. Nothing will keep Da from meeting with yer brother tomorrow."

She frowned. "Ye didn't answer my question. Yer Da can meet with my brother whether I am there or not."

"Don't worry, angel, everything will be fine."

"Stop it. I have sidestepped Davy and Mairi's questions about when I'm coming back all week. I can recognize when someone is avoiding an answer."

"Why have ye avoided that question? Would ye choose never to see them again?"

Anna stared at him in disbelief. "*I'm a MacKay*. The only reason I'm here is because ye've kept me prisoner. Nay, Andrew, once I cross that strait tomorrow I will never venture near MacLeod land again. Which brings me back to the question ye haven't answered, but I guess that in itself is telling. Ye won't take me with ye tomorrow if the weather's bad."

"Anna, be reasonable. Ye've been terribly ill. I think

this storm will pass by morning but ye're right, we will not risk yer health if it doesn't. Nevertheless, I swear to ye, everything will be resolved with yer brother tomorrow."

That was no consolation. She turned to stare out the window at the brewing storm for a moment.

Finally Andrew said, "Worrying about it will not change the weather, angel. Come and have yer evening meal. In the morning we'll decide what's to be done."

He was right. She nodded. "Aye, I won't worry about it now."

~ * ~

To Anna's dismay, a light rain was still falling at daybreak but it tapered off to a mist as the sun rose. When it had stopped altogether by terce, Anna gave in to her excitement. It wouldn't be long now.

Mairi and Davy knocked on her door before long. She called to them to come in. Anna's heart lurched a bit. Mairi looked as if she had been crying.

"Oh, Mairi, please be happy for me."

"But I don't want ye to go. I'll miss ye so much."

Davy said, "I keep telling her we'll see ye when ye visit us. Ye will visit us soon, right? Maybe ye can come at Easter."

"We'll see, pet."

Mairi sniffed. "I told Andrew I'd help ye get ready to go." She glanced around the room. "Have ye packed yer things?"

Anna smiled. "Mairi, I'm wearing the clothes I arrived in, and I have no other belongings."

"Ye have the clothes we made ye."

Anna didn't want to take anything with her from Curacridhe but she didn't want to hurt Mairi either. "Well, I was thinking maybe ye'd like to have them—as a way to remember me."

"But they're yers."

"Don't ye like them?" asked Anna, confident of the answer.

"Aye, they're lovely, but…"

"Then keep them.

Mairi smiled. "Thank ye Anna."

Andrew appeared at the door. "Anna, it's time to go."

Her heart leapt but she tried not to look too happy for fear of upsetting Mairi again.

Andrew took her hand, leading her downstairs with Mairi and Davy trailing in her wake. Cora joined them when they reached the great hall, walking with them to the bailey.

Anna expected to see Laird MacLeod and Graham prepared to go with them, but was a little shocked to see Father Ninian, as well as at least forty MacLeod warriors also mounted and ready to ride. A groom stood to one side holding the reins of Andrew's horse.

She frowned. "Where's my mount?"

"Ye'll ride with me."

"I am perfectly capable of riding alone."

"But ye'll ride with me anyway."

Anna didn't like this. She knew it would upset her brother if he saw her riding on Andrew MacLeod's lap. "I would really prefer to ride alone."

Andrew arched a brow at her. "Maybe ye'd prefer to stay here?"

"Andrew, I…please let me ride alone"

His voice grew stern. "I am not going to argue with ye about this. If ye intend on going to the strait, ye'll ride with me."

Just a few more hours, Anna, and ye will not have to submit to the will of the MacLeods. "Fine." She gave both Mairi and Davy a hug, said goodbye and let Andrew lift her onto his horse.

As she rode through the gates of Curacridhe Castle, she breathed a sigh of relief.

Anna remained silent and Andrew didn't push her to speak. The entire contingent of men was oddly quiet as they rode south.

After a little more than an hour, the meeting point

came into view, and there were an equally large number of mounted MacKay warriors, including all three of her brothers, gathered on the east side of the strait. Even from a distance she could tell Eoin was angry by his tense posture. She stiffened in response. More than ever she wished the MacLeods had let her ride alone. She was sure seeing her sitting in front of Andrew MacLeod with his arm around her did nothing to improve her brother's temperament.

When the MacLeod party neared the western bank of the strait, the bulk of them stayed well back, surrounding Andrew and Anna. Dougal, Graham and Donald rode closer to the shore. As the weather was warming, the ice on the straight had melted.

"I have nothing to say to ye, Dougal. I want to talk to Anna." Eoin called.

"Well, lad, that may be what ye want, but ye and I are going to chat first."

"What do we have to chat about, old man? Ye hold my sister prisoner and yet have made no demands. Until ye do, there is nothing to say."

"Nay, I haven't made any demands because *ye* have nothing I want."

"Then why are we here?"

"I thought I was doing ye a kindness, lad. I am allowing ye to see that yer sister is well and unharmed."

"I can see that one of yer sons has his filthy hands on her, so pardon me if I am not convinced she's unharmed. Let me speak with her," he demanded.

"Well as we are the ones who hold her, filthy hands or not, ye'd do well to mind yer tongue," Dougal snapped. "I'll let ye speak with her when I'm ready to."

This was the side of Laird MacLeod that Anna had first witnessed when Graham had dragged her half-frozen into the hall.

Eoin appeared to have a fragile hold on his temper. "What do ye want?"

"I want to keep yer sister."

Anna gasped and tried to twist out of Andrew's grip. "Ye lied to me."

Andrew held her firmly. "Wheesht angel," he whispered. "I never lied."

"Damn ye to hell, MacLeod. What's this about?" yelled Eoin.

"Calm yerself, lad," said Dougal, obviously pleased to see the effect he was having. "I understand that Anna is not betrothed to anyone."

"Not yet," he managed to grind out.

"Not yet, ye say. And do ye think arranging a betrothal now that she has lived with the 'thieving MacLeods' for a spell will be easy?"

"I'll manage," Eoin said, but the pain written on his face clearly revealed how his heart ached for her.

"Ye'll manage, will ye? Not if I don't give her back."

"Do ye want an all-out war, MacLeod? I'll give ye one if ye do."

"Nay lad, I don't want a war. In fact, I want this hostility to end for good. I want a betrothal between my eldest son Andrew and yer Anna."

Anna gasped again and spun around to look at Andrew, who only arched a brow at her and remained silent.

~ * ~

Eoin registered Anna's shocked expression. Tasgall and Aidan looked equally horrified.

The feud between the MacKays and the MacLeods was ancient; Eoin had learned to mistrust and hate them from the cradle. He would never have considered marrying his sister to one of them. "Not that Dougal. We can discuss a truce. I'll relinquish all claims to the disputed land, but I want my sister back."

"Eoin, ye can relinquish yer claim today and battle again tomorrow when I have no hold over ye." Dougal said more gently, "Ye know we need something stronger, more binding."

A fierce warrior, Eoin briefly considered signaling an

attack to take her back by force. He would have battled any MacLeod warrior with relish to protect his family and clan, but he could not fight his way out of this. Andrew MacLeod firmly held Anna on horseback and clearly visible strapped to his right leg was a dagger. If Eoin signaled an attack, Andrew could pull the dagger and slit her throat almost before the first sword was drawn. Dougal had cornered him.

"Let me pay a ransom then." Eoin knew he sounded desperate.

"I would never demand a copper from ye. Yer sister saved my grandson's life. She risked her own safety to pull him out of the loch after he fell through the ice and she became desperately ill as a result. I owe her more than I could ever pay. The only worthy gift I have to give is peace with ye, and the only way to bind that peace is with a marriage."

If this was true, surely Dougal wouldn't kill her. Again Eoin briefly considered attacking, however he didn't trust the MacLeods and wasn't willing to risk Anna's life. Finally he said, "Then give yer daughter to one of my brothers in marriage."

"Mairi's only fourteen. I will agree to a betrothal with one of yer brothers, but she's too young to leave home now. Furthermore, we both know that arranging a marriage for Anna after this will not be easy and that's my fault. I promise ye she will be cherished."

"Then let me speak with her."

"Nay, lad. It looks as if ye have at least half of yer garrison with ye. The temptation to take her and start a skirmish is too great. Ye will agree to the betrothals and sign the papers before ye speak to her, or we ride away—with Anna."

"My father asked me to consider her wishes in marriage. I must speak to her before I agree."

"I understand yer father's request. I would like to give Mairi the same gift, but I cannot. The good of my clan as well as yer own depends on this. I am not going to lie to ye,

Anna wants to come home and I did not discuss this with her. I have no doubt she's as angry as ye are right now. However, she is smart and compassionate and I suspect, if given enough time, she will see the wisdom in this."

Eoin didn't say anything. He ran one hand through his hair and stared at his sister. She did look furious. He hated being backed into a corner and yet, he knew it was the best solution. Sighing and shaking his head he said, "Fine. But I want a betrothal between Mairi and Tasgall and a solution to the border dispute."

"Agreed. Cross the straight and we'll sign the papers. Yer brothers and six other warriors can cross with ye." Dougal, Graham and Donald dismounted.

Shaking his head, Eoin motioned to his brothers and six of his guards and they urged their mounts into the straight, at its deepest the water reached well up to the horse's chests. They dismounted on the other side and Dougal approached, offering his hand. After a moment Eoin took it. "I don't like being cornered, MacLeod."

"No one does, lad.

"I swear to ye, if I learn that Anna is ever mistreated, nothing will keep me from killing ye."

"And I swear to ye I won't ever allow her to be mistreated. The MacLeods will die protecting her."

There were some minor changes that Eoin wanted made to the documents. Dougal agreed, calling Father Ninian forward to take care of them. Eoin asked, "Why did ye insist that I bring both of my brothers? I was fully expecting an ambush because of that."

"I know she doesn't believe it lad, but I am very fond of yer sister. I have no doubt she expected to go home today and as ye know, I can't allow that, but I wanted her to have the opportunity to see her family."

"I should thank ye for that at least," said Eoin grudgingly.

"We hold Anna in the highest regard. Although I know it's painful for her now, I'm doing this for her children and their children."

"I understand." Eoin frowned at him. "I'm not happy about the way it came about, but ye're right, these marriages will serve the best interests of both clans."

After they signed the betrothal agreements, Andrew dismounted and lifted Anna off the horse. She ran to her brother. "I'm sorry, Eoin."

"Anna," he said putting his arms around her, "I should be furious with ye."

"Ye aren't?"

"Nay, not really. If ye hadn't done what ye did, the child would have died. I wouldn't have wanted that. But ye know I can't fix this now, pet. Ye have to marry Andrew MacLeod."

"I know," she said sadly.

"Will it be that bad?" he asked, tipping her chin up to look into her eyes.

"Nay. He's better than Fearchar Morrison. At least I am close to home."

Eoin chuckled, "Sweetling, that's not saying much. It takes very little to be better than Fearchar. But I never would have sent ye to live on Lewis, even if it did mean ye'd be married to the laird's son. I was just angry with ye."

Aidan and Tasgall joined them, each hugging Anna.

"Are ye all right, pet?" asked Aidan.

"I'm sick of MacLeods telling me what to do, but I'm fine."

Aidan grinned. "Now, in fairness, Anna, ye wandered into this mess because ye were sick of Eoin telling ye what to do."

"Don't remind me."

Tasgall said, "Please tell me I won't regret this betrothal."

She smiled for the first time since they arrived. "Nay Tasgall, ye won't regret it. Mairi is lovely and sweet. She'll be a good wife when she's a little older, although like me, she manages to annoy her oldest brother no end."

"Then I like her already," Tasgall said and shot a glare at Andrew, who stood well away from them.

"Anna, the wedding will be in a little over five weeks at Curacridhe, on the Feast of St. Mark," Eoin said. "We'll see ye then, pet. I never actually imagined attending anything there except a siege, but so be it."

"Can't I go home with ye until then?" asked Anna. "The papers are signed, please Eoin, I want to go home."

"Nay, pet. I agreed that ye would stay at Curacridhe until the wedding, or I should say Dougal demanded it. I had very little choice."

Tears filled her eyes, "Eoin please…"

He hated seeing his sister like this and looked at Dougal who stood nearby. "Laird MacLeod, I give ye my word we will bring her back. She has been away from home for so long."

But the old laird shook his head. "Nay, lad. This is too important to take the risk. It has to be this way."

Anna turned on Laird MacLeod angrily. "Why are ye doing this to me? Ye have what ye want. After all of this, w-why can't ye l-let me go h-home?" Her voice caught. Clearly she was fighting desperately not to cry. She turned back to Eoin. "Please Eoin. Please, I want to come home, p-please," she sobbed, losing her battle against tears.

He wrapped his arms around her. "Wheesht, Anna. That's enough." Eoin had never felt so helpless in his life. He tried one last time with Laird MacLeod. "Let her come home. One of my brothers will go with ye in her stead. I swear I will honor the contract."

"Ye will honor the contract as it stands. She'll come back with us."

"Then let Tasgall go with her, so she's not alone."

"The absolute last thing I need is two MacKay's trying to escape. One of them could get hurt and we'd be right back where we started. Nay, she'll come alone and she'll come now."

She gripped Eoin tighter but there was nothing he

could do. "Ye need to go now, sweetling."

"But Eoin—"

"Nay, Anna, go back with the MacLeods. We'll see ye in a few weeks and we'll discuss a visit to Naomh-dùn after ye're married." He brushed her tears away and kissed her head. Andrew stepped forward and took her elbow to lead her away. She yanked her arm away from him and strode angrily toward his horse. He shook his head and followed.

"I almost feel sorry for him," said Eoin quietly to his brothers. At their affronted expressions added, "Nay, ye're right, I don't."

Chapter 8

Andrew lifted the very angry little MacKay onto his horse, mounted behind her, and the contingent of MacLeods headed back to Curacridhe. She sat forward, stiffly holding herself away from him, riding in sullen silence.

Finally she spoke. "Ye knew this was coming." It was an accusation, not a question.

"Aye, I did."

"And ye didn't have the decency to tell me."

"There's no need for ye to play the affronted maid with me. Ye think I don't know ye've plotted escape since the moment ye could lift yer head off the pillow? It only got worse after we found out who ye were."

"I couldn't escape. I could barely take a breath without a MacLeod knowing it."

"And why do ye think that was?"

She glared over her shoulder but said nothing.

"If ye'd had an inkling of what Da planned, angel, I have no doubt ye would have sprouted the wings Davy thought ye had and flown away."

"If the situation were reversed, wouldn't ye have expected Mairi to do the same thing?"

"Mairi would never have wandered off pouting in the first place, although I'm thankful *ye* did."

"Well it might be worth going back just to see if that's true when ye tell her she has to marry my brother."

"Is that such a terrible fate, Anna?"

In a milder tone she said, "Nay, Tasgall is a good man. She's lucky to have him."

"She might say the same about me."

"I doubt it."

He chuckled. "Ye're right, she probably wouldn't. But I *am* a good man and I will care for ye in spite of what my wee sister thinks about me."

Still upset Anna faced front again and remained silent for a time before asking crossly, "Why did he have to do this?"

"My father?"

"Aye, if ye were all so grateful to me for saving Davy, why couldn't he just let me go home?"

"Did ye listen to what he told Eoin?"

"About Eoin not being able to arrange a betrothal for me, thanks to the MacLeods? Aye I did. But I don't care."

"Not just that, angel. About seeking a lasting peace between our clans."

"After years of feuding, why does it matter now?"

"When Da first discussed this with me, he said peace between our clans was the greatest gift he could give Davy's angel. What would happen if we allowed the feud to continue?"

"Nothing. We would go on as we always have and I'd be on my way home."

"That's right. Nothing would change and maybe when ye have a grown son he would face Davy in battle and be killed." He heard her breath catch. "Da didn't think that was the best way to repay ye."

"Then just end the feud. Why must we marry to do that?"

"I asked him the same thing and, if ye remember, so did Eoin. This feud was too old and too ingrained to end it with a handshake. Only a powerful bond between our clans would ensure a lasting peace. That's why Da offered Mairi's hand too."

She frowned, but didn't say anything.

"Do ye hate me so much then? Is marrying me such a terrible fate?"

She didn't answer.

"Ye know, I had no choice in this either."

She cast a disbelieving look over her shoulder.

"Truly, Anna. I had absolutely no intention of ever marrying again. I loved Davy's mother. The idea of spending the rest of my life with a wife who hates me isn't exactly appealing."

"I don't hate ye." She paused for a moment. "Nay that's a lie, I do hate ye, but I don't expect I'll hate ye forever."

Andrew smiled to himself. "Well that's something."

They rode in silence for a while before he said, "There's at least one person who will be positively thrilled by this news."

"Who?"

"Anna, when ye marry me, ye'll be Davy's mother. I can think of nothing that would make him happier. He loves ye."

"I love him too."

"So, even if ye hate me at the moment, we come as a pair. Ye are getting him in the bargain."

~ * ~

Anna's anger hadn't subsided by the time they returned to the keep. She understood why Laird MacLeod forced the betrothals. But she didn't like it, and was sorely disappointed. As soon as she stepped into the great hall, David yelled, "Anna, you've come back!" and hurtled himself into her arms.

"Aye, Davy, I have."

Mairi too was in the great hall and rushed over with slightly more decorum than her young nephew. "Oh Anna, what happened? I thought ye were going home."

"She is home, Mairi," Dougal said.

Anna felt a lump form in her throat. At this moment she hated Dougal MacLeod with everything in her, but she did not want to cry in front of them again.

"What do ye mean, Da? Did yer brother not want ye back, Anna? Are ye staying with us after all? Are ye very sad?"

"Mairi, hold yer tongue. Of course her brother wanted her back, that has nothing to do with it," snapped Andrew.

"Andrew, she means well," chided Laird MacLeod. "Mairi, I wanted an end to the feud, so Laird MacKay and I came to an agreement: Anna and Andrew are betrothed."

"What? Ye're going to be my sister? That's wonderful! It is a shame ye have to marry Andrew, but I'm so happy. I really didn't want ye to leave." Mairi threw her arms around Anna.

As upset as Anna was, it was all she could do to keep from pushing Mairi away.

"Well Mairi, it's good to hear ye're happy to be Anna's sister, because Da has another bit of news that's sure to please ye," said Andrew.

"Andrew, enough," said Laird MacLeod.

"What's he talking about, Da?"

"Mairi, Laird MacKay wasn't particularly happy about Anna marrying Andrew and he wanted something in return, so I agreed to another betrothal."

"For Graham? I thought he was already betrothed. Anna, ye didn't tell me ye had a sister."

"I am betrothed," said Graham.

"And she doesn't have a sister," said Andrew.

Realization dawned and Mairi went pale. "The betrothal is for me? To a MacKay? Ye are marrying me to a *MacKay*?"

"I'm a MacKay, Mairi," Anna said quietly.

"Aye, but ye're all right. I know ye and ye saved Davy. Da, don't make me marry a MacKay!"

Still terribly angry herself, Anna had trouble keeping the irritation out of her voice. "Mairi, my brother Tasgall is good, kind man. I love him very much and I know ye will like him if ye give him a chance."

"But he's a MacKay," she moaned. "Da, how could ye?" She looked at David and said, "This is all yer fault, Davy! And yers, Andrew! If ye hadn't brought her here in the first place none of this would have happened."

"Actually, Mairi, I was the one who brought her here, and if I hadn't she would have died. Ye wouldn't have wanted that," said Graham rationally.

"Aye, I would if it meant I didn't have to marry a MacKay!" she cried, turning and running from the hall.

"That went well," said Andrew. "Da, I think it would be prudent to put a guard on Mairi, lest she decides to bolt."

His father frowned at him. "Andrew, why do ye goad yer sister? Ye didn't make this any easier. She's upset now, but she'll soon see the wisdom of it just as Anna has. Anna, dove, I am sorry for her rudeness. She didn't mean it. She'll come 'round soon."

Anna couldn't hold her temper in check. *She'll see the wisdom of it just as I have*? I'm not sure I've seen the wisdom of it yet. I don't want to be here. Ye let me think I was going home and I—" the words *hate ye*, were on the tip of her tongue but she realized David had been standing silently with his arms around her. She couldn't release the venom she longed to. She stood there trembling.

David tugged on her dress. "If ye marry Da that makes ye Mairi's sister?"

She nodded, stroking his head absently. "Aye, Davy."

"And Uncle Graham's sister?"

"Aye, son, when Anna marries me she will be a sister to Mairi and Uncle Graham and Aunt Ena also," answered Andrew.

"Will she be my sister too?" he asked hopefully.

Andrew knelt on one knee beside him and said, "Nay, Davy." He smiled at his son's crestfallen expression. "When I marry Anna, she'll be yer mama."

"My mama?" His face burst into a grin and he hugged her even tighter. "That's much better than a sister. My angel is going to be my mama! I have to go tell Cora, she keeps saying I need a mama and now I am going to get one!" He let go of Anna and ran from the hall.

Anna pressed two fingers to the bridge of her nose. She had to regain control.

Andrew stood and said, "I told ye he would be happy."

Dougal looked at her seriously. "Do ye really not understand this, Anna?"

"I understand it perfectly. I might have even 'come round' myself if ye had let me go home. And ye're all three fools if ye think Mairi will *come round* easily." It was hard to be a woman and to have very little control over one's life. She had learned that lesson all too often over the last few weeks. Mairi was young and sheltered and as much as she complained about Andrew, Anna knew Mairi believed her father and her brothers loved her. In spite of that, Anna suspected, at the moment Mairi felt betrayed. Anna felt the same way herself.

"I'm sorry ye're so upset, and I wish I could have let ye go home, but as I told yer brother, this is too important. When the wedding is over, ye and Andrew can go for a visit. It won't be long."

Anna clenched her teeth. She didn't want to go for a *visit,* she didn't want Andrew to go with her, and she certainly didn't want a wedding, but she had no choice. This was real. She wasn't going to wake up to learn it had all been just a nightmare. She was at Curacridhe, amongst the MacLeods, whom she had been taught to fear and hate since childhood, and she was going to marry the Laird's heir. Anna suddenly felt very tired.

Her consternation must have shown on her face because Dougal asked, "Anna, ye said ye understand why this wedding is necessary. Ye have accepted it, haven't ye?"

She looked down but didn't answer.

"Anna?" He gave her a questioning look.

"Aye," she said in little more than a whisper. "I've accepted it." She sighed. "I'm tired, I need to rest. I guess I haven't completely recovered my stamina. Please excuse me."

"Of course ye must go rest, little dove."

"I'll walk with ye, Anna," said Andrew, taking her

elbow as she walked to the tower stairs.

Anna wanted to escape and be alone but she didn't pull away. She didn't have the energy to fight. He didn't say anything to her while they climbed the stairs. When they reached her chamber he stopped outside. "I'm sorry it's been such a hard day for ye. But, Anna, ye didn't lie to my father did ye? Ye have accepted this?"

"Are ye trying to decide whether I need a guard?"

"Do ye?"

She glared at him. "Nay, Andrew. I didn't lie, I have accepted the betrothal, and whether any of ye believe it or not Eoin is honorable and absolutely true to his word. If I did manage to get away, ye can be certain he would bring me back for the wedding." She was unable to keep the sadness out of her voice.

Taking her hands he said, "Angel, I promise I'll try to make ye happy." His grim expression didn't quite match his vow.

"That's probably not a promise ye should make. Excuse me, Andrew." She entered her room and closed the chamber door. She had never felt so alone in her life. She sat on the window seat, pulled her knees to her chest and gave in to the tears that had threatened all afternoon.

~ * ~

Andrew stood for a moment outside her door. He heard her heart-wrenching sobs. He probably should just walk away; she clearly wanted to be alone, but he simply couldn't. He opened the door. There she was, on the window seat, weeping uncontrollably.

"Oh, Anna, please don't cry," he crossed the room and rested a hand on her back. "Ye'll make yerself ill."

"Just l-leave me alone. S-stop pretending ye care about me."

"But I do care about ye."

"Do ye? If ye gave a f-fig about me, ye wouldn't have let him do this." She raised her head from her knees and looked into his eyes. "I h-hate him."

"Nay, ye don't. Ye have too big a heart to hate anyone. And I know ye understand why peace between the clans is necessary."

She put her head on her knees, giving over to sobs again. "I thought I was going h-home."

"I know ye did, angel, and I'm sorry ye're so very disappointed." Her tears tore at his heart. He knew his father's decisions were sound, but it seemed the only person who kept being repeatedly hurt was the one who most deserved their kindness. Wanting to comfort her, he lifted her into his arms. She didn't fight him, on the contrary, she buried her face in his léine and wept. He sat down, continuing to hold her. "Wheesht, now." He kissed the top of her head. "Wheesht, angel."

When her tears were spent, she rested her cheek on his chest, accepting the comfort he offered. "I wanted to go home," she whispered.

He stroked her hair. "Maybe ye can try to start thinking of Curacridhe as home."

"But it *isn't* my home. Home is Naomh-dùn with the people I love and who love me."

"Ye're loved at Curacridhe too, ye know. Although ye've tried valiantly not to accept it."

Her brow furrowed. "What do ye mean?"

"Angel, ye're the one who has been holding yerself apart. Everyone here wants to embrace ye."

"Only because I saved Davy, not because of who I am. Yer da threw me in the dungeon because of who I am."

"Nay, ye've got it backwards. Da threw ye in the dungeon because of yer name. Ye saved Davy because of who ye are. There's a huge difference. We love ye because of who ye are, in spite of yer name. And probably more importantly, the MacLeods are learning that the MacKays are not the devil's spawn *because* of who ye are."

Her lips twitched into a half smile. "There is at least one person who believes we're the devil's spawn."

"Mairi will get over it."

"Why are ye so sure?"

"Because, I am holding a wee angel in my arms who will press her relentlessly until she does."

"Ye think I'm going to fix this?" she asked, her tone incredulous.

He chuckled. "I know ye're going to. It's part of who ye are. Ye love Tasgall, ye love Mairi and ye won't rest until they love each other."

She sighed but didn't argue the point. Who was going to fix the mess she was in?

"Are ye feeling better now?" he asked.

Was she? "I still want to go home, but aye, crying about it won't change anything."

"Anna, please don't do this again."

"Cry? I know I can't make that promise."

"That's not what I mean. Ye were upset and ye shut me out. I don't ever want to find ye curled up sobbing yer heart out again. I'm going to be yer husband, the least ye can let me do is comfort ye when ye weep and dry yer tears."

"If that's the least I let ye do, this will be a terrible marriage."

Andrew laughed. "Well, it's a place to start."

~ * ~

When he finally lay down in his bed that night, Andrew was more tired than he ever remembered being after a hard day of training. He hadn't done anything physically exerting but the stress of the day had taken its toll. The ride to the strait and back with Anna on his lap had been excruciating. Not that he minded Anna on his lap, but sensing her nervous excitement on the way to the meeting caused his heart to ache. He had expected her disappointment to be profound and it certainly was.

In fairness, it took her less time to accept it than it had him. From the moment his father first mentioned the plan for their betrothal Andrew had not stopped thinking about it. Initially he was every bit as angry as Anna and then Mairi had been. He didn't like being forced into anything but he truly did not want to be married again. He had loved Joan and losing her hurt so damn much he never wanted to feel that again. Even now, four years later, anything that reminded him of Joan renewed the pain and he avoided it.

After his initial anger cooled, he had decided he was taking the betrothal issue much too seriously. His father's decision didn't mean Andrew had to let the little copper-haired angel into his heart. He would do his duty, she would do hers, they could live together congenially—it was the way of things. He could still protect his heart. He had to admit it was certainly a boon that she was lovely. The fact that his son adored her and she loved him too was quite frankly both a blessing and a relief. David needed a loving mother. Andrew was certain Anna could be that for him.

But today as he held her in his arms while she experienced the full emotional spectrum, he realized he was in real danger. He felt the pain of her disappointment, sharp and deep. Going forward, he had to do a better job of protecting his heart.

Having made that decision, he tried to relax into sleep. Just as he began to doze off, he was jarred awake by a knock at his door. Alert and on his feet in a flash, he wrapped a plaid around his waist and opened the door to find Rory.

"Andrew, I'm sorry to bother ye, but ye were right, Mairi is trying to run away."

"God's breath, I may strangle her." Beyond irritated, Andrew grabbed his clothes and dressed.

"We did as ye asked, just watching and following her, but Andrew, Anna has gone too."

"What? Damn, she said she had accepted this."

"I don't think she's running away, I think she's following Mairi."

"Where did they go?"

"Into the stable. I left Cormag and Finlay to watch for them. The men have orders not to let them leave the walls."

"Let's go."

When they reached the courtyard, Cormag and Finlay

stood watching the stables.

"Are they still in there?" Andrew asked.

"Aye, Mairi's in a fine fettle. I would have tried talking to her myself, but Anna MacKay was on her heels," answered Cormag.

"Thank ye, Cormag. Ye've always had more patience with my wee sister than I have."

"That's because I've been around her more."

"Well, if ye hear screaming, come fast. I may need ye to keep me from killing her."

Cormag chuckled. "Andrew, go a bit easy. This has been a hard day for Mairi."

"It has been for all of us, but, aye, I won't kill her. Not tonight anyway. The men chuckled as he slipped quietly into the stable. He heard Mairi talking so he remained still, just listening.

"But ye don't understand, Anna," sobbed Mairi. "It's not the same for ye."

"Now how did ye arrive at that, Mairi?"

"Ye know us now. We're nice people. Ye have nothing to fear from the MacLeods."

"Do ye think the MacKays are different?"

"Of course they're different," sniffed Mairi, "they're MacKays."

"But, Mairi, I'm a MacKay. The MacKays are nice people too."

"They can't be. They're MacKays," she wailed.

"We're getting nowhere with this, pet. Let's go inside and we can talk."

"Nay, I'm leaving. I won't let Da force me to marry a complete stranger, *a MacKay*." By the tone Mairi used, one would think she was naming the foulest vermin on earth.

To her credit, it sounded as if Anna took no offense, saying gently, "Mairi, sweetling, ye can't run away from this any more than I can. Besides, ye aren't marrying a complete stranger. He's my brother, I love him and I know ye will too once ye get to know him."

"But the wedding is in five weeks," she cried.

"Mairi, *my* wedding is in five weeks, but ye won't be getting married for several years at least."

Mairi sniffed, "What? I thought…"

"Nay, pet. Is that what ye've been so upset about? Ye'll have plenty of time to grow up a bit and to get to know Tasgall first."

"Ye're sure?"

"Aye, I'm positive. I'm the one who is practically marrying a stranger."

"Nay, ye're marrying Andrew."

"Sweetling, less than a month ago, the MacLeods were *my* mortal enemy. I thought ye all were monsters and then yer Da proved it by throwing me in yer dungeon."

"But that was a mistake, Anna."

"I know it was, but can ye see how I might not be terribly happy about being forced to marry a MacLeod in five weeks?"

"Well ye should be happy. Anna, ye're marrying *Andrew* and he'll be the laird someday. Ye'll be Lady MacLeod. Ye know he's a good man. Even if he is bossy and doesn't like me very much, I know he loves me and I love him most of the time."

"Mairi, this conversation is hopeless." Anna laughed. "Let's go back inside the keep. I'm cold."

"Oh, Anna, Da will kill me if ye get sick again. Aye, ye must go inside now."

Andrew smiled, made some noise near the front of the stable and yelled, "Mairi MacLeod, are ye in here?"

"Aye, Andrew, what business is it of yers? I am allowed to be in the stable," said Mairi petulantly.

"This is the brother ye love most of the time, remember?" whispered Anna loudly, her voice filled with amusement.

"Mairi, ye're allowed in the stables during the day. God's teeth, lass, even horses have to sleep," said Andrew as he walked towards them. "And ye dragged Anna out here too? Ye should know better. The night air is damp and cold and Anna has been ill." He threw his plaid around Anna's shoulders. "Come now, back to the keep with both of ye."

"Oh all right," said Mairi and, pouting, she pushed past him and out of the stable.

"Let's get ye back inside too," he said to Anna.

"How much of that did ye hear?" Anna asked.

"How do ye know I heard anything?"

"Because I suspect when Rory woke ye, ye were planning to do more than just scold Mairi for keeping the horses awake."

He chuckled, "Ye knew she was being watched?"

"Andrew, ye've had me watched for weeks now and ye'd have to be a fool not to guess she'd do this. However, just in case, I was listening for her to sneak away too. So what did ye hear?"

"I heard my illogical little sister tell ye why it is so much worse for her to have to marry a MacKay in a few years than it is for ye to marry me in five weeks."

"Well of course it is because ye're Andrew MacLeod and, even though ye're bossy, she loves ye most of the time."

He chuckled and said, "I also heard ye say ye were cold, but she was wrong about one thing, Da won't kill her if ye take a chill, because I'll do it first."

Anna laughed and he put his arm around her as they walked to the keep.

When they reached her chamber Andrew said, "Good night, angel. And if by chance Mairi changes her mind and tries to sneak away again tonight, leave her to me this time. It's cold out and ye need yer rest."

"I don't think she'll leave again—not tonight anyway. Tomorrow I intend to ask her to stand with me for the wedding and make her promise not to leave before then."

"Will we have to put her under lock and key after the wedding?"

"Of course not."

"Why are ye so sure?"

"Because by then she will have met Tasgall and she'll love him."

"And how do ye know that?" he asked teasingly.

"Because he is Tasgall MacKay, he isn't nearly as bossy as ye are, and *I* love him *most of the time*," she said with a grin.

Chapter 9

Anna was home. She was at Naomh-dùn with Grizel, her old nursemaid.

"I can scarcely believe I'm here. I thought Laird MacLeod said I couldn't leave. I've missed ye Grizel. I've missed everyone at Naomh-dùn."

"Oh, my lovely child, I love ye so and I've missed ye too. Ye've grown into a fine woman. I know what ye did to save that wee lad. I'm very proud of ye."

"I'm glad I was there. Davy is a sweet child. But Grizel, Laird MacLeod wanted me to marry Andrew. I don't want to do that. I don't want to live at Curacridhe. Maybe Eoin won't make me go back; maybe I can stay at home forever, especially since ye're here again."

"Lass, this isn't yer home anymore, just as it isn't mine."

"Of course it's my home."

"Nay, pet it isn't. Ye have another home and ye have work to do. Ye have to pass it on."

"I'll do whatever is needed, if I can just stay here to do it."

Grizel chuckled. "The work isn't here. I gave it to ye, sweetling, but ye can't keep it. Ye have to pass it on."

"I don't understand, Grizel. I have nothing of yers, nothing to give."

"Oh, but ye do. I gave ye love. I poured all the love I had into ye and yer brothers. But ye were never intended to keep it. Ye have to pass it on."

"Why can't I do that at Naomh-dùn?"

"Because that isn't where it's needed."

"Please don't ask me to do this."

"Anna, if Davy were alone and falling through the ice again, what would ye do?"

"The same thing I did before."

"Well sweetling, ye're needed just as much now. And ye're the only one who can help. I was with ye when ye needed me—now someone needs ye. Don't let me down, lass."

"But, I can't—"

"Of course ye can. Remember, ye can do all things in Him who strengthens ye."

"But, Grizel—"

"Give me a hug now, sweetling, it's time to go."

Grizel wrapped her arms around Anna in the kind of hug only Grizel could give, all warmth and love and comfort.

Anna held onto her. "Don't leave me yet, Grizel, I don't understand. Please don't leave me yet."

"I have to go back home and so do ye. It's the rules, but ye'll be fine Anna. Just remember to pass it on, child."

~ * ~

Anna woke just as dawn was pinking the sky. It had been a dream unlike any she had ever had before. She could almost feel Grizel's arms around her still. Anna felt the keen pain of loss, but oh how wonderful to have seen Grizel again and know her love, even if it was only a dream.

In her dream, Grizel had said *ye have another home.* Yesterday Andrew had asked her if she could start thinking of Curacridhe as home. From her first moments here she had had one single goal—to go home. Was she home?

Aye. The decisions had been made and the betrothals signed. Her fate was sealed. No matter how she might wish otherwise, this was now her home. Andrew had also said *Angel, ye are the one who has been holding yerself apart.* This was true. Anna had only allowed herself to think of them as hated MacLeods, not people. On the night Laird MacLeod had discovered who she was, she had chided Colin for thinking the MacKays were terrible enough to allow a child to drown. *We are just people, just like the MacLeods.*

We laugh, and we cry, and we show compassion, and we make mistakes! And yet, she herself was willing to believe the worst from the MacLeods and let fear rule her actions.

She needed to listen to her own admonition. Like it or not she was marrying Andrew MacLeod. Someday she would be Lady MacLeod. Fighting against it, or curling up and giving into tears over it was not going to change things. She was nineteen, a woman by all standards, but even though she hated to admit it to herself, she had been behaving like a child.

She also remembered Davy's horrified expression on the night when she and Andrew had fought during the evening meal. *Anna, don't ye like us?*

Last evening Andrew had promised to try to make her happy, but that wasn't in his power. The choice to be happy or not was Anna's. If she didn't try to make things work with Andrew, accept the MacLeods as her clan, and at least try to make Curacridhe her home, no one would be happy. She vowed to spend the weeks before the wedding trying to do just that.

I can do all things in Him who strengthens me. This is what it meant: with faith she could handle the circumstances in which she found herself.

So, with new resolve, she got up, dressed and did something she had never done at Curacridhe. She went down to the great hall alone for breakfast. She hesitated in the arched doorway of the stairwell. There were a good few people there but not nearly as many as at an evening meal. The only person she recognized was Laird MacLeod who sat across the room at the refectory table.

She hesitated a moment, glancing around at the people seated at the trestle tables. She didn't see the mistrust or hatred she had feared. Those who looked at her gave her warm smiles and wished her good morning. She smiled back, took a deep breath and walked across the hall to where Laird MacLeod sat.

His smile was broad and welcoming. "Good morning,

Anna. Come sit with me and break yer fast."

She swallowed hard. "Aye, Laird, thank ye."

"Did ye sleep well?"

"Aye, and ye?"

"Well enough that I didn't hear about Mairi's little escapade until this morning. I'm sorry about that."

Anna smiled. "It was rather a lot for her to take in."

"No more that it was for ye."

Anna flashed him a grin. "But I've had weeks to become accustomed to living amongst the devil's own."

Laird MacLeod laughed heartily. "Anna MacKay, I didn't know ye were such a cheeky lass, but I quite like that about ye."

Anna blushed. "I suspect I'll have to remind ye of that someday."

Laird MacLeod only laughed harder, "No doubt, little dove, no doubt."

Looking to change the subject, Anna said, "Mairi mentioned ye have another daughter. Where does she live?"

"Ena is my oldest and she's married to the Chisholm heir, Fearghas."

Just then Andrew entered the hall. The concerned look he wore faded when he saw Anna. "Good morning, Anna."

Graham came rushing in behind him, "Do ye think— oh there ye are, Anna."

Anna smiled to herself. Clearly they thought she had gone missing.

"Good morning, lads. I was just telling Anna about yer sister Ena, and it occurs to me, since I've announced the betrothals to the clan, I should send word to her. Perhaps she'll plan to arrive a few days early to help with the wedding…and Mairi."

Andrew frowned. "Da, do ye really think we should expect her to help? She has her hands a bit full."

Graham snorted. "Andrew, ye know that nothing will keep her away when she hears this news. Ye'll like our older sister, Anna. She can teach ye how to handle a husband," said Graham, at which Dougal laughed heartily.

"What do ye mean?" asked Anna.

"Fearghas Chisholm is as big and frightening a Highland warrior as ever drew breath, and he is besotted with our sister Ena. He would deny her nothing."

"They have three daughters, the poor man. Two is more than I can handle. But it's decided. I'll send for Ena, she'll be a great help and ye're right, Graham, she's likely to arrive weeks before the wedding, whether I send for her or not."

As Anna listened to them discuss planning the wedding, it occurred to her the task of running this keep would rightly fall to her even now, but she wasn't sure what Laird MacLeod expected. But there was no better time to find out.

"Laird MacLeod…I was wondering…well, I do know how to run a keep. I've helped Fiona—Eoin's wife—manage Naomh-dùn for several years now."

"Ye needn't worry about that, Anna. Brenda has taken care of things here for years," Dougal said.

"But I—"

"Anna, there are plenty of people assigned to tend Curacridhe. Ye don't need to work," said Graham. "Besides, just yesterday ye said ye hadn't completely recovered yer stamina."

Anna couldn't spend her days doing nothing—she would go mad. "Nay, ye misunderstand. I'll be Lady MacLeod soon enough and I need to learn how things are done here."

Andrew shook his head. "As Lady MacLeod, ye'll be Davy's mother and the best thing ye can do, what I need most, is for ye to care for him so I don't have to…worry."

Anna frowned. "I thought Cora has been seeing to Davy."

"She has been, but she is elderly and looking after a wee lad is a challenge. She only agreed to do it until someone more suitable could be found, but that has been difficult over the last few years. The truth is, if someone had been minding him properly the day he fell through the ice, neither of us would be facing a wedding we don't want."

She smiled, trying to hide the sting from that comment. It was true, but hearing him say that he didn't want her still hurt. "Aye, well then, I'll mind Davy. I'll just go find him now."

"But ye haven't had yer morning meal yet, lass," said Laird MacLeod.

"Davy will need to break his fast as well. I'll eat with him."

As Anna went to find David, she tried to brush away Andrew's comment. She knew he hadn't wanted to marry her any more than she had wanted to marry him. Just because she had decided to do her best to be happy with him didn't mean that he had made the same choice.

That the MacLeods didn't intend for her to actually do the things for which the lady of the castle would normally be responsible bothered her a bit more. It seemed despite Andrew's declarations about how the MacLeods loved her because of who she was, and that Curacridhe was her home now, he and his father didn't trust a MacKay with the running of her new home. She suspected that as much as they said she belonged here and the clan was prepared to respect her, she would always feel like an outsider if she was destined to be Lady MacLeod in name only.

Still maybe her whole purpose for being here was to be a mother for Davy anyway. Perhaps that's what the dream meant.

~ * ~

Mairi woke that morning feeling no happier about the betrothal. It simply wasn't fair, and no one seemed to recognize that. Not even Anna. Anna couldn't see how different it was for her to be betrothed to Andrew while Mairi had to marry *Tasgall MacKay*. Her father only wanted to end the feud and her brothers certainly didn't understand or even care about her feelings.

Oh she believed her brothers loved her—they had to, they were her brothers. But she didn't feel particularly close to either of them. While they had come home occasionally over the years, they were away training during most of her childhood. Andrew had already begun training with the Macraes before Mairi was born and Graham went to train with Laird Gunn when she was just a bairn of two. When Andrew came home seven years ago, he was a grown man with a wife and, soon thereafter, a son of his own. He took little notice of his young half-sister other than when she annoyed him. Graham had only been home two years. He wasn't as bossy as Andrew, but he too was a stranger to her.

Mairi felt closest to the lads who had come to live and train at Curacridhe. She had essentially grown up with many of them. Some had lived here as long as she could remember. Cormag MacKenzie came to train with the MacLeods when he was twelve, the year Mairi had been born. He had always treated her like a sister—a sister he was fond of, not impatient and bossy with, like Andrew. Mairi had been thrilled when Cormag fell in love with a MacLeod lass, married her and stayed on.

Boyd Sutherland came to train when he was ten and Mairi was seven. He was a serious lad with dark hair and eyes. He taught her to play chess but would never let her win, like some of the other lads. She would pout and beg, but he refused. When she finally won her first game against him, she was overjoyed. He had given her a rare smile. "Ye see, Mairi, how much sweeter victory is when ye it comes solely from yer own skill?"

She still played chess with him regularly and he nearly always trounced her, but when she won, it thrilled her like nothing else. And she was always rewarded with his warm smile.

Perhaps her best friend, the person to whom she felt closest to, was Darach Morrison. Mairi had been a lass of four when Darach came to begin training at the tender age of seven. That was the year Mairi's mother had taken ill. Near the end, there were many days when Mama was so very sick, Isla and the other women who cared for her wouldn't let Mairi see her. "Yer Mama loves ye pet, but she's sleeping and needs her rest to get better."

Mairi remembered one maid or another would be set the task of minding her, but there were times when she wanted her mama so badly she would cry for what seemed like hours. The only one who could console her, who could find ways to distract and entertain her, was Darach, her father's young page.

When Mairi's mother died, Andrew was too far away to come home for the funeral. Graham was there, but Mairi barely knew him. It was Cormag and Darach who held her hand and dried her tears that day and the many days that followed.

She needed to find Darach today and talk to him. He would understand.

~*~

"That was surprising news last night, Mairi. I knew ye had to be upset by it. I'm so very sorry."

Aye, Darach understood. Mairi shook her head. "They all think I should just smile and accept this. But how can I? He's a *MacKay*."

"I know. I don't understand how yer da could do this to ye. Surely Andrew marrying Anna is enough to end the feud if it's so important to him."

"I want to run away. I would have last night, but Andrew had set a guard on me. *Me!* I'm his own sister and he treats me like a prisoner. Why doesn't he just chain me in my room and be done with it."

"Mairi, now ye're being ridiculous, and in fairness, ye *did* try to run away. I know ye're upset, but that was foolhardy. Where would ye have gone? Who would have protected ye? Nay, ye can't do that again."

"I couldn't even if I wanted to, because I'm being watched like a criminal."

Darach laughed. "Don't be so dramatic. Yer brother is concerned for yer safety, and I am as well. Ye can't go running off in the middle of the night."

"Surely ye don't think I should marry Tasgall MacKay."

"It doesn't matter what I think, but even so, ye have plenty of time to figure out a way around it. Yer da said yer wedding wouldn't be for three years or so."

"So what are ye suggesting?"

"Accept things for now. Bide yer time. Anything can happen in three years. Maybe yer da will change his mind, or you'll decide ye like Tasgall." He laughed at her affronted look. "Don't look so shocked. It could happen, but even if it doesn't, three years is a lot of time to come up with a better plan than sneaking off alone in the night."

"I suppose ye're right, Darach."

He grinned. "Of course I'm right."

She threw her arms around him in a quick hug. "I wish ye were my brother. Ye're a better brother than Andrew or Graham."

Chapter 10

After her discussion with Andrew and his father in the hall, Anna made her way to Davy's chamber. Cora was already there. Both Cora and Davy were thrilled when Anna told them she had been given the responsibility to mind the lad.

"Och, my lady, I love the wee rascal but truthfully, he wears me out with all his comings and goings. Still, I know ye'll have other responsibilities, so I'll help ye where I can."

Anna tried to keep the bitterness from her tone. "Thank ye, Cora, but Andrew and the laird don't wish for me to have other responsibilities."

Cora nodded sagely. "Aye, I suppose that is best, at least until ye're fully recovered and have become Lady MacLeod, but after that, if ye need me, just ask."

Anna didn't think that was what Andrew meant, but she didn't disavow Cora of that notion. "Thank ye Cora. Perhaps I can join ye and Davy for your morning meal and ye can tell me how ye spend yer day and what rules Davy is expected to follow."

"Rules?" asked Davy.

Cora frowned. "Very little has been expected of Davy since his mother passed away." Her tone clearly conveyed her disapproval.

"But that's been..." Anna realized she didn't know when Andrew's first wife passed away, "how long has that been?"

"Four years," said Cora.

Looking at Davy, Anna frowned. "The maids caring for ye have just let ye do whatever ye wished? All day?"

"Aye," said Davy, nodding happily.

"Well, I think we need to change that a bit."

"Why?" asked Davy

"We want ye to learn to be a fine man when ye grow up."

"But I won't be grown up for ever so long," Davy said.

"Once ye're grown up it's too late," said Anna. "And ye do want to be a fine man, don't ye?"

Davy frowned. "I suppose."

Cora patted Anna on the shoulder. "I told Davy he needed a mother. I'm glad to see he is getting one."

The men had left the hall by the time Anna returned with Davy and Cora. Over their morning meal Anna learned that other than using good manners at mealtimes, just as Cora had said, very little else was expected of Davy.

"Don't get me wrong, he's a good lad. An absolute joy in many ways—very much like his mother. It's really more that he needs to be someone's priority. He has largely been left in the care of one maid or another, all of whom were very young women with little experience in raising a child. When he was a wee thing, that wasn't really a problem but once he grew a little older, he became more independent and didn't need quite as much attention. So, not really knowing any better, the young women tasked with minding him largely left him to raise himself. The only thing that was expected was that he not leave the walls alone."

"What does *raise myself* mean?" asked Davy.

Cora smiled at him. "It means just what Lady Anna said, the maids caring for ye have let ye do whatever ye wished all day."

He furrowed his brow but nodded. "Oh."

Anna laughed and ruffled his hair. "Well then, that explains a few things. So, Davy, we are going to start with just one rule. I must always know where ye are."

"How can ye always know that?"

"Because ye'll tell me."

"But what if I want to go to the stable to see Grieg or

my pony?"

"Ye'll ask me if ye may do that and then I'll know where ye are."

"But what if while I'm there, Uncle Graham says he'll take me riding?"

"Then ye'll tell Uncle Graham ye have to ask me first."

"But what if it's Granda who wants to take me riding?"

"Then ye'll tell Granda ye have to ask me first."

"But Granda is the laird."

"I know that, but yer da and granda have made me responsible for ye, so they'll understand."

"Well Da never takes me riding anyway, but as long as Granda knows the rule, I guess it's all right. But why do ye need to know where I am?"

Andrew never took him riding? How odd. She wanted to ask why, but helping Davy understand the reason for the rule was more important. "Davy, if ye had told Nessa where ye were going, would ye have fallen into the loch?"

"Nessa didn't want to hunt dragons with me."

"Sometimes that might happen, but ye must never wander off without telling me where ye intend to go."

"Why?"

Anna laughed. "Because bad things can happen."

"But falling through the ice turned out to be a good thing, because ye're going to be my mama."

Anna shook her head. Clearly whether it was good or bad depended on one's perspective in this case. "I know ye're happy about that, but I became very ill as a result. And what if I hadn't been there?"

Davy frowned. "But ye were."

Anna seized on this. "Aye, I was. And if I always know exactly where ye are, I can know ye're not doing something that might put ye in danger, like walking on thin ice."

"Oh." Davy seemed to consider this for a moment

before asking, "Do ye have rules ye have to follow?"

Anna sighed. "Aye, Davy." *Don't walk northward on the bluff Anna. You must never venture that close to MacLeod territory.* "Do ye understand the rule?"

"Aye."

"Good. Now, Cora said ye haven't begun to learn to read."

"Nay. I expect Father Ninian will teach me someday."

"I'm going to start teaching ye this morning."

Davy laughed. "Lasses can't read."

Anna assumed this statement meant that Mairi couldn't read. She needed to learn too, but one challenge at a time. "Some can. I can read. This morning we are going to start learning letters and numbers."

"I don't know any letters or numbers."

"That's why we are going to start learning them."

"I'd rather go see people and maybe hunt dragons."

Anna laughed again. "I know. But after ye've spent some time learning a bit, perhaps we'll hunt dragons."

"Ye'll go with me?"

"Aye, Davy. But I haven't hunted dragons in years. Ye'll have to remind me how it's done."

They spent at little more than an hour learning letters and numbers. Anna didn't want it to feel like a chore, so she made things into games, which Davy seemed to love. When they were through, Anna said, "We can go hunt dragons now if ye wish."

"Nay, I have a few other things to do first. Can we go to the kitchen?"

Anna cocked her head and looked at him. "What other things?"

"I have to go see people. Like Dallis."

"Who is Dallis?"

"Ye don't know Dallis? She's the head cook and sometimes she makes sweet buns. Ye have to meet Dallis. I love her."

"Because she makes sweet buns?"

"Aye, but she is nice too. Come with me."

This suited Anna quite well. She wanted to meet the staff, and clearly Davy could help her do that. He took Anna's hand and practically dragged her downstairs and out to the kitchens, chattering the whole way about Dallis.

He pulled her into the busy kitchen but before the first word was out of his mouth a tiny, reed thin woman saw him. Her angular face was suddenly wreathed in smiles. "Davy, lad, I thought ye weren't going to come see me this morning."

"I had to learn some letters first. Anna says it's important." The tone of his voice led Anna to believe he wasn't convinced.

"Well, lad, 'tis very important for a young laird to learn such things." Dallis gave Anna a look of such pure affection, it startled her. "And it's about time someone remembered that."

"Well Anna did. But she says she hasn't met ye so I brought her with me. Anna, this is Dallis. Ye know, Dallis, Anna's my angel."

"So I've heard, lad. My lady, 'tis truly a pleasure to meet ye."

"It's lovely to meet ye as well. I hope we're not interrupting." Anna responded.

"Nay, of course not. Ye're always welcome and if there is ever anything ye need, just ask."

"Thank ye, Dallis."

In a loud whisper Davy said to Anna, "Tell her ye need some sweet buns."

Both Anna and Dallis laughed.

"Come, sit at the table here and I'll give ye both a wee bite to eat."

Dallis brought them sweet buns before sitting down at the table with them. "My lady, I know ye've heard this before, but we are so very grateful to ye."

Anna never knew what to say to that. "Anyone would have done it."

"Perhaps. But ye were the one who did." Dallis put her hand over Anna's where it rested on the table. "And I'm fairly certain ye never bargained for this betrothal."

"It's...I..."

"I know, lass. I'm sure it's all a bit overwhelming. Ye'll be fine and I promise ye, I will do whatever I can to help ye adjust. 'Tis good to have a lady in the keep again." Sorrow touched Dallis' features for a moment. "The laird married Lady Kenna less than a year after Lady Arabella died. Ena, Andrew and Graham were not without a mother long, and Lady Kenna was wonderful. Sir Andrew married Lady Joan just two years after Lady Kenna passed away and she too was an absolute joy. She lit up a room just like wee Davy does. Aye, 'Twill be good for everyone, but especially for Davy and Mairi. It's better when there is a lady seeing to things. If ye wish, we can go over the meals for the rest of the week now."

Anna looked down for a moment.

"What is it, lass?"

"I'm not...that is...the laird...well, I won't be managing the household."

"Ye won't? Lass, we can teach ye what ye need to know."

Anna looked her in the eye. "I'm certain ye could, and it's not as if I have no experience, it's just the laird said Brenda was to keep handling things. My only responsibility is David."

Dallis frowned. "Perhaps he just doesn't want to overtax ye until ye're fully better."

Anna didn't think so, but she said, "Perhaps."

They chatted about other things until Davy had finished his sweet bun. When he was through, he stood up, wiped his hands on his léine and announced, "Now we need to go see Grieg."

"Davy, ye need to thank Dallis for the nice treat."

He grinned. "She knows I liked it. I come every day and I always eat what she gives me."

Anna shook her head but a smile played at her lips. "Even if Dallis knows ye like yer snacks, ye must still thank her for making them for ye."

He looked stunned. "Really?"

Anna nodded. "Really."

"Dallis, is that so?"

"Aye, Davy, it's considered good manners."

"Then why have ye never told me that before?"

Dallis tried to hide her amusement. "Because it wouldn't be good manners for a cook to point that out to the Laird's grandson."

"Really?" He sounded incredulous.

Dallis chuckled. "Aye Davy, really."

"But Anna can tell me I have bad manners?"

Anna shook her head. "I didn't say ye had bad manners, I just told ye what would be polite."

Dallis smiled broadly. "And she can do that, because she is going to be yer mama."

Davy grinned. "Aye she is. Thank ye for making the sweet buns I like, Dallis."

Dallis gave a small bow. "Ye're very welcome, Davy."

"Did I do that right?" he asked Anna.

"Aye, that was very nicely done. Thank ye for taking a bit time for a chat, Dallis. I enjoyed it."

"Ye're most welcome, Lady Anna."

Davy took Anna's hand and pulled her out the door. "Now we have to go see Grieg."

"Who is Grieg?"

"The stable master."

"Why do we need to see the stable master?"

"Because I go see him every day."

As it turned out, Davy had a series of people he visited each day, and each person seemed genuinely delighted to see him. Some, like Dallis, had treats for him, but it wasn't always food. The stable master stopped his work to let Davy have a brief ride on his pony. The cooper let him pick a tool to practice using for a while. The fletcher let him smooth arrow shafts with a waxed cloth. But others, like the weavers, the laundress, the chandler and the brewer just stopped to chat with him for a few minutes. He even introduced Anna to Brenda, the woman who had run the household for the last four years, and to Fergus, the steward.

Just as Dallis had said, Davy seemed to be a welcome bright light everywhere he went. Anna slowly began to realize why the MacLeod's had been so willing to accept her solely because she'd saved him. He was loved, but not just because he was the laird's grandson, a child they saw from a distance. He was loved because he had endeared himself to each clan member. Few adults had the kind of charisma that Davy displayed and she couldn't help but wonder how he had become so adept at reading and responding to people. Anna had told him she wanted him to *learn to be a fine man* when he grew up. Clearly in some areas he was well on his way.

After the midday meal, Davy grinned at her saying, "Now we can go dragon hunting."

Chapter 11

Over the next week Anna's eyes were opened to more than just why Davy held such a special place in the clan's hearts. Davy always seemed to be in a hurry to get downstairs to the great hall for the morning meal. Although Andrew was often just leaving as they arrived, Davy seemed overjoyed and hugged his father enthusiastically. If Andrew was still seated at the table, and the seats near him were unoccupied, Davy climbed into one and chattered away happily.

On the other hand Andrew never seemed to be quite as pleased to see Davy. A brief look of what appeared to be pain crossed Andrew's face the instant he saw the lad run towards him. He covered it so quickly Anna thought she might have imagined it the first time, so she watched more carefully after that.

She hadn't imagined it.

Not only did Andrew almost cringe every morning when Davy found him still at the table, he never stayed long after his son arrived. And while Davy was full of suggestions about things they might do together, Andrew was equally full of reasons why he couldn't do them.

Davy usually sighed and accepted Andrew's refusals without argument. Anna found his restraint remarkable. She remembered whining and pleading with her own da when he refused to let her do something. Of course, he had doted on his only daughter and very seldom denied her anything. Anna could only assume that Davy was used to being rebuffed by his father.

The only attention Andrew seemed to give his son was during meals, and even then, it was minimal. As Anna thought back to the first meals she had with them in the hall, she realized it had always been Mairi and Davy who had kept conversation going. Andrew had interacted very little with his son.

This truly puzzled Anna. She knew Andrew loved David, so why did he so assiduously avoid the lad?

Of course, Andrew treated her no differently. While she had hoped to get to know her betrothed better during this time before the wedding, she saw considerably less of him than she had before. Like Davy, she really only saw Andrew during meals, and he paid no more attention to her than he did to his son. For someone who had asked her not to shut him out, he was doing a fairly good job of that himself.

After a week of this, Anna decided something had to change. On the day before Holy Thursday, she arose earlier than usual to ensure they did not miss Andrew. Even so, he was rising to leave the table as she and Davy entered the hall.

"Good morning, Andrew, I'm sorry we missed breaking our fast with ye."

"Aye, well as the next few days start the Triduum and little work will be done, I wanted to make certain the men trained hard today."

True to form Davy asked, "Da, can I come with ye for a while?"

"Nay, Davy, ye know it's too dangerous for a wee lad on the lists."

"All right, but could we go riding later? Just for a little while?"

"Nay, Davy, perhaps another time."

As always, Davy nodded resignedly. "Aye, Da."

But Anna didn't accept the answer. "When will ye?"

"When will I what?"

"Go riding with Davy."

"I am very busy, Anna. I will find a time to go riding...soon."

Anna looked thoughtful for a moment. "Ye know, Davy, I love to go riding. Perhaps ye and I can go out for a bit."

Andrew frowned. "I don't think so."

"Why not?" Anna asked. She tried to sound innocently curious although she had expected this answer.

"Because ye've been ill."

Anna laughed. "Oh nay, I'm fine. Clearly I was well enough to ride all the way to the straight and back over a week ago. A brief ride today will not overtax me."

"I said nay, Anna."

"What ye actually said was that I couldn't ride because I have been ill but ye were mistaken in that."

"Even so, ye and Davy cannot go riding alone."

"Oh, is that all? Ye've no need to worry about that. I'm sure we can find someone to accompany us."

"Uncle Graham might," offered Davy, "or maybe Granda—he takes me riding a lot."

"Then we'll ask them. Even if neither of them are free, yer granda will certainly find someone to accompany us."

Davy nodded vigorously. "Aye, he will. Maybe Cormag, or Gavin or even *Donald*." His tone when he spoke Donald's name was something akin to awe. Clearly he admired the captain of his grandfather's guard.

Anna smiled at Andrew. "See, no need to worry. You can see to training and we will find someone else to ride with us for a bit." She turned to Davy and took his hand. "Let's eat so we can go find yer granda or Uncle Graham."

"What do ye need to find me for?" asked Graham, having just walked in on the conversation."

"Nothing," said Andrew.

"Davy and I were hoping ye'd go riding with us," said Anna.

"I'd be happy to," said Graham.

"Anna, *I said nay*," growled Andrew.

Anna shook her head as if dealing with a slow child. "Ye said we couldn't go alone, but Graham can go with us, so we won't be alone."

Andrew's frustration was clearly at its limit. "Ye cannot go at all. I'm tired of arguing about this. In fact, I forbid both of ye to leave this keep today."

Graham stared, speechless, while Andrew turned to stalk out of the hall.

Anna had intentionally pushed him, but she had only wanted him to realize other men were willing to fill the role he should have in David's life. Andrew's vehemence both surprised and angered her. She called, "At the risk of sounding like Mairi, ye aren't my da, my laird or my husband…yet. And I'm fairly certain if I ask *the laird*, he'll see things my way."

Andrew turned around slowly, glowering at her.

Anna crossed her arms over her chest and arched an eyebrow in challenge.

"Andrew, it isn't a problem for me to escort them on a wee ride," said Graham, trying to diffuse the situation.

"That isn't the point," Andrew ground out through gritted teeth.

"And exactly what is the point?" asked Anna.

He strode back towards her, took her by the elbow and walked to the stairs. "Excuse us for a moment." He pulled her along at his side, up the stairs and down the hall until he reached an empty chamber. "What is this about?" he demanded.

"Maybe ye should tell me. Yer son asked ye to go riding with him—a perfectly reasonable request."

"And I said I was too busy today."

"Aye, ye always seem to be too busy to go riding with him, or to play fox and geese of an evening or to go fishing as he wanted to last week or to do any of the other perfectly reasonable things he asks ye to do with him on a daily basis. What's the matter with ye? He just wants to be with his da. Why do ye keep him at arm's length?"

"Ye don't know what ye're talking about."

"Ye think not? When was the last time ye did anything with yer son, other than sit at the same table?"

"I do things with my son."

"When, Andrew? When was the last time?" she demanded.

He scowled and didn't answer.

"I'll tell ye when it was. It was the day he fell through the ice almost five weeks ago, and that happened because ye only spent a few hours with him in the morning, before giving him to someone else's care. I'll warrant I've spent more time with that sweet child in the last five weeks than ye have in the last few years."

"I have a great many responsibilities, Anna. You couldn't possibly understand."

"Clearly, I don't. I thought one of a father's responsibilities was to raise his child. Davy loves ye with all his heart. I would have thought nearly losing him would have reminded ye of how precious he is to ye.

"This is none of yer business."

"Did ye actually just say that to me? We're to be married. Ye told me ye came as a pair, didn't ye?"

"Aye, we do. And I'm glad ye care about Davy. He needs a mother, but that doesn't give ye the right—"

"He needs a father too, and ye're doing everything in yer power to avoid being that."

"Ye don't understand."

"Don't I? Let me ask ye this, how difficult was it for ye not to have a mother? Oh wait…I forgot, yer da married Kenna when ye were younger than Davy is now. From what I hear she was a wonderful mother."

"Aye she was."

"Mairi was at least old enough to remember her too. Davy and I don't remember our mothers. I had Grizel, but she wasn't exactly a mother, and I had my da. Davy has had no one for the last several years."

"He's had me."

"He hasn't. Andrew, he only wants a tiny bit of yer time once in a while, and yet ye rebuff him every day. To his credit he simply accepts it with no argument or pleading. But every day I see how much it hurts him and how he increasingly seeks love and approval elsewhere. Ye have given me one task and I am trying to do it. But do ye remember what ye said? Ye told me that the best thing I could do, what ye needed most, was for me to care for Davy so that you didn't have to."

Andrew's eyes narrowed and he clenched his fists at his sides. "I said I wanted ye to care for Davy so I wouldn't have to *worry*."

"As it turns out, it's pretty much the same thing. So, pardon me, I have a wee broken heart to go tend." She turned to walk out of the room.

Andrew grabbed her arm, "We aren't finished."

She yanked her arm away from him. "Yes we are. Since ye'll neither go riding with us nor allow us to go with anyone else or even leave the keep, I'll find something else to occupy Davy's time today. Go train yer men. Yer son is no longer yer problem. I'll see he doesn't bother ye again."

~ * ~

Andrew fairly trembled with suppressed rage as he watched his betrothed stride angrily toward the door again. "Don't take another step."

She spun back around. "Nay, Andrew. Ye don't have the right to—"

"And don't tell me what rights I have. Ye have levelled a serious accusation. How dare ye suggest I don't love my son?"

Anna squared her shoulders. "I suggested no such thing. I know ye love him. I said ye *avoid* him."

"I don't avoid my son either." Even as the words left his lips, he knew they weren't completely true. He avoided anything that reminded him of Joan.

Immediately after she died, he moved out of the chamber they had shared because the memories were too raw. He hadn't attended the celebration of Bram Sutherland's wedding to Joan's cousin several years ago because her family would be there in force and he didn't want to be reminded of his loss. Likewise, he hadn't wanted them invited to his upcoming wedding to Anna, but his father had overruled that, not wishing to insult either the Sinclairs or the Sutherlands.

Davy was little more than a bairn when Joan died, but as he grew older and lost his soft, baby features, he resembled her more and more. Truth told, it caused Andrew's heart to ache with loss each time he caught sight of his son.

"Aye ye do avoid him, Andrew." Her tone had become soft and gentle. "Help me understand why."

Anna was painfully perceptive. He did avoid Davy, but, and he couldn't deny that she was right. But he didn't want to discuss this with her. "Leave it, Anna."

"Nay. Ye asked me not to shut ye out. Now I'm asking ye the same thing. Davy is doted on by every member of this clan except the one person whose attention he most seeks."

"Ye can't possibly understand."

"Perhaps not. But here's what I do understand. The day Davy fell through the ice, ye were terrified at the thought of losing him. And yet, what ye don't realize is, ye are losing him bit by bit anyway. He grows older and farther away from ye as each day passes. If things keep going as they are, someday he'll stop seeking yer time and attention altogether, and on that day ye will have lost a thing of great value." Anna looked down for a moment, blinking as if she held back tears. When she looked at him again she said, "And he will have as well."

Andrew stared at her in stunned silence as the truth washed over him. Had he wanted to avoid the pain of his own loss so completely that he shut the dearest piece of Joan remaining to him out of his life? *Dear God what have I done?*

Perhaps reading his silence as stubbornness or anger, Anna sighed. "Excuse me. I'm sorry if I angered ye. It was for Davy."

She started to leave and once again he stopped her.

"Nay, Anna, wait. Please…wait."

She turned back to face him again but said nothing.

"Ye're right. I've been a coward."

"I never said that."

"I know ye didn't, but it's the truth. I've told ye before that I loved Davy's mother. The truth is, Davy grows more like Joan each day, and not just in looks. He is as full of life and joy as she was. My heart aches for her every time I look at him…and so until now I suppose I have done whatever I could to prevent that pain."

"I'm sorry. I shouldn't have pushed."

"Nay, I needed to be pushed. I have been so wrapped up in my own sorrow, I held myself away from the only person who will ever be as precious to me as Joan was. I can never give my heart to anyone like that again. I thought solely of my own pain and, as a result, denied a motherless lad his father too. Even coming so very close to losing him didn't change anything." He reached out and took one of her hands in his. "Thank ye, Anna. Now that I look back, I realize others may have tried to tell me the same thing but ye're more relentless than the Highland winds in a winter gale."

She blushed. "I—I…"

"I know. Ye did it for Davy and I'm grateful."

"Ye're welcome. I…uh…I should get back to Davy."

"I'll walk back to the great hall with ye. And, I'll take ye both out riding this afternoon."

"Perhaps ye should just take Davy today."

"Whatever ye think is best."

Once they reached the great hall Davy was thrilled to learn they would be able to go riding later. Andrew's heart caught a little—his son's glee so resembled Joan's. But at that moment Andrew knew he needed to embrace their similarities instead of hiding from them. He had to focus on what remained to him rather than what he had lost.

~ * ~

Anna had needled Andrew intentionally that morning.

She wanted him to see how he had been ignoring his son. She thought maybe, if over the course of days or weeks he realized that other men were filling the role that he should have in Davy's life, he too would spend a little more time with his son.

She hadn't expected him to become so angry.

She hadn't expected to become so angry herself.

And she really hadn't expected to hear the reason he seemed to ignore his son.

But perhaps the thing that took her most by surprise was how much it hurt to hear him profess the profound love he held for his first wife. Of course Andrew had already told Anna that. He said until his father forced the betrothal, he "had absolutely no intention of ever marrying again." She knew it had to be devastating to love someone so profoundly and then lose her.

However, when he said, "I held myself away from the only person who will ever be as precious to me as Joan was," the pain she felt was surprisingly sharp.

It was foolish really. Once Anna had decided she would do what she could to make the best of the situation in which she found herself, she had allowed herself to imagine loving Andrew. Perhaps worse, she had allowed herself to imagine receiving his love in return. But it seemed Andrew had already ruled out that possibility. *I can never give my heart to anyone like that again.* Rather suddenly, Anna realized she was destined to marry a man who would do his duty by her and perhaps even be kind and affectionate towards her, but would never love her.

That prospect seemed shockingly bleak.

When they returned to the great hall that morning, her heart had been heavy. Seeing Davy's joy at learning his father would go riding with him that afternoon truly pleased her, but nevertheless, a terrible shift had occurred. She had lost the shred of hope to which she had been clinging—the hope that she and her husband might grow to love each other.

Chapter 12

Once Andrew had been forced to admit to himself that he had intentionally avoided Davy to protect himself from the pain of loss, he vowed to make amends. The next morning after addressing some clan business for his father, he went in search of his son. Davy had asked so many times for Andrew to allow him to watch the men train—Andrew intended to do just that. He entered the great hall and called to one of the maids who was cleaning in preparation for the Easter celebrations. "Janet, do ye happen to know where David is?"

"Aye, sir. Well, that is I'm not certain, but he's usually in Lady Anna's chamber this time of the mornin'."

"What is he doing there?"

Janet laughed. "Did ye not know? Lady Anna is teaching him letters and numbers. After the first day or so she convinced Mairi to join them too."

"Anna can read?"

Janet shrugged. "I expect she can, seein' as how she's teaching them to."

Andrew smiled at her. "Thanks for not just coming right out and telling me that was a stupid question."

"I'm happy to serve, sir," she said giving him a mischievous grin.

He chuckled as he left the hall, climbing the stairs to Anna's chamber. The door was open and he heard their voices, so he stopped for a moment to listen.

"H" said Davy, gleefully.

After a moment Mairi said, "B."

There was another pause and Davy said, "F."

Then he heard Mairi sound puzzled. "Eh...Eh...I

don't know elbow."

"Elbow begins with an 'E'," said Anna. "I'll give ye the point if ye can guess what the next letter in 'elbow' is."

"But we haven't done second letters," said Mairi petulantly.

"Nay, we haven't, but say the word and think about it," said Anna. "I bet you can figure it out."

"Hmm. Elbow. El…el…oh, the next letter in elbow is 'L'!"

"That's right. And what do ye think is next?"

"Elb…buh…buh…it's a 'B'," Mairi said confidently.

"Aye, it is."

Andrew smiled with pride in his little sister.

"Can I guess the next letter?" asked Davy.

"All right. The first three letters are 'E-L-B' what do ye think comes next?"

His son repeated the word "elbow" several times, very seriously, until he said, "Is it 'O'?"

"Aye, very good, Davy."

Andrew didn't want to be caught eavesdropping so he stepped forward, tapping on the door as he entered the room. "What's going on here?"

"Da!" squealed Davy as he jumped up from his chair and threw his arms around his father.

"Anna is teaching us to read," said Mairi.

"Is she? That's wonderful." He smiled at Anna. "I didn't know ye could read."

Anna's smile didn't quite reach her eyes. "There might be one or two things ye don't know about me."

He canted his head. "Aye, I expect there are."

"Look, Da, I can write my name." Davy proceeded to show him a parchment on which he had written "David" in a blotchy, slightly crooked hand.

"Well done, son. Mairi, can ye write yer name too?"

Mairi gave him a brilliant smile—something she almost never did. "Aye, I can." She showed him the parchment on which she had written her name in a slightly neater script.

"Very nice, Mairi."

Mairi beamed.

Andrew chanced a glance at Anna, who stood quietly to one side. She looked rightfully proud of her students. "Anna, I didn't realize ye were teaching these two to read but 'twas a very good idea. Thank ye."

She nodded but didn't meet his eyes. "Ye're welcome."

"I'm sorry to have interrupted."

"Ye didn't."

He arched a brow at her.

"What I mean is, we were finishing up for the morning."

"Well, in that case, I thought Davy might want to go with me to watch the men train for a bit."

"Do ye mean it, Da?"

Andrew ruffled his hair. "Aye, Davy."

"Can I go too, Andrew?" asked Mairi.

There was no way he was taking Mairi to the lists, but before he said so, Anna stepped in.

"Nay, Mairi. Andrew, I don't care what ye say, the lists are absolutely no place for a young lady."

Andrew stared at her for a moment, speechless. "Anna, I—"

"Nay, Andrew. Absolutely not."

What was Anna doing? He certainly had no intention of taking Mairi.

Mairi pouted. "Anna, that's not fair."

"I'm sorry, Mairi. It cannot be allowed. Go now and get your tapestry frame. We will work on that a bit."

Mairi frowned and stomped out of the room.

Andrew was perplexed. "Anna, I—"

She put up her hand and shook her head, saying very quietly, "Andrew, ye don't always have to be the bossy one."

By all the saints. "Ye did that on purpose?"

"Ye weren't planning to take her too, were ye?"

"Nay, but now she's mad at ye."

Anna grinned. "Aye, but she won't stay mad long. Ye and Davy go on before she realizes that not only am I not her father or her laird, I'm not even her brother."

He laughed. "Aye, we'd better make our escape." Then for some reason he could not fathom, he brushed her cheek with a kiss before leaving with Davy.

~ * ~

Anna touched her cheek where he had kissed her, slightly confused by the unexpected show of affection. Then she chuckled to herself thinking of how astonished Andrew had looked when she had forbidden him to take Mairi to the lists. Sometimes Anna saw so much of her relationship with Eoin in Mairi's interactions with Andrew. Maybe it was simply because the difference in their ages was similar. Mairi had seemed inordinately pleased when Andrew complimented her. Anna smiled, knowing she would have reacted exactly the same way to praise from Eoin. Knowingapproval like that from one of her brothers had meant to her when she was Mairi's age, Anna couldn't stand seeing the moment ruined.

Very soon, Mairi returned with her tapestry frame— pouting. Anna tried to hide her amusement. Mairi was beginning to love needlework as much as Anna did. If Andrew had refused to take his sister, and there was no doubt he was going to, Anna would have consoled her with the offer of working on her tapestry. She, so she had simply skipped a step. And while Mairi continued to pout for a while, she soon forgot her pique and was back to her talkative self again.

~ * ~

Andrew continued to make time for Davy and after what Anna had done with Mairi, he looked for ways to include his little sister occasionally too. On Saturday afternoon before Easter, he was teaching them both to play quoits. It was an easy enough game to learn, even if it took practice and skill to master. Mairi was actually getting rather good at it for a young lass.

"That was close, Mairi. Don't forget to let yer arm keep going after ye release the quoit. It will fly truer."

As his sister prepared to throw her next quoit, her brow furrowed as if she were pondering some great problem. She took careful aim, tossed the quoit and, exactly as he had instructed, she followed through with her arm. The iron ring landed over the spike in the ground just as it was supposed to.

"I did it!" Squealed Mairi.

Andrew smiled at her. "Well done." Her face lit with pleasure.

"Aye Mairi, that was perfect," said Graham as he joined them.

"Did ye see me do that, Graham?"

"Aye, sweetling, I did."

"Mairi, can I show Uncle Graham how I can throw them?" Davy asked.

She smiled. "Aye go fetch them. It's yer turn anyway."

Andrew and Graham stood back to watch Davy and Mairi play for a few minutes, calling the odd instruction and offering praise when it was warranted. Mairi particularly seemed to blossom with the slightest compliment.

"Has it always been this simple to make her happy?" Andrew asked.

Graham snorted. "Aye, Andrew, it doesn't take much, just a bit of attention."

"I guess I'm guilty of not paying much attention to either of them."

"Aye, ye've been a bit wrapped up in yer own problems for a while. But the important thing is that ye know it now and ye are changing things."

"Why did ye never say anything?"

"Well, I've tried to make subtle suggestions before but I guess we all understood how much ye'd lost. At what point do ye tell someone ye care about that they have mourned long enough?"

"*We* all understood?"

"Andrew, surely ye can't think ye were alone in this?"

Andrew shook his head. "I guess I never realized. I'm sorry."

"There is nothing to apologize for. I'm just glad that wee fireball ye're marrying stood her ground on this. Heaven knows, no MacLeod would have done it."

Andrew chuckled. "Aye, she's bold and too hardheaded by half."

"Have ye realized how fortunate ye are yet?"

"Fortunate? Nay, Graham. I'm not fortunate, but if I have to marry someone, she's better than most."

Graham sighed. "And ye have the nerve to call *her* hardheaded."

Chapter 13

As Easter approached, Anna noticed the change in Andrew had a ripple effect across the clan. It was as if an invisible pall, one they hadn't even realized enshrouded them, had been lifted. Davy was obviously ecstatic, and for that she was glad.

On the other hand, Anna herself had trouble coming to terms with the things Andrew had said about never loving anyone as he had loved Joan. Just as she hadn't regretted pulling Davy from the frozen loch, she certainly did not regret pushing Andrew back into Davy's life.

Andrew seemed fond of her at times, and Anna wasn't sure why having his love suddenly mattered to her. An arranged marriage with no guarantee of love or even mild affection had always been in her future. When had she added love to her expectations?

She knew the answer to that. Eoin and Fiona were very much in love and Anna wanted that too. Maybe it's the reason she had been so resistant when Eoin had been seeking a betrothal for her. In spite of it being a completely unrealistic expectation, it was becoming increasingly difficult to bear the realities of the loveless marriage that lay ahead of her.

During the Easter feast, she maintained as cheerful a front as she could, but in addition to everything else, she had never been away from home on a feast day and she missed her family desperately. The jubilation around her only made things worse. Andrew asked her to dance occasionally and she couldn't easily refuse. She also danced one obligatory dance each with Dougal and Graham, but otherwise she tried to blend into the background and simply endure until she could excuse herself.

Eventually, while the celebration was still in full swing, Anna found her opportunity just as she finished a dance with Andrew.

"Anna, excuse me for a moment and I will find us some refreshment."

"Oh, nay, thank ye, Andrew, none for me. I am tired and if ye don't mind, I will say good night and seek my bed."

"Don't leave yet. It's early." Andrew grinned. "Even Davy is still holding his own." Davy was indeed winding through the dancers, playing a chasing game with other children.

Anna smiled. "Aye he is, and he seems to be having a wonderful time, but I am truly exhausted."

"I'll walk with ye to yer chamber then."

She put up a hand. "There is no need to. Stay and enjoy the fete. I'll see ye in the morning."

He cocked his head to one side, "If ye're sure…"

"I'm sure. Good night Andrew."

"Good night, angel." He kissed her forehead before letting her go.

As she made her way up to her chamber her thoughts roamed to her first days here at Curacridhe, when her one goal had been simply to go home. At the time she had looked for any possible avenue out of the MacLeod stronghold, but escape was impossible because she had never been left unobserved. However at this moment, no one guarded her, the great hall and bailey were packed with merrymakers. Slipping out of the keep and through the gates amidst the crowd would be simple. Because she had accepted the betrothal, no one would be expecting her to leave, so if she truly wanted to escape, she would never have a better opportunity.

It was tempting. While Anna no longer hated the MacLeods, she still longed for her family and Naomh-dùn. Furthermore, the opportunity to avoid marriage to a man whose heart would never be hers was beyond enticing. With one quick turn of her heel she could be back down the stairs, out of the keep and on her way home.

Anna sighed wistfully. Aye, it was tempting, but it was also pointless. If she ran away now it would cause a terrible uproar and she would only have the solace of home briefly; the marriage was inevitable. Eoin would not break the agreement unless the MacLeods committed some grievous offence, which they certainly had not. Nay, nothing could be gained by running away. She needed to set silly dreams aside and fulfill her obligations as had always been expected of her. Resigned to her future, even if not terribly happy at the moment, Anna continued on to her bed chamber.

~ * ~

That Easter was the first great feast in which Andrew had truly participated in, in the years since losing Joan. Experiencing the celebration around him, particularly Davy's uninhibited delight, unearthed wonderful, happy memories. Andrew experienced joy and real comfort in the connection he and Davy shared.

He also had quite relished dancing with Anna, and felt no small amount of disappointment as he watched her leave the feast early.

"Where is Anna going? Is something wrong?" his father asked.

"I don't think so. She's going to bed, she says she's tired."

Dougal frowned. "Are ye sure nothing's wrong? She's been a bit subdued recently. She hasn't had a smart, cheeky thing to say to me in days."

Before Andrew could respond, Mairi too approached. "Where's Anna going?"

"She says she's tired and going to bed."

Mairi frowned.

"What's wrong, Mairi? Do ye know something?" asked their father.

"Nay, Da. It's just…well, I don't think she's tired. She doesn't really get tired, at least not since she got better.

She looked sad to me."

"Sad?" Andrew hoped that wasn't it.

"Why do ye think she's sad?" asked Dougal

Mairi rolled her eyes. "Honestly have ye both forgotten? She's away from home, away from her family. I bet she's never been away from home on a feast day. I'd be sad if I wasn't here with all of ye."

Andrew scrubbed his face with his hands. "Dear God, Mairi, ye're right."

She put her fists on her hips. "Don't sound so shocked."

His father swore. "Aye, Mairi's right and it never crossed my mind. She seems to have adjusted so well. Andrew, ye'll take her to Naomh-dùn for Pentecost, or better yet Roodmas—it's right after the wedding. We told her she could visit once ye were married."

"Aye. I should go after her now and talk to her."

"Nay, what ye should do is make sure she hasn't left the keep," said Mairi.

Andrew and his father stared at her with disbelief.

"Why do ye think that?" asked Dougal.

Mairi smiled triumphantly. "Because it is what I would do."

"God's bones." Andrew worked his way through the crowded great hall and took the stairs two at a time. He needed to be sure she actually had gone to her chamber and sighed with relief when she called, "Who's there?" in response to his knock.

"It's Andrew."

She opened the door. "Andrew, I said I was tired. I'm going to bed."

"I know ye said that, angel, but I can't help think something's bothering ye. Mairi thought ye might be missing home."

She smiled. "Aye, Mairi would think that."

"Is she right?"

"I suppose she is."

He took her hands in his. "I'm sorry I didn't realize it earlier. Ye know it won't be long now until we're married. Ye'll see yer family then and we can visit Naomh-dùn for the Roodmas celebration there."

"That will be nice Andrew. Thank ye."

He dipped his head to look directly into her eyes. "That doesn't really make it better, does it?"

She shook her head, giving a half-hearted chuckle. "Nay. I do appreciate yer concern, but ye needn't worry, I'll get over it."

She sounded…defeated, and it tore at his heart. He wrapped his arms around her. "I'm sorry, angel. I wish I could make it better."

She rested her head on his chest, but to his great disappointment, after only a moment, she took a deep breath and pulled away. "It's all right. I'll be fine. Really, I will. This is my home now. I'll get used to it eventually, but it's still all very new."

Her unhappy tone belied her words, but he didn't know what to say. "Ye've been so brave and so strong." He caressed her cheek, wanting more than anything to hold her in his arms and kiss her until he banished the sorrow in her eyes. *Dear God, where had that come from?* Nay, he couldn't do that. He couldn't.

Almost as if she sensed his inner conflict, she stepped back. "Andrew, I…I'm tired. I'll feel better in the morning. Good night."

She went into her chamber, closing the door on him.

He stood there listening, remembering how she had crumbled once before. This time, he heard nothing, so after a few moments he left, returning to the festivities.

As soon as he stepped into the great hall, Davy barreled toward him. Andrew grinned. His son glowed with happiness and youthful exuberance.

"Da, where've ye been? Where is Anna?"

He ruffled Davy's hair. "Anna is tired and has gone to bed. I was just checking to make sure she was well."

Davy frowned. "She never goes to bed before I do. She always tells me a story and tucks me in."

"Does she?" Andrew wasn't sure why that surprised him. Anna took excellent care of Davy. "Well, since she is a bit more tired than usual and ye are up a bit later than usual, I'll see ye tucked in tonight."

"Will ye really, Da?"

Davy looked as if Andrew had offered him a priceless treasure. He remembered Anna's words from a few days ago. *If things keep going as they are, someday he will stop seeking yer time and attention altogether and on that day ye will have lost a thing of great value.* She had been right.

"Aye, son, I will. Are ye ready to go to bed now?"

"Can I just find Granda and Uncle Graham and say goodnight to them first?"

"Of course ye can. I'll wait here for ye."

When Davy returned a few minutes later, he put his hand in Andrew's and they went up the stairs to the lad's room. Davy removed his plaid, washed his face and hands and climbed into bed. "Will ye tell me a story, like Anna does?"

Andrew chuckled. "Aye, Davy. Is there one ye'd like to hear?"

"I like all stories. Tell me one ye like."

"Hmm. Have ye ever heard of a trow?"

Davy nodded eagerly. "Aye. They are wee folk, like faeries."

"Well this is a story about a trow and a poor widow named Mallie."

Andrew proceeded to tell his son the story of the generous woman, who although she had only a handful of meal left to feed her children, shared it with a stranger in need—a tiny old man dressed all in gray.

When Andrew had finished the story, Davy smiled. "Anna would have done that. She would have helped the old man."

"Aye, I suspect she would have."

"I *know* she would have. I like that story."

"I've always liked it too." Andrew remembered how Joan would cuddle Davy on her lap and tell him stories even when he was too young to understand them. Mallie and the Trow was one of her favorites. It was a good memory.

"Ye look happy, Da."

He smiled at his son. "Aye. I am happy. I was just remembering how yer mama loved to tell ye that story."

"Did she? I don't remember."

"I expect ye don't. Ye were very little when yer mama died."

"Would she have done what Mallie did and give away her last bit of food to someone who needed it?"

"Aye, son, she would have."

"Can ye tell me another memory before I go to sleep? What's something else mama liked?"

Could he? Could he bear the pain of remembering? In truth, remembering how she told Davy stories hadn't hurt at all. It filled him with warmth. "Aye Davy. Let me see...well, yer mama loved to go riding. Before ye were born, I tried to take her riding every day."

"But ye didn't after I was born?"

Andrew chuckled. "It's a little harder to find time to go riding when ye have a wee bairn to care for, but aye, we still went riding when we could."

"I like riding too."

"I know ye do. Perhaps we can go tomorrow afternoon if the weather is fine."

"I'd like that. Can Anna come too? I think it might make her happy."

Andrew grinned at his thoughtful son. That was so like Joan as well. She took joy in pleasing others. "Aye, we'll take Anna too, if she wishes to come."

"I hope she does."

As Davy said that, Andrew realized that he hoped she did too.

"Now, son, it is time for ye to go to sleep. Andrew

kissed Davy on the forehead, and tucked the covers snuggly around him. "I'll see ye in the morning."

"And we'll go riding if the weather is fine."

Andrew chuckled. "Aye, son, if the weather is fine."

~ * ~

When Andrew finally found his bed on Easter night, he prayed for fine weather the next day. To his consternation, when he woke in the morning, later than he normally did, it was to leaden skies and a steady rain, that promised to last through the day. He dressed and ventured down to the great hall. Graham and a rather sleepy looking Mairi sat at the table.

"Good morning, brother," called Graham.

"Good morning. Where is everyone else? Have Davy and Anna not risen yet?"

Mairi yawned. "Anna and Davy were up ages ago."

"And Da is taking his morning meal in his chamber," added Graham. He grinned "Da always enjoys himself well at a feast. I expect he needs a bit of time to recover."

Andrew laughed. "So where have Anna and Davy gone?"

"Perhaps her chamber?" suggested Graham.

"Nay, they've gone dragon hunting," said Mairi.

Andrew's heart caught. Davy was "dragon hunting" when he fell through the ice. "Surely they didn't go out in this downpour."

Mairi yawned again. "Nay. Anna wouldn't allow that. Davy wanted to go dragon hunting down in the caves—that's what he calls the storage rooms."

Andrew frowned. "I'm not sure that's a safe place."

Graham shrugged. "I don't see a problem with it. It is just a series of rooms filled with supplies. There isn't even much in them this time of year. It seems like as good a place as any to hunt dragons."

"I think I'll just check on them anyway." Andrew grabbed a bannock, eating it as he headed for the stairs. He hadn't been down here since the day of the accident when he carried Anna, blue with cold, up from the dungeon.

As he reached the bottom, he heard his son's voice say, "Stay back, Anna, this is a nasty one. Watch that he doesn't get ye with his tail."

Anna's soft chuckle floated to him. "Aye, Davy. Don't forget, aim for his eyes or his nostrils. That's where they are most vulnerable, ye know."

Andrew peeked around the edge of the doorway. A torch held in a wall sconce provided light for the intrepid warriors. Davy was whacking fiercely at his invisible foe, driving it ever back, closer to the end of the hallway.

"Nay! He is escaping into his lair. We need to follow and finish him off." Davy headed for the stairs to the dungeon at the end of the hall.

"Nay, Davy," came Anna's panicked voice. "Ye can't go down there. It's dark."

"Ye can hold the torch for me. He can't get away from us now."

"I said nay, Davy."

His son must have heard the dread in Anna's voice. He turned around. "Are ye afraid Anna? It's not really a dragon's lair. It's just an old empty dungeon, but we won't go down there if ye're scared."

"I don't like it down there."

"How do ye know, ye've never been down there, have ye?"

"I…I…just don't like dungeons. Let's go upstairs and I'll tell ye a story about two dragons named Magni and Asgre."

Andrew shook his head. Anna always managed to surprise him. Even after her awful experience, she chose to protect Davy from the truth of it. He took a step back calling, "Davy…Anna, are ye down here?" before stepping out into the corridor.

Davy rushed toward him. "Da!"

Andrew swung him up into his arms. "What are ye doing down here?"

"Anna and I were hunting dragons."

Andrew glanced toward her. She looked slightly shaken. "I see. It's very brave of her to come with ye, don't ye think?"

Davy grinned and whispered, "They aren't real dragons, Da."

"I certainly hope not. If we had real dragons in the cellars they might eat all our food and drink our fine ale."

Davy giggled. "Anna knows stories about dragons and now she's going to tell me one.

Andrew looked at Anna again. "That sounds like a very good idea." He offered Anna his free hand. "Come, Anna, let's go back upstairs now that the great beast has been driven back."

She nodded, taking his hand. He guided her in front of him, put Davy down and grabbed the torch from the wall to light their way back up the stairs. When they reached the top, Davy ran to the head table, where Graham still sat, and proceeded to tell him about the dragon hunt.

Anna started to follow but Andrew placed a hand on her shoulder, stopping her. "Are ye all right?"

"Aye," she answered a little too brightly.

He arched an eyebrow at his betrothed but said no more.

Chapter 14

On the Thursday after Easter, just before the evening meal was ready to be served, Andrew sat with his father and Graham, discussing which crops had already been planted and what was still needed, when Colin knocked on the solar door.

"Laird, Donald told me come and tell ye, a large party bearing the Chisholm banner approaches."

Dougal grinned. "Thank ye, lad. Run and tell Dallis there will be more mouths at dinner, and then tell Brenda to ready rooms for Lady Ena and her family. After ye've done that, see if ye can find Mairi and tell her Ena's here…oh and tell Davy too."

"He knows. He was in the stable with Grieg and is already waiting in the bailey."

"Well then, just tell the others."

"Aye, Laird." Colin hurried to do as he had been bid.

"Well, lads, it looks as if Ena has arrived, a full three weeks early. I knew she'd take pity on us and come to help."

"Aye, it'll be good to have her here." Andrew was truly happy that Ena had arrived. She was five years older than him, and he had always adored her. She married Fearghas Chisholm the year Andrew went to train with Laird MacRae. The Chisholm holding was not terribly far from the MacRae's land and they were allies, so Andrew saw his sister frequently throughout his training. But it had been nearly a year since she had last visited Curacridhe.

When they reached the bailey, Davy was jumping up and down excitedly. "Aunt Ena's coming, Da."

"So I hear."

"Look, there she is now."

Sure enough, his sister was riding through the gates with her husband, children, and a retinue of servants and guardsmen in tow.

Ena was off her horse and hugging her father and brothers before the rest of the Chisholm party had come to a full stop.

Standing a little to one side, Davy smiled broadly until it was his turn.

Ena crouched down in front of him, hugging him close and just holding him for a moment. When she released him, her eyes sparkled with unshed tears. "It is so good to see ye, Davy, and ye're growing so big."

"Anna—she saved me when I fell in the loch and she's going to be my mama—she says I get bigger every time she blinks."

"I'm sure ye do. Where is Anna? I would like to meet her."

"I'll go find her," Davy offered enthusiastically. "She might be in her solar." Before anyone could stop him, he turned and ran into the keep on his mission.

Ena smiled at his retreating figure. "Andrew, I can't believe how close we came to losing him. Were it not for Anna MacKay…"

"Aye. I can't let myself think about it. Davy thought she was an angel, and for certain 'twas only by the Grace of God that she was there to save him.

"My thoughts exactly." Ena turned to her father. "So, Da, I'm not sure forcing her to marry Andrew was the best way to thank her, even in the name of peace."

"Ena, love, let's at least get into the keep before ye launch an attack on yer da," said Fearghas.

"Thank ye, Fearghas. I fear I'll need fortification before I face my daughter down over this," said Dougal.

Andrew said nothing, but he too was thankful for the reprieve.

Ena and Fearghas' daughters, Allison who would be eight in a month, Lara who was three years younger, and the baby Rhona, who had been riding in a wagon with maid servants, were lifted out, hugged by their uncles and grandfather and ushered into the hall.

Mairi burst into the great hall with a squeal of glee. "*Eeeeenaaaaaaa!*" She launched herself at her sister.

Ena laughed and returned her hug. "Mairi, sweetling, it's good to see ye too."

Somewhere in the midst of the uproar, Davy returned, pulling Anna by the hand.

Andrew frowned. Something seemed to be amiss. Anna looked…he couldn't quite put his finger on it. He watched as Davy practically dragged her towards Ena.

"Aunt Ena, this is Anna." Davy sounded as if he were presenting his aunt with a rare and priceless jewel. "Anna, this is my Aunt Ena."

Anna curtsied. "Good evening, my lady."

"Don't 'my lady' me, precious lass. I'm just Ena." Ena gave her the same warm hug with which she had greeted the rest of the family before linking arms with Anna and introducing her to the *Chisholm invaders* as she called her family.

~ * ~

Ena took one look at the sad, tense, copper-haired lass Davy dragged towards her and was filled with dismay. She understood why her father had forced the betrothal, at least she did intellectually. But her heart told her Anna was hurting and either no one noticed or cared. Ena maneuvered to surround the little MacKay with Chisholms during the evening meal.

"Aunt Ena, Anna always sits with me and Mairi," said Davy.

Ena laughed merrily. "I'm sure ye quite like that, pet, but I thought ye might like to sit with Allison and Lara tonight and let me get a chance to know Anna better."

"Ooh, Ena, ye'll love her. I'll sit with ye both," said Mairi.

"Mairi, sweetling, I was hoping ye'd keep a bit of an

eye on my wee lassies for me, and they have been looking forward to seeing *Aunty Mairi* all day."

Mairi smiled proudly. "I'd be happy to."

Ena knew her sister liked being entrusted with a bit of responsibility. She also knew Mairi was one of the most overwhelming members of her family, and if she wasn't much mistaken, Anna had been overwhelmed by MacLeods from the first moment she stepped foot on their land. She suspected the lass could use a respite, which was Ena's real purpose for sequestering Anna for the evening. Ena was so very proud of her husband. He had caught on to what she was doing instantly and ensured that Chisholm guardsmen created distance between Anna and Andrew, Graham and Dougal.

Ena had been right. When Anna was insulated from the family, she appeared to relax ever so slightly and chat a little.

Nothing was said outright, but the things Ena pieced together shocked her. Anna was marrying Andrew and would someday be Lady MacLeod, but had been given no real position in the household, except to be a nursemaid to Davy. None of the wedding plans had been discussed, or even shared with her. Her father and brothers insisted that Anna was loved and respected by the MacLeods, and Ena was certain she was, but the lass needed to be allowed to step into a leadership role or she would always be *the little MacKay who saved Davy*. Worst of all Ena suspected her brother might have done something that had deeply hurt Anna. While she didn't know exactly what it was, she had her suspicions.

Ena could only imagine the pain of losing a beloved spouse. Losing their mother had been terrible and losing Kenna had nearly been worse. But as much as losing a mother hurt, Ena knew it was different than losing a wife.

When she arrived at Curacridhe after Joan had died, the brother she knew was gone. He appeared strong, never allowing himself to break, but Ena saw his stoicism for what it really was. Withdrawal. It was as if Andrew had put all emotions into a box, sealed it and set it aside. It wasn't just his sorrow that he locked away, it was everything: joy, hope and even love. What remained was detachment, emptiness. Ena suspected it was an act of self-preservation—it was easier for Andrew to feel nothing than to risk feeling overwhelming grief ever again. It hadn't really gotten better over time.

Ena knew it would take strength and persistence to break through Andrew's defenses. Perhaps Anna was perfect for the task, but Ena vowed to do what she could to help.

There was one issue Ena could take steps to fix tonight, and woe be to the father or brother who stood in her way. At the end of the meal, Ena called Brenda over. "Brenda, 'tis so good to see ye again."

Brenda nodded. "And ye, my lady."

"I don't want to be a bother, or be in the way, but I suspect Anna might need a bit of extra help taking care of the household with the upcoming wedding. I'll meet with ye both in the morning and we can begin to make plans."

Brenda grinned broadly. "Aye, my lady. That will be perfect."

Ena took Anna by the hand and gave her a sly wink. "Is that all right with ye?"

Anna smiled the first genuine smile Ena had seen. "Aye, Ena, I would love it."

~ * ~

Andrew sat at the table the next morning with Davy and Anna. He had felt oddly out of sorts the previous evening when Ena had occupied Anna throughout supper. Of course he realized his sister wanted to get to know her but still, he missed Anna's company.

When Ena, Fearghas and their brood arrived downstairs, she was her usual, direct, efficient self. She announced immediately, "Davy, Uncle Fearghas doesn't get to go fishing very often and intends to spend the morning with his squire at the loch doing just that. Would ye like to go?"

Davy nodded happily. "Aye, I would. Can Anna

come too?"

"Actually, there are some things to be done that Anna needs my help with. Yer da can go if he wishes." She smiled warmly at Andrew.

Andrew wasn't sure what Anna needed help with, but he thought it better not to ask.

"Da will ye go with us?"

Andrew chuckled. "Aye, Davy, that sounds like fun."

When the meal was over, Ena linked her arm through Anna's. "Now, shall we go find Brenda? I suspect there is much to be done."

Andrew frowned. Is that what Ena had meant? "Wait, Ena, there is no reason why Anna has to be bothered with any of that. Brenda manages quite well and Anna has other responsibilities."

Ena flashed him a brilliant smile, which he knew didn't bode well. "Does she?"

"Aye, she minds Davy."

"But Davy doesn't need minding this morning. He's going fishing with his Da and his uncle. Besides, what could possibly be more important that the running of her household?"

"But it isn't her household."

His sister's arched brow told Andrew it had been the wrong thing to say. "That is to say, she isn't Lady MacLeod yet, and Brenda has things well in hand anyway. There is no need…" his voice trailed off as he realized Ena was only growing angrier.

Her eyes narrowed. "Andrew, now that I think on it, there is something I wanted to discuss with ye and Da. I believe he's in his solar. Excuse us, Anna, Fearghas, we won't be long." She headed for the tower stairs, glancing back when she reached them. "Are ye coming, Andrew?"

Andrew sighed and looked heavenward. He had no clue what had Ena irritated, but he knew he would get no peace until it was sorted out, so he followed his older sister up the stairs.

He wasn't left wondering for long. Ena pounced the moment they reached the privacy of the solar.

"By all that is good and holy, can either of ye tell me why ye are treating that sweet lass so poorly?"

Their father looked incredulous. "Ena, sweetling, what are ye talking about? She is treated like an honored guest."

"But, Da, she isn't an honored guest—at least not anymore. She is betrothed to Andrew and will be Lady MacLeod in a matter of weeks. Someday she will be leading this clan at yer side Andrew. But the message ye both are giving to her and the clan is that ye feel she is incapable of anything except minding a child."

"Nay, ye misunderstand me. I didn't want to risk her health. She was so very ill."

"I'm sure she *was* very ill, but she isn't anymore."

Andrew tried to reason with his sister. "Ena, she's quite young, and it's only been a little more than a fortnight since the betrothals were signed. She needs time to become used to the idea."

"She's older than I was when I married Fearghas and she's older than Joan was when ye married her, not to mention the fact that she has been equally as well-trained to run a household as Joan and I were. While I'll grant ye, the poor wee thing has a great deal to adapt to, and I still think it was wrong of ye to force this marriage," Ena glared at their father, "she seems to be trying to accept it and adjust. I think she wants to find her way amongst us and ye both have tied her hands by not allowing her to assume the role that is her right.

Andrew tried again. "But she isn't Lady MacLeod yet, and…well…the household staff might not take too kindly to accepting orders from a MacKay."

Ena shook her head. "That is exactly what I thought ye'd say. In spite of everything, ye still see her only as a MacKay. Well, I have news for ye both, tis the *household staff* that fear ye have no intention of ever letting her assume the role of Lady MacLeod. They are fond of her, they want to help her and see it as an insult to her. I see it the same way. But perhaps worst of all, I suspect she does too. If it were Graham's betrothed who came here to live before the wedding, you would absolutely expect her to begin learning the workings of this keep. The only reason ye hesitate with Anna is because of who she is."

Andrew didn't know what to say. Ena was right, of course. His own words to Anna came back to him. *Nay, ye've got it backwards. Da threw ye in the dungeon because of yer name. Ye saved Davy because of who ye are. There's a huge difference. We love ye because of who ye are, in spite of yer name.* After all this he still continued to think of her as Anna MacKay, a guest and an outsider, rather than the woman who would become Lady MacLeod.

Their father sighed. "We didn't intend to insult her. I truly didn't want her overworked and she is so very good with Davy. Not to mention she…ah…*encouraged* Andrew to spend more time with him too."

Ena smiled. "Did she? Well, good for her. Don't underestimate her—she will be able to manage both Davy and a household. Most noble women do."

Dougal nodded. "Aye, ye're right, sweetling."

"So, I'll get no arguments from ye on this? Either of ye?" She glared at Andrew.

Andrew put up his hands. "No arguments."

~ * ~

Since Anna had not been allowed to do anything but mind Davy, once Andrew started paying more attention to the lad, she had even less to occupy her time. She often retreated to her solar alone to do needlework. Frankly, she was thankful for the hours she was able to spend in seclusion. When she was with the MacLeods, particularly Davy, she worked to maintain a pleasant, happy demeanor, but it wasn't always easy. As each hour passed, she dreaded her wedding more and more. The days and years that seemed to stretch out before her promised to be dismally empty. When she was alone, she didn't have to pretend a cheerfulness she didn't feel.

She had retreated into this solitude the previous evening when Davy burst in with news that the Chisholms had arrived. She had no time to compose herself before he had pulled her down the stairs and across the hall towards his Aunt Ena.

Ena Chisholm had blond hair and blue eyes just like all of Dougal's children, and while she was taller than Anna, she was dwarfed by the tall, bearded warrior beside her. He had long dark hair that was beginning to show some gray at the temples. This must be Fearghas Chisholm, Laird Chisholm's heir, and he was every bit as frightening as Graham had said.

Even though Ena was only thirteen years older than Anna, when Ena had embraced her, it felt like she imagined a mother's embrace would. And for a moment Anna had the profound sense that everything would be all right.

Before she had been fully aware of what was happening, she was at the table, and surrounded by Chisholms. Ena pulled her into conversation and some of the strain she had been feeling began to ease. She was floored when the meal was over and Ena simply included her in the plans for the next day. Frankly, Ena she left Anna a little in awe.

When Anna had awakened this morning, for the first time since that fateful trip to the strait, she was excited about what the day would bring. That was until Andrew interfered. So crestfallen was she that she found herself blinking back tears at the thought of another day locked away in her solar. But to her surprise Ena appeared ready to do battle with him, all but dragging him from the hall.

Fearghas Chisholm's rumbling chuckle drew Anna's attention. He flashed her a huge smile. "Anna, pet, ye have a new champion, and yer betrothed is about to be eviscerated by her."

"What do ye mean?"

"Ena is not overly happy that her da and brothers are not letting ye assume the role ye deserve in the clan, and when Ena isn't happy, there's no one happy."

"I'm sorry."

Fearghas laughed richly. "There's no need for ye to be sorry—they deserve it. Frankly, it's only fair that Dougal get a taste of her wrath once in a while. After all, he raised her."

Anna smiled at him but was still worried. When Ena reappeared in the hall she looked completely unruffled. "Well now, Anna, shall we find Brenda?"

Fearghas laughed until tears rolled down his cheeks. "Aye. Go," he said between chuckles. "I'll tend the wounded if she left any survivors."

Ena snorted in a most unladylike fashion. "My husband exaggerates. I was just helping them recognize a minor error in judgement."

Anna smiled, but didn't know what to say, so she just followed Ena.

The morning sped past. Ena directed work subtlety, deferring often to Anna. It wasn't long before the MacLeod women turned first to Anna for a decision on something. By time for the midday meal, Anna realized she wasn't having to force her cheerfulness and she certainly didn't feel isolated.

~ * ~

Andrew went fishing with Fearghas, Fearghas' squire Tadhg, Davy, Graham and several guardsman. He didn't see Anna until the midday meal and wanted to sit with her to find out how things were going. He had hoped his sister was right—that the staff would accept Anna's leadership, but he wasn't completely sure. He would feel awful if they did anything to hurt Anna. However, once again Ena pulled Anna into a seat near her family and well away from him. After the meal they disappeared again.

He frowned, thinking maybe he would follow them, just to be sure all was well. But as he rose from the table his father called. "Andrew, come to my solar. I want to go over some accounts."

Andrew sighed. He would seek Anna out later.

He followed his father to the solar, but before long they were interrupted by Colin.

"Laird, two Morrison guardsmen have arrived and wish to speak with ye."

Dougal frowned. "Show them in."

Two older men stepped into the solar and bowed. "Good afternoon, Laird MacLeod. My name is Gordon and this is Conan," he gestured to the other guardsman, a fearsome looking warrior with a scarred face. "We bring a message from Laird Morrison."

"Laird Morrison sent guardsmen to deliver a message?" asked Laird MacLeod.

Gordon nodded. "I fear we bring distressing news from Laird Morrison. He suffered an apoplexy two evenings ago. He still lives but cannot move the right side of his body. He fears he may die soon and would like to see his sons. We have come to escort Darach home."

"Ah, poor man. Of course he wants his children with him. I believe he has a daughter too?"

Gordon nodded. "Aye, Laird, he does."

Andrew's father frowned. "He hasn't sent for her?"

"Not as yet, Laird."

Dougal's frown deepened. "That's unfortunate. Poor lass." He gave a heavy sigh. "Well, I'll go find Darach."

"I can go, Da."

His father shook his head sadly. "Nay, Andrew. I should be the one to tell him. Show these men to the hall and see they're given refreshment." To the Morrison guardsmen he said, "I expect ye plan to return to Lewis as soon as ye can."

"Aye Laird," answered Conan. "If we leave within the hour, we can make Durness before dark and sail on the morning tide. We'll reach Castle Morrison tomorrow evening."

Chapter 15

Darach and his father's guardsmen arrived at Castle Morrison the next evening as planned.

Gordon said, "It's good to be home."

"Aye," agreed Darach, but the truth was Castle Morrison hadn't felt like home since he was a wee lad. He had lived at Curacridhe for most of his life. He barely knew his oldest brother. Fearchar was thirteen when Darach was born and had already been training with Frasers for several years. He didn't return until after Darach had been sent to the northern Highlands to train with the MacLeods. He spent a bit more time with his brother, Coll, who was only six years older. Darach remembered following him like a puppy when he was little. Coll hadn't minded having a little brother under foot. He affectionately called Darach his *wee beastie*. Darach had been heartbroken when at the age of eleven, Coll went to train with the Macauleys. Still, given that the Macauleys were less than a day's ride away, at least Darach had seen him frequently over the next two years.

He was probably closest to his sister Claire. She was only a year older and he remembered her being fun and always up to some mischief.

That was until Da had married again. His father's new wife, Gavinia, had encouraged Da to send Claire to be educated at an abbey and Darach into training immediately. Neither of them had wanted to go, and he'd thought Da wouldn't want them to either. He idolized his Da, and had spent a great deal of time with him after Coll left. Darach still remembered overhearing the argument between his father and Gavinia.

"Gavinia, I'm not ready to send Darach away. Seven

is too young."

"Tyree, ye baby yer sons. Many lads are sent off to train as young as six."

"I know they are, but I still think that's too young. And I see no reason to send Claire away at all."

"Her behavior is atrocious. She needs to be reined in immediately, and there is no better place for her to learn discipline than an abbey."

"But I had hoped ye would—"

"Is that why ye married me? So that I would take care of the children ye have let run wild?"

"Nay, Gavinia, but—"

Gavinia sniffled, as if in tears. "I think ye care more for them than ye do me."

"Lass, it isn't a case of more or less. They are my youngest children. Ye're my wife."

"Aye, I'm yer wife, the one who is carrying *yer youngest child* at this moment. I want to be able to focus all of my energy on raising *our* children."

"Are ye carrying?" His father's voice had sounded excited.

"Aye, I am. And I do not need the stress of an uncontrollable lass and a boisterous wee lad. If ye care about me and yer new child, ye'll do as I've asked."

So Da chose his new wife over his children, or at least that is what Darach believed at the time.

Darach remembered Claire's heart-wrenching sobs as Da's guardsmen rode away with her. He also remembered begging Da if he had to leave home, to let him go to the Macauleys to train, so at least he would be with Coll and not so far away.

"Nay, lad. I need to establish better ties with some of the clans on the mainland. Laird MacLeod will be a strong ally, and many of the ports we use to ship goods are in MacLeod territory."

So praying that his father would change his mind, Darach left his home to go live with strangers. Thankfully, they didn't remain strangers long. Laird and Lady MacLeod made all of the young men training there feel welcome and even loved. Darach had never experienced a mother's love, and he adored Lady MacLeod. Perhaps that is why it was so important to him to help wee Mairi as her mother was dying. He missed his own sister, and he knew all too well how it felt to live without a mother.

Nay Castle Morrison wasn't his home.

When he entered the great hall, both his brothers sat near the hearth, drinking tankards of ale. There was no denying that all three of them were brothers or that Tyree Morrison was their father. They were all tall with dark hair and gray eyes, but there were distinct differences as well. Coll perhaps looked most like Darach remembered their father looking, strong and lean with a close-trimmed beard. Fearchar wore a heavy beard, had a thicker upper body and a bit of a paunch. At only seventeen, Darach was thin, lanky and clean-shaven, the hair on his face still too sparse to have a beard that wouldn't be laughed at.

Coll rose immediately, crossing the hall to greet Darach. He looked weary but his smile was warm as he shook Darach's hand. "Little brother, it's good to see ye."

"Ah, it looks like yer *wee beastie* is nearly grown," called Fearchar from where he sat. "Come, sit with us, Darach, and refresh yerself with a tankard of ale."

"Thank ye, Fearchar, but I should really see Da first."

"That can wait 'til morning. Da isn't going anywhere, not even to the garderobe—trust me."

Coll, whose back was to Fearchar, rolled his eyes in disgust. "Nay, Fearchar, ye know Da wanted Darach sent up as soon as he arrived." To Darach he added, "I'll go with ye."

Fearchar grunted. "It's pointless, but suit yerselves."

As he and Coll climbed the tower stairs, Darach said, "I expect yer training is done now isn't it?"

"I suppose so, although before this, I hadn't planned on coming home just yet."

"Have ye returned for good then?"

Coll frowned. "Aye, it seems I must. Da is very frail. He won't live long, Darach. He knows Fearchar is a fierce warrior, but our brother has never been as attentive to the other skills needed to lead a clan. Da is worried we'll not prosper long without someone to help mind clan business."

"What does Fearchar think of that?"

Coll snorted. "He quite likes the idea of having all of the power of a laird, with none of the responsibility."

"What about Claire? Have ye sent for her?

Coll shook his head sadly. "Nay, and we won't. Da doesn't wish to see her."

Darach could scarcely believe his ears. "Why not?"

"I don't know, Darach. I think maybe he feels guilty. As I understand it, he tried several times to convince Gavinia to let Claire return home. Gavinia always fought against it and he always gave in to her."

"Did Claire decide to take vows?"

"Nay, and for that reason, please don't mention her in front of Fearchar. It's better that he not think about her for now, else he'll see her as a pawn. I hope to be able to learn her wishes. If she wants marriage, maybe I can put things in place before Fearchar pays too much attention to her. Perhaps I can find a husband for her who Fearchar will see as an advantageous match and who will also treat her well."

~ * ~

Fearchar shook his head in disgust as Coll and Darach left the hall. "Wasting their time. Da's nothing but a shell," he muttered to the fire.

Well at least his poor health returned the beastie from MacLeod clutches.

"Why do I care? As long as he's there, he's out of my hair."

It should try ye sorely. After all they were the ones who stole yer bride.

"Shut up."

Why? Ye know it's true. Ye know she'd be yers if MacLeod hadn't stolen her.

"Aye. She'd have been mine.

Yer little brother bends the knee to Dougal and yer bride'll be forced to spread her legs for Andrew. And all because she did them a kindness.

"It isn't fair. He doesn't deserve her."

And ye do. Ye're not going to let this pass are ye?

"Go away."

"I'm sorry, sir, I just thought ye might like more ale."

The feminine voice startled him until he realized it was just a serving maid. He glanced at her. She was one he'd enjoyed before. "Aye, I'd like more ale. And I'd like to be served in my chamber. Ye ken?"

"Aye, sir. But I still have work to do tonight."

"And ye can finish it when we are done."

"Aye, sir."

~ * ~

When Darach and Coll reached their father's chamber, Coll knocked and they entered. Their father appeared to be asleep. He looked old and frail, nothing like the Da who Darach remembered. His squire sat next to the bed but stood when they entered.

"Sawny, this is our youngest brother, Darach," said Coll.

Sawny gave a slight bow. "Good evening, sirs."

"How fares our father tonight?" asked Coll.

Morrison opened his eyes. "Same," he croaked. His gaze swept the room, landing on Darach. The left side of his mouth turned up in a smile, his rheumy eyes filling with tears. "Darach, ye're here." His voice was slow and slurred. Tyree lifted his left hand, reaching towards his youngest son.

Darach took his hand. "Aye, Da."

"Missed ye."

What could he say? In truth, over the years his father had become a stranger Darach seldom thought about. "I've missed ye too, Da."

"Stay."

"Of course, Da," said Darach, releasing his father's

hand and taking the chair Sawny had vacated. "I'll stay as long as ye wish."

His father shook his head, appearing agitated. "Stay. Stay."

Coll stepped forward, patting his father on the shoulder. "It's all right, Da, I'll explain for ye." Turning to Darach, he said, "Da is asking ye to stay here for good."

"Leave the MacLeods?" Leave his real home and the people he cared about to stay here with the shell of the man who had sent him away ten years ago? "But my training isn't finished."

"I know," said Coll. "Da wants ye to finish yer training here at home with me...and Fearchar."

It took a concerted effort for Darach to keep the bitterness from his voice. "I'll stay as long as ye need me to, Da." At least it wasn't a promise to stay forever, a detail his brother didn't miss.

After their Da was settled for the night, the two brothers returned to the great hall. Fearchar had evidently retired too. Coll filled tankards with ale and they sat by the hearth, talking for quite a while before Coll raised the issue.

"Darach, when Da asked ye to stay, ye do know he meant for good? Not just until...well until he doesn't need ye anymore?"

"Aye, that was my impression."

"But...?"

"I want to finish my training with Laird MacLeod."

"But ye can finish it here. Ye've been away a long time."

Darach shook his head. "Coll, ye were eleven and Fearchar twelve when ye were sent to train. But Gavinia wanted rid of me and Claire, and Da let her have her way. We were sent away at seven and eight to make room for the children she never had. At the time, Claire—dear God, her heart was broken. When they took her away...well, I'll never forget the sound of her sobbing." He scrubbed his face, as if trying vainly to wipe away the memory. "If I had to leave home, I wanted to train with ye. Da said he needed the alliance with MacLeod, and so off I went. I barely remember my life here."

Coll looked away for a moment. "I'm sorry, Darach. I know it was hard and it certainly wasn't fair to ye, but ye were always meant to come home."

"I was meant to come home when my training was done. It isn't."

Coll sighed heavily. "Da loves ye. Can't ye do this for him?"

"Da has a funny way of showing his love. His new wife's preferences and his desire for an alliance with Laird MacLeod came before the needs of his youngest son and only daughter. God's bones, Coll, until tonight I had only seen him twice in the last five years. Once when I came home for Gavinia's funeral and once when he came to Curacridhe for Lady Joan's funeral. And I haven't seen Claire since the day she left."

"Da did miss ye. He missed ye terribly."

"And Claire? Did he miss her terribly too?" His voice dripped with sarcasm.

"I've already told ye, he tried."

"But he didn't even bring her home after Gavinia died."

"Claire was but thirteen then. Da had no idea how to manage a daughter, and over the years, Gavinia had convinced him the abbey was a better place for her. He did have every intention of bringing ye home when he went to Lady Joan's funeral. But ye seemed to be happy and doing well under Laird MacLeod so he left ye there."

"I'm glad he did. I was happy. I'm happy now. If he was truly concerned about me, he wouldn't ask me to stay on here longer than necessary."

"I'm sorry ye feel that way, but think on it. A decision doesn't have to be made tonight."

As far as Darach was concerned, the decision was made already. He would never choose to return to Lewis permanently.

Chapter 16

It had been nearly three weeks since Andrew had returned from the strait with the brokenhearted angel on his lap and had vowed to protect his heart. However, over the days since then, his betrothed had dragged him through a range of emotions equally as broad as those she had experienced on that day. From helping Mairi in accepting her betrothal to Tasgall, to determinedly shaking him from his self-pity and grief, Anna hadn't held back. And once Ena pointed out the need to let his betrothed begin managing the household, Anna approached her new responsibilities with the same energy and good humor she brought to everything. For some illogical reason—for he had nothing to do with it— he felt pride in her accomplishments.

Admiration. Anger. Grief. Determination. Pride. His resolve to stay detached was slipping.

Perhaps he should have been pleased that his sister kept Anna away and occupied, but he wasn't. He had begun to look forward to seeing her and talking with her, especially at mealtimes. For three nights, Ena had ensured that Anna was nowhere near him during meals, and Andrew grew more irritated daily.

Tonight, he would not allow that to happen. He had been hunting earlier in the day, but. Then after returning late in the afternoon, found Davy to take him for a brief ride. He fully intended to be in the great hall for the evening meal earlier than usual, so he could claim Anna himself. As soon as Ena entered with her daughters, Mairi, and a laughing Anna, he made his move.

"Good evening, ladies, ye all seem to be in a very fine mood this evening."

"Aye, brother, it has been a most productive day. Fearghas tells me the hunt went well too."

"Aye, to be sure."

"Anna, we had fun riding, didn't we, Da?" said Davy.

"Aye we did, son. Perhaps Anna will sit with us during the evening meal and ye can tell her all about it." Even as he said it, he took Anna by the elbow and guided her to the seat she had always occupied until Ena arrived.

"I've missed ye," he whispered, smiling at Anna's puzzled expression.

"I didn't go anywhere."

"Aye ye did, angel. Perhaps it was just to the other end of the table, but Davy and I had gotten used to dining with ye. I fear my sister has completely stolen ye away."

"Oh. I suppose I have spent a little less time with him recently, but he truly seems to be thriving, the more time he spends with ye."

"Aye he does, but he adores ye as well."

Anna nodded, but he sensed a shift in her mood.

"Andrew, I know ye didn't want me to help run the household—"

"I was wrong about that."

Anna looked surprise. "Ye were?" She shook her head a little. "I mean, I'm glad ye changed yer mind—"

"So am I. Ye seem to be thriving as well."

"I am. That is to say, I like having purpose and being able to contribute to the life of the clan. But I swear to ye, it's equally as important to me to see to Davy. I'm sorry if ye think I haven't been doing that."

It was Andrew's turn to be puzzled for a moment until he realized she had misunderstood him. "Anna, I'm not upset with ye, and I see that ye are able to balance things quite well. Frankly, I'm impressed. I just realized that ye and I spend very little time together—usually just at mealtimes. I've missed yer company over the last few evenings, that's all."

She drew her brows together, looking wary. Andrew

chuckled, took one of her hands in his and kissed the back of it. "It's the truth."

As the evening meal progressed, Andrew realized that it was truer than he'd realized. He enjoyed being with Anna, and he had nearly from the start. He smiled, remembering the first night he sat with her after her fever had broken. Too weak to lift her head from the pillow and knowing she was being held by her family's worst enemy, she had openly referred to Curacridhe as "hell."

Aye, he enjoyed her company and he would not let his sister rob him of it again.

~ * ~

With Brenda and Ena's help, Anna's life was settling into a comfortable rhythm. As she had promised Andrew, Anna still ensured that Davy was well cared for. Davy had followed the one rule she had given him perfectly. She always knew where he was and what he was doing, even if she wasn't with him.

Anna also still devoted time every morning to teaching Davy and Mairi, but now Davy often spent afternoons doing something with his father.

She was even beginning to think Andrew might be softening a bit. The previous evening, she had been both surprised and pleased when he said he "missed" her. When he kissed the back of her hand, she felt a little flutter stir deep within.

It wasn't a declaration of love, but it was nice.

As she entered the hall for the midday meal with Davy and Mairi, Anna felt the same thrill when Andrew met them halfway across the room.

He took her hand and walked with her to the table. "Has yer morning gone well, angel?"

Slightly better prepared for his attention than she had been the previous evening, she smiled. "Aye, it has."

"I can write all my letters now and I know the sounds they make," declared Davy with pride.

"That is quite an accomplishment, son. Ye should be

very proud."

"I can write all the letters too," said Mairi.

Andrew smiled at her. "Well done, Mairi. Very few young women can say that. Ye should be proud too."

Mairi beamed.

Andrew turned his attention to Anna. "That being the case, how is it that *ye* learned to read and write?"

"My da taught me." Anna smiled at the memories of her beloved father.

Andrew squeezed her hand.

"He started teaching me after Tasgall went away to train. Aidan was gone too and I know Da missed them. Eoin had just returned home but he and Da butted heads." Anna gave a wry smile. "Eoin was a bit full of himself."

Andrew chuckled. "I might have been when I first came home after training too."

Mairi threw her head back and laughed outright. "*Might have been*? Sometimes ye still are."

Andrew smiled, simply shaking his head at his audacious little sister. "So ye think he taught ye to read because Eoin tried his patience and he missed Tasgall and Aidan?"

"All of those things might have been a part of it, but I think it was mostly because he missed Tasgall. He had taught all three of them to read, but Aidan and Eoin had always considered it a necessary chore, while Tasgall loved it. Our father had a small collection of books, as did our priest. Tasgall reread them over and over. He loved to talk about them with Da and I think that's what Da missed most."

"Did ye discuss books with yer da, once ye learned to read?"

She nodded. Again poignant memories of her father nearly took her breath away.

Andrew put a finger under her chin, lifting her gaze to his. "I didn't mean to make ye sad, angel."

Although she knew tears had filled her eyes, she smiled. "I'm not sad. I loved my da and I still miss him, but my memories are happy."

After they were seated at the table, Mairi leaned forward and asked quietly, "Is that why ye want me to learn to read? Because Tasgall likes to read?"

Anna chuckled. "I want ye to learn to read because it's a good skill to have. But, aye, I thought it might also be nice if ye enjoy reading as he does."

~ * ~

As they ate their midday meal, Andrew was struck again by what a truly remarkable woman his betrothed was. She was smart and capable—the servants now deferred to her rather than Brenda or Ena. Not only had she already embraced the role of mother to Davy, she had firmly taken Mairi under her wing too.

And when she laughed—something he had seen far too little of—she practically sparkled.

He had the sudden strong desire to spend more time with her.

Near the end of the meal he said, "Davy, don't ye think it would be a good idea if Anna went riding with us this afternoon?"

His son nodded exuberantly. "Aye, Da."

"Anna, will ye join us?"

Her face lit with a smile. "I'd love to."

Fearghas Chisholm called from the other end of the table. "Davy, lad, the weather is perfect to go fishing. Would ye like to come with me and my squire?"

"Fishing? I love fishing." Davy exclaimed. "Oh, but Da and I were going riding with Anna."

"Don't worry about me. We can ride another day. Ye'll both enjoy fishing."

Andrew frowned. At the moment, riding with Anna was a much more appealing prospect.

Ena shook her head. "Nay, Anna deserves an outing. She's been working very hard." At her husband's mock frown she added, "But Uncle Fearghas seldom gets to go fishing and even when he does, he has no wee lad of his own to fish with."

Her comment was made to the table at large, but she fixed Andrew with a piercing look.

He had to force himself not to laugh. "I have an idea. Davy, you go fishing with Uncle Fearghas and maybe Uncle Graham too, and I'll take Anna for a ride."

Ena smiled broadly. "That is an excellent idea. I should've thought of it myself."

Andrew arched an eyebrow at his interfering sister. Clearly she *had* thought of it herself—for which he was very thankful.

In no time at all, the meal was over, horses were saddled and Andrew was riding through the gates of Curacridhe with Anna at his side and several guardsmen at a discreet distance.

Surprisingly, Anna, who was never at a loss for words, seemed to have gone very quiet.

"Ye do like riding, don't ye Anna?" He knew she did. "I didn't think to ask."

"Aye, I love it."

"What else do ye like to do?"

She glanced sideways at him. "That's an odd question."

"Ye think? Rumor has it we are to be married. Learning a bit more about ye doesn't seem so very odd to me."

She grinned. "Rumor has it?"

"Well, perhaps it is more than a rumor. There may be the odd contract signed, but still, a groom should know a bit about his bride."

"And shouldn't the bride also know a bit about her groom?"

He nodded. "Now that ye mention it, I suppose she should. I'll make ye a deal—ye answer a question about yerself and then I'll do the same."

"That seems fair."

"So my question was, other than riding, what do ye

like to do?"

"Hmm. Well, I actually do love needlework. That's probably why I told yer da I was a seamstress right after I was captured. It was the first thing that popped into my head."

Damn. He didn't want her mind to linger on the events of that day. "Aye, Mairi has mentioned how very skilled ye are. Now I believe 'tis yer turn to ask me a question."

She thought for a moment and then shrugged. "I guess I'll ask the same thing. What is something ye like to do, at which ye are very skilled?"

"Hmm. Well, I like to go hunting—I am deadly accurate with a bow."

"Are ye?" There was a note of awe in her voice. "I've always wanted to learn to shoot a bow. Da wouldn't let me. He said I was too small."

"Well it is true, the taller ye are, the longer yer arms are and the longer yer draw will be, but ye could still learn. It's just yer arrow won't fly as far or have the same force behind it as a taller archer's would." He considered her for a moment. "Would ye like to learn?"

She grinned. "Aye, I would."

"Well then, things are a bit hectic now with the wedding pending, but after that, I'd be happy to teach ye."

She beamed at him, pleasing him beyond measure. It took a moment to remember it was his turn to ask a question. "Next question. What is—"

"I believe the next question is mine."

"Nay, I don't think so. Ye asked me what I was skilled at."

"Aye, I did, and then ye asked me if I wanted to learn archery. So it's my turn again." She gave him a cheeky grin.

He chuckled. "I beg yer pardon, my lady. Ask away."

She thought for a moment. "All right, I have one. Who is your most trusted confidant?"

He arched a brow at her. "That's hard to answer. I am

probably closest to my father and Graham. I guess it would depend on this issue. If it was something that concerned the whole clan, I would seek my father's counsel."

"But what if it didn't concern the whole clan? What if it was something personal?"

"Hmm. Well, I suppose Graham. He would be more likely to consider what was best for me alone. My father's decisions will always be tempered by what is best for the clan."

She looked down. "Like forcing us to marry?"

Damn. When would he stop putting his foot in his mouth? Andrew reached out and grabbed her horse's rein, pulling her to a stop. He looked into her beautiful green eyes, which moments ago had sparkled with laughter. "Anna, I didn't mean to hurt ye. Still, now that ye mention it, I firmly believe Da's decision was the best one for both of our clans. This will be a good marriage. Things have changed so much since that first day. Ye don't fear us anymore. By all that's holy, ye practically run Curacridhe singlehandedly, and I don't think ye hate me anymore. It isn't still the terrible fate ye thought it was, is it?"

She smiled, but it didn't quite reach her eyes. "Nay, it isn't a terrible fate and I certainly don't hate ye."

"Good, because I find I quite like ye." He let go of her mount and started moving again. "It's my turn for a question. What's yer favorite food?"

She chuckled. "That's hard, I like to eat. I like quail but I suppose my favorite is lamb."

He gave a small sigh of relief, having successfully steered her towards safer topics.

When they reached a heath beyond the village, he gave the horses a chance to run. It seemed to delight her. By the time they returned to the keep, her cheeks were flushed and the distressing topics seemed forgotten. He stopped in the bailey, dismounted, and lifted her from her mount.

"It's turned a bit chilly. Go inside now and warm yerself. I'll see to the horses." But even as he bid her leave, he couldn't take his hands off her waist.

"Thank ye, Andrew. I enjoyed the ride."

He smiled down at her. "I did too." Staring into her eyes, he was surprised to see…was it longing? Or was he simply seeing his own longing reflected there. It was something he hadn't felt in years. He couldn't deny that right now he longed to take her in his arms and kiss her.

Her voice broke through his desire. "I, uh…I should probably…well it is a bit chilly." She seemed as befuddled by his nearness as he was by hers—and that pleased him.

"Aye, ye probably should." His lips brushed her cheek and he let go of her, stepping aside so she could enter the keep. "I'll see ye at the evening meal, angel."

~ * ~

Andrew had expected Ena and her family to arrive well in advance of the wedding but was shocked when, while he tended their horses, the watch announced the arrival of the Sinclairs. Joan's parents were nearly a fortnight early.

He finished caring for the beasts before joining his father in the courtyard a few minutes before the visitors reached the gate. "Da, did ye know about this?"

"Aye, I invited them."

"I knew ye'd invited them to the wedding, but did ye know they were coming so soon?"

"Aye, son. I wasn't certain of the exact day but I thought they might like to spend a bit of time with Davy before the wedding. It'll be so hectic after the other clans begin to arrive."

Andrew frowned. "Ye could have warned me."

His father raised his brow. "Warned ye? Why on earth would ye need a warning? They're Davy's grandparents. Do ye begrudge them a visit?"

Andrew shook his head. "Nay, Da." His father was right. Davy's grandparents saw him so rarely, Andrew knew his son would be thrilled. How could he explain to his father that the Sinclairs were just another painful reminder of the love he had lost?

Moments later, Anna hurried out of the keep with Davy at her side. "I'm sorry, Andrew, I would have brought Davy down sooner, but he was a bit of a mess after fishing with his uncles. I wanted him to clean up a bit before greeting his grandparents."

Dear God. Andrew didn't want Anna here. He wasn't sure how the Sinclairs would react to her…or how he would react to the Sinclairs. "Ye needn't have worried. In fact, ye're probably still chilled from the ride. Ye can go back inside where it's warm if ye wish. Da and I can handle this."

Anna smiled, but canted her head, looking a bit confused. "I fetched my mantel before coming out. I don't mind greeting our wedding guests, and I'd like to meet them. The MacKays had no feud with the Sinclairs but they weren't allies. Besides, once we heard they were arriving, Davy insisted that I come down with him."

Her presence here was perfectly reasonable. Still Andrew would have suggested again that she return to the keep, except the Sinclairs were already riding through the gates. Their sons Eller and Nivan accompanied them. Thankfully, their daughter Annice had not joined them. She was expecting a child soon and while Andrew hadn't seen her since Joan's funeral, again he feared the resemblance between them would stir unwelcome memories.

His father called, "Ranulf, Lara, welcome to Curacridhe."

As soon as Ranulf Sinclair had lifted his wife off her horse, before Andrew or Dougal could say anything, Davy ran to her. She crouched down and caught him in her arms.

To his shock, Andrew didn't feel the searing pain he expected. Aye, there was an undeniable ache and a warm memory, but nothing more.

"Granma, Granda, I want ye to meet my angel, who's going to be my new mama."

Andrew stiffened, worried the Sinclairs might be upset that Anna was replacing Joan in Davy's life. He didn't want her hurt.

Anna curtsied. "Good afternoon, my Lady, Laird, I'm pleased to meet ye.

Lady Sinclair rose gracefully and, giving Anna a brilliant smile, opened her arms to her. "My precious lass, we owe ye so much, formality will not do. I'm Lara."

Anna blushed, as she always did when someone alluded to her having saved Davy, but returned Lara Sinclair's hug.

When Lara released her, Laird Sinclair took her hands in his and kissed her cheek. "Thank ye seems so very inadequate, but they are the only words I have."

Andrew gave a small sigh of relief and stepped forward to welcome the Sinclairs. "Davy robbed me of the opportunity to introduce her, but this is Anna MacKay, my betrothed."

His father introduced Anna to Eller and Nivan as well. Both young men smiled appreciatively at her and greeted her with a kiss on the cheek, which somehow irritated Andrew. He should be happy that Joan's family accepted her without reservation, but their sudden arrival left him feeling uncomfortable.

~ * ~

Anna had ridden back to Curacridhe after spending the afternoon alone with Andrew, with a bit of hope burgeoning once again. Ever since returning from the strait that day, she had seldom experienced more than cool detachment from Andrew. But over the last few days, things seemed to be changing. Perhaps no one would ever be as precious to him as Joan had been, but Anna didn't think she imagined the warmth and affection that was beginning to grow between them. Maybe she couldn't expect the extraordinary love Fiona and Eoin had, but it seemed as if there was a bit of room in Andrew's heart for her.

She hadn't been in her chamber long when Davy had come rushing in. "Anna, come quick! My grandparents are coming. In fact, they're almost here. I want ye to meet them."

When she and Davy joined Andrew and Laird

MacLeod in the bailey, Anna had the vague sense that Andrew hadn't wanted her there.

The Sinclairs had greeted her for the first time with grateful affection as most people who loved Davy did. It always made her a bit uncomfortable. She'd done what had to be done at the time—just as anyone would. Still it was always nice to be met so warmly.

As the visitors were led inside, Anna was a little surprised when Laird Chisholm's squire all but ran to Lara Sinclair as they entered the keep, giving her a huge hug.

"Aunt Lara, I didn't know ye were coming so early."

Lady Sinclair returned his hug. "Tadgh, 'tis good to see ye lad. My, ye're very grown now. Do ye like being a squire?"

Anna smiled. She knew the lad was only about ten years old, but he stood a little taller under his aunt's praise. "Aye, I do."

Once inside Anna stepped smoothly into the role of hostess, ensuring that the Sinclairs were given comfortable guest chambers and the evening meal was held until they had the opportunity to refresh themselves. As they had not been expected to arrive this evening, she also had a quick chat with Dallis to make her aware of their additional guests.

By the time everything was done and she too had had a moment to freshen up, Anna returned to the great hall. Laird MacLeod was carrying on a lively conversation with Fearghas Chisholm and the newly arrived Sinclairs. Andrew stood to one side, appearing to be listening, but he seemed distracted.

His odd mood continued through dinner. The comfortable rapport that had been developing between them seemed to have fled. Anna tried to ignore it and focus on their guests. Still, she felt a keen disappointment. She feared that the Sinclair's arrival had brought Joan to the forefront of Andrew's thoughts, and any growing affection he might have for Anna had been firmly quashed again.

Chapter 17

Ena had been thrilled when it appeared Andrew was coming around where his betrothed was concerned. Anna was absolutely lovely, she had every skill necessary to serve as lady of the castle. As soon as she had been allowed to, she seemed to be happier.

Yet after the Sinclairs had arrived the previous evening, Ena once again sensed the underlying sorrow Anna clearly tried to hide.

Had she fooled everyone into believing she had accepted the situation? Ena couldn't deny the way in which the betrothal came around was unpleasant, to say the least. Still, many noblewomen married strangers and often the only goal for those arranging the union was the political advantage it represented. Did Anna hide her true feelings while only trying to assimilate into the clan because it was expected of her?

Nay. The lass was more open and forthright than any she had ever met.

Ena had also ruled out simple incompatibility as the cause. Anna was open and loving—she seemed to like Andrew. Perhaps it was Andrew who didn't care for Anna.

Ena chuckled at this thought. Over the last few days, Andrew looked like a man who was clearly smitten. His eyes followed Anna whenever she was in the room. Ena had intentionally kept his betrothed away from him during mealtimes for several days and was thrilled when he put a stop to it.

Things seemed to be improving, until last night. Andrew had become cool and distant even as the spark of joy Ena had begun to see in Anna flickered and died.

Ena could only guess that the Sinclairs' arrival had stirred up painful memories and Andrew had once again withdrawn.

If that was the case, it had to stop, and Anna herself stood the best chance of accomplishing that, but someone had to encourage her a bit. Ena smiled.

After the morning meal, when the household staff had been set their tasks, Davy was with his grandparents and Ena's littlest ones, Lara and Rhona were in the care of their nursemaid, Ena said, "Anna, we haven't decided what ye'll wear to yer wedding. It's less than a fortnight away now, let's go see what we have to work with."

"I don't really have much to choose from." She smiled apologetically. "I have what I was wearing the day I arrived and have made a couple of léines since then."

"Nay, pet, I didn't mean to choose from the clothes ye already have. I thought yer options might be limited, so I brought several pieces of beautiful fabric. We'll be able to make ye something lovely."

"Ooh, can I help?" asked Mairi.

"Me too?" asked Ena's oldest, Allison.

Ena smiled. "Of course ye can. Mairi, does Janet's mother still weave flax?"

"Aye, she does."

"Excellent. I think Da is in the bailey. Go and ask him to send someone with ye to the village and bring me several lengths of the finest white linen she has."

Mairi nodded eagerly. "Aye Ena. Do ye need anything else?"

"See if she has any dark green thread and perhaps some gold."

"I will. Will we come to yer chamber when we get back?"

"Nay, pet, if we aren't already in Anna's solar when ye return, we will be soon. Meet us there."

Mairi grabbed Allison's hand and practically ran to the door. "Allison, let's go find my dal. We'll be back soon," she called over her shoulder.

Ena smiled. "Ye needn't rush so. It's a lovely day. Enjoy the walk." But the lassies were already out of the hall. She shook her head after them. "That sister of mine. She's almost fifteen and one minute she's poised and mature, but then ye blink and the wee lassie comes bubbling up."

Anna laughed, knowing how very true those words were.

Ena gave an exaggerated sigh. "Ah well, come with me to my chamber and we'll decide what to use."

As Anna followed her up the stairs, she asked, "Ena, have I done something wrong?"

Ena laughed. "Goodness, lass, of course not. What would make ye ask that?"

"Well, since ye've been here, I've noticed if ye make a point of getting someone alone, it's because ye need to, how is it ye put it?"

"Help them recognize a minor error in judgement?"

Anna laughed. "Aye, that's it. Since ye sent the lassies away, I thought perhaps ye might be planning to help me *recognize a minor error in judgement*."

By this time they had reached Ena's chamber and she ushered Anna in. "Nay, Anna, ye've done nothing wrong, but I did want to speak with ye privately."

"About what?"

Ena considered her for a moment. She probably should make certain that Anna herself was not the problem. "Anna, ye seem very sad and I want to know why."

Anna looked a bit taken aback. "Ena, I'm not—I mean—there isn't anything…" As Anna's voice trailed off, she looked away.

Ena smiled gently at her. "Ye're unhappy, Anna. Ye try very hard to hide it and ye do rather well most of the time. None of the men seem to notice, eejits that they are, but I do. I thought it was getting better but…well, I know ye're still sad."

"I'm just missing my home, I suppose."

"There's more to it than that. I thought at first it might be that ye didn't like Andrew and dreaded marrying him, but I think ye do…like him that is."

Anna smiled sadly. "I do."

"So, I figure the problem is that ye believe he doesn't like ye."

Anna shook her head. "He doesn't."

"Nay, ye're wrong. He clearly adores ye."

Anna met her gaze unflinchingly. "Nay, Ena, he doesn't. It isn't that he dislikes me. In fact I rather thought he was beginning to enjoy being with me until last night. He changed almost instantly when the Sinclairs arrived. I suppose it's because he loved Joan so. He's made it very clear, nearly from the start, he does not wish to love anyone else."

Ena frowned. "No one's that stupid. Ye must have misunderstood him."

Anna gave a chuckle followed by a sigh. "I don't think so. I believe his exact words were, 'I can never give my heart to anyone like that again'."

Ena was dumbstruck. "The roaring arse. Oh, Anna, I'm sorry he said something so hurtful and I'm not sure why he did, but he's wrong. He may think he can control his heart, but that isn't possible."

"But…"

"Nay, I'm right. I know him better than anyone. For some absolutely asinine reason, he may be trying to convince himself that he doesn't love ye, or can't love ye because of what he felt for Joan, but I tell ye, he's wrong. He already loves ye. I know he does. It looks like someone needs to apprise him of his *major* error in judgement immediately."

"Please don't."

"Why? Do ye plan to?"

"Nay, Ena, but—"

"Anna, if ye weren't his betrothed and ye knew he had spouted such nonsense to the lass he was marrying, what would ye do?"

Anna just shook her head.

"Don't deny it to me, pet. I know what ye'd do. Ye'd go nose to nose with him." Ena smiled. "Of course ye'd have to stand on a block to reach his nose, but ye wouldn't let him believe something so ridiculous, for his sake as well as hers."

"Is it ridiculous? Maybe he can't love me as he did her."

Ena huffed, exasperated. "Of course he can't. He loves ye as he loves *ye*. Anna, love isn't quantifiable. Just because he loved Joan doesn't mean he can't love ye completely and just because he loves ye, it doesn't mean he didn't love her completely. It isn't an issue of more or less."

Anna canted her head. "But it feels as if he has built a wall to keep me out."

"Well then, ye shall just have to break that wall down. Ye've done it before, but always for someone else."

"I haven't—"

"Don't even try to deny it. I know how ye pushed him about Davy, and ye are relentless with Mairi."

"Mairi? I haven't done anything to her."

"Anna, my da and brothers might be blind but I'm not. I notice what ye do. Ye find ways to mention Tasgall when she's around. Ye reveal bits and pieces about him, about how kind, and smart, and funny he is. Ye're wearing her down. Before long, she'll be starry-eyed about meeting yer 'brother Tasgall' instead of dreading the arrival of 'the MacKay she's being forced to marry someday'."

Anna blushed and smiled.

Ena laughed. "I knew ye were doing it with a purpose. So now lass, ye must use yer considerable powers of persuasion on my hard-headed brother." Before Anna could argue, Ena wielded her most powerful argument. "Can ye do that for him, Anna? Ye gave him back his son. Can ye finish mending his heart and bring him happiness again?"

~ * ~

Finish mending his heart? Hours later Ena's words still echoed in Anna's mind. Could she do that? During the midday meal she sat with him as was normal, but she paid closer attention to him than she ever had. His mask of cool indifference was back in place. It made Anna wonder if his sister had been wrong, but as the meal progressed, it was clear she hadn't been. His actions and responses were forced, as if he wasn't allowing himself to become engaged or enjoy anything overmuch. It was exactly how he had behaved around Davy weeks ago.

The meal was over before she could do anything about it. She needed more time with him—alone.

"Andrew, would ye care to go riding again this afternoon?"

"Nay, Anna, there is business I need to attend to."

"Perhaps just a brief walk then? On the shores of the loch?"

He shook his head. "I really can't today. Another time perhaps."

She smiled to herself. It was just as he had been with Davy. She decided not to push today. Gentle persistence was called for. "Aye. Another time. Ena and I were working on my dress for the wedding anyway."

She kissed his cheek before leaving the table to seek out her sister-in-law. She would try again later.

~ * ~

Andrew stood by the hearth in the great hall, waiting for the evening meal, staring broodingly into the flames, but his eyes were pulled to Anna the instant she entered the room. She had kissed him as she left the table that afternoon. She had never done that. He had kissed her chastely before, on the head, hand or cheek. She had never pulled away from his touch. He smiled to himself; that wasn't quite true. When she was ill and barely had the strength to move she had tried. And there was the day coming home from the straight when she was hopping mad, but later that same evening she had clung to him as she sobbed.

He liked holding her in his arms.

He liked her kiss.

He imagined how it would feel if she clung to him in passion instead of sorrow.

He had to stop this line of thinking.

After greeting several people, Anna's eyes found his. Her face lit with a warm, happy smile.

For him.

It nearly took his breath away.

After a moment, she looked away, her attention drawn to Davy, who rushed into the hall followed by his Sinclair uncles. She crouched down, giving him her full attention. The sight of her with Davy had warmed his heart from the moment Andrew had found his son asleep in her arms before she had even recovered from her illness. He could have searched the earth over and never found a better mother for his son than Anna MacKay.

Davy's voice drew him from his musing. "Anna, do ye mind if I sit with Uncle Nivan and Uncle Eller tonight? I don't get to see them often."

"Of course I don't mind," Anna assured him.

"Ye could sit with us too."

Nay. Andrew didn't want that. He wanted her to sit with him and her next words pleased him no end.

"But then who would yer da sit with? We wouldn't want him to be lonely would we?

Davy shook his head. "I didn't think about that."

"Well don't worry, I'll see he doesn't get lonely. Ye have fun with yer uncles."

Dear God. He had been lonely for so very long.

Anna stood smiling after Davy as he led his uncles to the table. Then she joined Andrew where he stood near the hearth.

"Good evening, Anna."

"Good evening." She smiled up at him and slipped her hand in his. "Did ye have a good day?"

Did he have a good day? Everything seemed washed from his memory but the feel of her small hand in his, and that made it a very good day. He smiled at her. "Aye, I suppose so. Did ye?"

"Yesterday was better."

"It was?" Yesterday they had spent the afternoon alone together. She had asked him to go riding again this afternoon, but he declined. He had refused to even take her on a short walk. Why would he have done that?

She smiled. "Aye it was. But Ena and I made quite a bit of progress on my dress."

"I'm looking forward to seeing ye in it."

For the next few minutes, she kept him engaged in small talk, never letting go of his hand. This pleased him until he realized he was holding her onto it so firmly she couldn't have pulled her hand away even if she had wanted to. Still she hadn't tried.

During the evening meal Andrew fought an internal battle. One moment Anna's smile, laugh or casual touch would draw his attention and he allowed himself to become intoxicated by her nearness. He told himself there was nothing wrong with enjoying her company. After all, he was marrying her in less than two weeks. Why had it been so important to keep her at arm's length?

Then a glance at Lady Sinclair would remind him. He loved Joan. How could he love anyone else or risk that pain again?

When the meal was over, Andrew's mental war had exhausted him. He offered his apologies, intending to retire early. "It's been a long day, I will wish ye all good night."

"It has been," agreed Anna. "Will ye walk me to my chamber?"

"Aye, of course, Anna."

She slipped her arm through his as they left the hall.

It felt as if she belonged there, as if a part of him had been missing and now he was whole.

Neither of them said anything until they reached the door of her chamber. There she turned to face him, looking deeply into his eyes. Her brow furrowed. "Andrew, is something wrong?"

"Nay, I'm…nay, nothing's wrong."

She reached up and caressed his face. He could only lean into her delicate touch. He put his hand over hers and turned his head to kiss her palm, then folded his fingers around her small hand.

She was gentle and sweet and so very beautiful.

"Andrew, ye confuse me."

Not to mention forthright, he added to the list of her charming attributes.

He chuckled. "Ye confuse me too." Letting go of her hand, he raised her chin to peer into her eyes. He saw a deep yearning there—so like one he had fought all evening. He caressed her cheek and just as he had done, she leaned into his touch.

She was there, in front of him, lips parted and trembling. Putting his other hand on the wall, behind her, he leaned in, tilting her head back ever so slightly. In the instant before his lips touched hers, voices drifted to them from the stairwell.

Startled, he straightened. *What was he doing? He couldn't.* "Anna, I…goodnight, Anna." He turned and walked away, his brain scarcely registering the stricken look on her face.

~ * ~

Anna stood for a moment, watching him stride away, barely able to process what had just happened. Graham emerged from the stairwell, glancing first toward Andrew's retreating figure, then back at Anna. A look of realization crossed his features, replaced quickly by anger. He turned and strode after Andrew.

Anna spun away, entering her room, mortified. She had all but begged him to kiss her, and he'd simply turned away. Ena was wrong. Andrew did not love her. He couldn't possibly love her and have humiliated her like that.

After a moment her embarrassment and disappointment morphed to anger.

Embarrassment ached, but righteous anger didn't, and

she had every right to be angry.

She paced as memories of the last six weeks came crashing down on her and she began a litany in her head. *Captured, accused of horrible things, thrown in the dungeon, allowed to freeze. By all that's holy, I was so ill, they gave me the Last Rites in this very room.*

They wouldn't let me go home, even after the precious betrothal was signed. I have accepted everything, I have tried my best to find happiness here. But what is the result? What can I look forward to? I don't expect all-consuming passion, but at least consistency would be nice. One minute it seems as if he reaches for me—the next he pushes me away. It hurts more each time he does.

She could no longer keep it in, saying to the empty room, "I will not accept that. I've had enough. No priest will preside over a wedding if I refuse to consent…and I refuse." She grabbed her mantle, charged out of her chamber and down the stairs. She took a deep breath to calm herself before stepping into the great hall.

Laird MacLeod was still there, sitting near the hearth with Lairds Chisholm and Sinclair, tankards of ale in their hands. "Anna, my little dove, where are ye going? Why do ye have yer mantle on?"

She forced a smile to her lips. "I need to speak with Father Ninian."

"It's a bit late isn't it? Surely this can wait until morning."

"Nay, Laird, I assure ye, it cannot." She strode to the door and out into the bailey before he could respond. She knew the quiet priest chose to say the liturgy of the hours, at least those from prime to compline, in the chapel. If he wasn't already there, he would be arriving soon—it had to be nearly time for compline.

She slipped inside the chapel. It was bathed in soft candlelight as Father did indeed stand before the altar reciting the Divine Office.

She sat on a bench near the back of the church, bowed

her head and let his words wash over her, calming her.

When he had finished, he turned towards her, a small smile forming on his lips. "Anna, child, what brings ye here so late?"

"Father, I seek sanctuary."

He blinked at her. "Surely ye don't mean that. Ye haven't committed any crime."

"Nay but I refuse to marry Andrew MacLeod."

"Ye don't mean that. Come sit with me and tell me what has upset ye so."

"I do mean it, Father."

More seriously he said. "Anna, ye can't just refuse. The betrothal is signed."

"But ye need my consent to marry us do ye not?"

"Aye, but lass, a betrothal is binding. It cannot be set aside."

"It can if I chose the religious life, can't it?"

"Aye, but—"

"Nay, Father, I am asking for sanctuary until I can be taken to an abbey. Will ye deny me?"

Chapter 18

Andrew had barely reached the confines of his chamber before Graham charged in.

"By the Almighty, Andrew, what have ye done?"

"Get out, Graham."

"Not until ye tell me what ye did to crush Anna."

"I didn't crush her."

"The hell ye didn't. I saw her as ye were walking away, and I've never seen her look like that. She was shattered."

"It's better this way. She shouldn't have any romantic notions about me. I cannot love her."

"Ye're an idiot. Why are ye so dead set against letting her into yer heart?"

"It's none of yer business, but I've told ye before, I loved Joan. I don't want to love anyone like that again."

"Get yer head out of yer arse. I never knew ye were such a selfish coward."

"Ye don't know what it's like to lose yer beloved, and until ye do, ye have no right to call me a coward." But even as he said it, Andrew knew Graham was right. Hadn't he admitted as much to Anna when she confronted him about Davy?

"Perhaps I don't know about that kind of loss, but I know a bit about courage. I have witnessed a wee lass, a reviled MacKay, who, when she saw a child in danger, gave no thought to herself, to what might happen to her, or even to the possibility that her actions might have resulted in her own death. She simply acted. If she had turned around on the bluff that day, none of us would have known and no one in her clan would have blamed her. But I'll warrant it never occurred to her to protect herself. Then she did it again the morning she challenged you over going riding with Davy. Ye were enraged and ye practically dragged her out of the hall."

"I would never have hurt her."

"Of course ye wouldn't, but I doubt she knew that. And yet she clearly stood her ground because whatever it was she said awakened ye to the fact that ye had been pushing yer own son away for years. I've already told ye, the rest of us knew it, but we also knew how badly ye were hurting and none of us were bold enough to call ye on it. Andrew, she gave ye back yer son...twice."

"I know she did, but—"

"Nay, there is no but. That wee lass has a heart bigger than the Highlands and she gives her love freely, without worrying about how she could be hurt. She deserves yer love in return."

Andrew shook his head in frustration. Everything Graham said was true. He tried again to make his brother understand. "There is more to it than fearing the pain of loss again, and it isn't that I don't want to love her."

"Then what is it? Do ye not desire her? That's hard to believe."

Andrew scowled darkly. "Of course I desire her. That has nothing to do with it."

"Then I am at a loss. She cares for yer clan, she adores yer child, and she loves ye. What could possibly keep ye from loving her in return?"

There was only one answer Andrew could give. "Guilt."

"What? What do ye have to feel guilty for?"

"If I allow myself to love Anna, I fear I'm letting Joan go."

"Of course ye're letting her go!" Graham practically shouted. "She's dead, Andrew, *ye must let her go*, but it doesn't mean ye love her any less. If I'm not much mistaken, she would be furious over this. She loved ye too, but she was as loving and generous as Anna. Joan wouldn't want ye to lock yer heart away, and she certainly wouldn't want ye to eschew Anna's love out of some foolish devotion to her."

Andrew was silent as he let the things Graham had said sink in. It was true. Once again he had been focused only on himself, on what he had lost. Furthermore, with his misguided notion of loyalty he hadn't allowed himself to see any other perspective. Graham was right about Joan too. She wouldn't begrudge him this. She would be thrilled that another woman cared so deeply for her son, and she wouldn't want Andrew to live the remainder of his days without love either.

"Do ye still think ye can't give Anna yer heart? Because if ye do, I'll go now, take her to Naomh-dùn tonight, beg her brother to break the betrothal and face Da's wrath in the morning."

"For the love of all that's holy, Graham, don't do that. I fear I gave her my heart the moment I carried her from the dungeon. I just didn't…I couldn't…"

"Don't tell me. Tell her—if she'll even speak to ye."

Andrew nodded and left the room.

When he reached Anna's chamber he knocked. Hearing nothing, he knocked again. "Anna, please."

She didn't respond.

"Anna, we need to talk." He frowned when she didn't answer. He knocked again. "Anna, I'm coming in."

He opened the door only to discover the room was empty. He left her chamber and practically ran down the stairs.

He burst into the great hall and, on seeing his father, asked, "Da, have ye seen Anna?"

Obviously concerned, Dougal frowned. "What's happened?"

"We had a…misunderstanding. Did ye see her?"

"Aye, she was here not long ago. She said she was going to the chapel to speak with Father Ninian."

Without another word, Andrew left the keep, crossing the bailey to the chapel. Someone was there; the windows glowed with candlelight. He took a deep, calming breath before stepping inside.

There sat Anna, her back to the door, speaking earnestly with Father Ninian.

The priest looked up. "Ah…Andrew…good evening."

Anna's back went rigid. "Leave me be."

"Anna, I'm sorry. Come back to the keep with me, there are things I need to tell ye."

"Nay, Andrew. I said leave me be."

"Anna, please, it's late. I'm sure Father Ninian is ready to retire. Come with me now."

"I said nay."

Andrew was growing frustrated. He knew she was angry and she deserved to be, but he didn't want to discuss this here. "Anna, I threatened to throw ye over my shoulder once before. Don't make me do it again."

Father Ninian stood up. "I'm sorry Andrew, I can't allow that. Anna has asked for sanctuary and I have granted it."

"Sanctuary? From what?"

"From marriage."

"Ye can't be serious. Anna, the betrothals are signed. They can't be broken. Isn't that right, Father Ninian?"

The priest shook his head. "That's not precisely true, Andrew. A betrothal can be broken in some circumstances, if both parties agree."

"Well, I don't agree."

"And," continued Father Ninian, "a betrothal can be broken unilaterally if one party seeks to make religious vows. Anna has requested sanctuary and safe passage to an abbey. I cannot deny her that."

This couldn't be happening. He had to change her mind. "Anna, please, give me the opportunity to explain."

Finally she turned around. The hurt and anger in her expression gutted him.

"There's nothing to explain. Ye've made yerself

abundantly clear."

Damnation. He needed to talk to her…alone. "Father, I accept that ye've granted Anna sanctuary. I swear to ye that I will not force her to leave. However, there are things she needs to hear. Would ye give us privacy?"

The priest appeared to consider the request for a moment before drawing Anna's attention by putting his hand on her shoulder.

"Anna, clearly something happened this evening to upset ye. The decision to enter the religious life is a serious one. I believe it would be best if ye discussed whatever has happened with Andrew. I also believe that he will honor yer request for sanctuary, but whether I stay or leave is your choice."

"I'll speak with him alone," she said softly.

He nodded. "Well, then, I'll leave ye for now. Andrew, if she decides to remain in sanctuary, please let me know. She'll need blankets if she's to sleep here tonight."

"That won't be necessary, Father. If she still chooses the religious life when we're done, I'll not stand in her way."

"I'm sorry, my son, but ye do not have the power to release her from the betrothal. Only Laird MacLeod can do that and I am certain that he will not. Lady Anna, if you choose sanctuary, do not leave this chapel."

She nodded. "Aye, Father."

They waited in silence until Father Ninian had left.

"Anna, I—"

She put her hand up. "Don't. Ye said ye have things to tell me, but I am tired of being told. I was told I couldn't go home. I was told I had to marry ye. I was told to accept that it was the best thing for our clans. I was told that ye could never give yer heart to anyone again."

"Anna—"

"Wheesht!"

Andrew was taken aback by her vehemence.

"I have been told a lot of things. Right now I am going to tell ye a few things and I don't care if ye find what I have to say hard to hear.

"Ye've been greatly blessed, Andrew. Yer father arranged a marriage for ye to a wonderful woman who ye came to love passionately and who by all accounts loved ye in return. Few noblemen are given that blessing even for a little while. Ye were blessed to have her in yer life for almost five years. Ye were blessed with a wonderful child from that union. And yet for too many years, ye've focused on your loss rather than the blessings ye were given. Ye feared the pain of that loss so much ye even locked yerself away from yer son and vowed never to marry, never to take a risk with yer heart.

"Then another blessing came into yer life. Me. *I was a blessing*. Right now I'm the slightest bit irritated about that, but it is true. Aye, I was where Davy needed me in order to save him, but it's more than that.

"Neither one of us wanted this betrothal, but my reticence was born from fear. Fear of my clan's enemy and fear of the unknown. But that isn't why ye didn't want to marry me. Ye're life would hardly have changed. Ye still live in yer home, among yer clan, and ye are still the laird's heir. Marrying one little MacKay might be an annoyance, but nothing more. Ye certainly didn't fear me. But make no mistake, Andrew, ye were afraid."

"Aye, I was."

She continued as if she hadn't heard him. "Ye were afraid of risking yer heart again, afraid of loving me and perhaps losing me as ye did Joan. Yer life had become all about protecting yourself, ensuring that ye didn't ache with loss again. But tell me this, if before ye married Joan ye'd known how brief yer life together would be, would ye have chosen not to love her? Would ye have chosen never to experience her love for ye. If ye could have avoided all of this pain, would ye have?

"Nay."

"Of course not. But ye're willing to shut me out. Well, I'm sorry Andrew. I didn't ask to be brought here or betrothed to ye. I didn't ask to fall in love with a wee lad who fights dragons or a clan I thought was my enemy. And I certainly didn't ask to fall in love with a man who was too scared to love me back. But I did. I had no choice in any of this, but now I do. I deserve better."

"Aye, ye do, and ye won't be happy in a convent."

"I've learned that happiness is a choice. I refuse to spend my life lamenting what I can never have. I will be happy wherever I decide to be happy."

"Then decide to be happy with me."

She stared at him, stunned. "I tried, and ye just keep pushing me away."

He stepped towards her and took her hands. "Ye're right. But as much as I've tried to guard against loving ye, I failed miserably. I think I've loved ye from the start. I also think part of me felt guilty loving ye. I worried that somehow I was setting Joan aside. I was wrong. I'm sorry I hurt ye, but please, Anna, if happiness is really a choice, I'm begging ye, choose to be happy with me."

"Why should I?" she asked warily.

"Because I love ye and ye love me too. Ye just said so."

Her brow drew together. "I did, didn't I?"

He chuckled, pulling her in his arms. "Aye, angel, ye did. And ye love Davy. And ye love my clan."

"I said all of those things?" But as she looked up at him a small smile played around her lips, suggesting that her hurt and anger were evaporating.

"I assure ye, ye did."

"And ye promise to stop pushing me away?"

"I promise."

She sighed. "Then, aye, I suppose I'll choose to be happy with ye."

He cupped her face in his hands and finished what he had started early in the evening. He kissed her, deeply and passionately, and she returned his kiss with ardor. For several moments nothing existed but the two of them. When he finally broke the kiss they were both left breathless. He continued to simply hold her close, resting his cheek on the top of her head.

Realizing they were still in the chapel, Andrew breathed a silent prayer of thanksgiving. She was indeed a blessing, an incredible gift from the Almighty that he had nearly lost through his own blindness.

"Come back to the keep with me now?"

He held her hand as they left the church and walked across the quiet bailey. When they entered the hall, his father sat by the hearth, watching the door, looking ready to do battle. Lairds Chisholm and Sinclair had evidently retired.

Andrew called, "Goodnight, Da. I'll see Anna to her chamber before I retire."

He had hoped to avoid any questions, but nothing else this evening had gone as expected, so it was no surprise when his father said, "Stop right there. Neither one of ye are going anywhere until ye tell me what's going on."

A hot blush rose on Anna's cheeks. "Laird, I…"

Andrew put one finger to her lips. "Anna just had to help me *recognize a minor error in judgement*."

"And did ye?" his father demanded.

"Aye, Da. I did."

"Good. See that it doesn't happen again."

"I will."

His father harrumphed. "I believe ye, thousands wouldn't."

~ * ~

From the moment Anna had arrived at Curacridhe, her first thought on waking was some version of, *I miss home*. Even as she had worked to fit in and find happiness, she couldn't quite suppress her longing for Naomh-dùn. However, when she woke the next morning, she was happy and content. Her first thoughts were of Andrew and Davy and the things that needed to be accomplished that day.

She was looking forward to her brothers arriving for the wedding, but not simply because she had missed them.

Now she was excited to show them her home and help them see the MacLeods as she did.

When she entered the great hall for breakfast, Andrew looked up from where he sat and gave her a smile, so filled with love and adoration, it made her knees go weak.

He didn't wait for her to reach the table but met her halfway, caught her in his arms, spun her around and kissed her full on the lips. If there had ever been any question whether the MacLeods were happy with this union it was laid to rest that morning. The cheer was deafening.

When he broke the kiss, he looked around at his obviously happy clan before asking quietly, "Ye haven't changed yer mind about the abbey have ye? I don't think I could face them. They love ye almost as much as I do."

"Nay, I haven't changed my mind."

Anna firmly believed that happiness was a choice, but this morning she had to admit, it was a much easier choice when wonderful things happened.

Chapter 19

Ten days after the messenger arrived from Lewis with news of Laird Morrison's illness, another arrived during the midday meal.

"Laird MacLeod, I fear I bear sad tidings. Laird Tyree Morrison suffered another apoplexy yesterday, which took his life. God rest his soul."

Laird MacLeod made the sign of the cross. "God rest his soul. He was a good man and will be missed. I'm certain his sons are grieving. We think very highly of Darach and have missed him these last days."

"The requiem Mass will be three days hence, Laird."

Dougal rubbed his forehead. "Under other circumstances, I would want to be there myself with the lad. However, my oldest son's wedding will be held on the Feast of St. Mark, but ten days away. I am expecting allies from all over the Highlands to begin arriving soon. I cannot leave."

The messenger nodded. "I understand, laird, and will offer yer regrets to the family on my return."

"Nay, lad, ye misunderstand. I cannot go myself, but, I look upon Darach as a member of my family. My son, Graham, will represent me. He'll leave for Lewis today with a contingent of men—Darach's comrades—to pay our respects and offer any assistance which may be needed."

Graham nodded and rose from the table. "I will make preparations immediately. If we leave this afternoon, we can sail on the morning tide and reach Castle Morrison tomorrow afternoon."

~ * ~

Darach had done what was asked of him. He stayed

and attended his father faithfully. After his discussion with Coll the night he arrived, Darach never revealed the deep hurt he felt to anyone else. His father seemed grateful and truly happy that Darach was home. When the second apoplexy claimed Tyree Morrison's life, Darach was saddened as one would be to lose an acquaintance, but he was not grief-stricken.

Although it was rare for clans from the mainland to send representatives to a funeral on the island, Darach was beyond pleased when Graham arrived along with several guardsmen and men-at-arms. To Darach, these men felt like brothers. Graham greeted him more warmly than Fearchar had.

"Da sends ye his deepest condolences. He would have come himself, but Andrew's wedding is a little over a week away."

"Aye, Graham. I know that. I'm just glad ye could come."

Having Graham and the other MacLeod guards there was a blessing Darach hadn't expected, and it made the whole ordeal tolerable.

The day after the funeral, during the evening meal, Graham said, "Darach, we'll be leaving at high tide tomorrow morning. Ye can travel with us or come later, if ye wish."

"I'd like—"

"He won't be returning to Curacridhe," said Fearchar.

Graham looked from Darach to Fearchar and back. "He hasn't finished his training."

"Nay, I haven't," said Darach.

"He belongs here. He'll finish his training here," said Fearchar flatly.

"Fearchar, perhaps it would be prudent to let him go back for a while at least," said Coll. "This has been a shock for all of us. He can return at the end of the summer."

"I don't want to stay now and I don't want to come back at the end of the summer."

Fearchar rose to his feet, growling. "I don't care what ye want. I'm yer laird now and I said ye're staying here."

Darach rose to his feet as well. "Ye aren't my laird yet. I've not sworn fealty to ye."

"Is that the kind of disrespect the MacLeods are teaching ye? It was yer Da's dying wish that ye stay here."

Coll inserted himself into the argument. "That's enough. It was certainly not Da's dying wish for the two of ye to go at it like this, or for ye to insult the MacLeods, Fearchar." To Graham he said, "My apologies, Graham. I'm sure ye understand the last few days have been trying ones."

Graham nodded, but said nothing.

Darach knew he needed to tread carefully here. "Fearchar, the MacLeods are our allies."

"Then they will understand that things have changed."

Again Coll interjected, "Fearchar, Darach, let's give it a little time. Graham, we appreciate yer willingness for Darach to accompany ye back. However, perhaps it's better if he stays here for a while until we've the opportunity to make some decisions."

Fearchar grunted and emptied his tankard. Darach was prepared to argue but Graham caught his eye and shook his head ever so slightly.

Then Graham stared at both of Darach's brothers. "The MacLeods would like to maintain an alliance with yer clan. We very much hope ye feel the same way and that ye will send Darach back to Curacridhe to finish his training."

Graham's voice was unemotional, even genial, but Darach understood the underlying threat. *If ye do not allow Darach to return, our formal alliance is over*. Darach hoped that would be enough to change his brothers' minds.

~ * ~

Later that night, Fearchar jumped from his bed, burning with fury. "Get out, wench."

"I'm sorry, Laird. I know ye're virile. Maybe if I—"

"I said get out. I'll take a strap to ye if ye don't leave

this instant. And if ye utter a word of this to anyone, I'll have ye beaten for lying."

The wench grabbed her clothes and was out the door before she pulled them on.

This is their fault, ye know. The MacLeods. Ye wouldn't have this problem with yer intended bride.

"Aye. Their fault."

They have no respect for ye at all. As if stealing yer bride wasn't enough, MacLeod insulted ye by sending his youngest son.

"Insulted me."

He would have come himself—if he didn't have wedding guests arriving for a wedding to yer woman.

"It's not fair."

Andrew MacLeod doesn't deserve her.

"Nay he doesn't. She should've been mine."

Then do something about it.

~ * ~

Darach rose early to see Graham and the MacLeod guardsmen off. Coll too was present to say farewell. Fearchar showed no such respect for the rules of hospitality.

"Graham, thank ye for coming. I know having close friends here helped Darach during this time of mourning," said Coll.

"He is a fine young man. I do hope Fearchar changes his mind about allowing him to return to Curacridhe. I still firmly believe it is in the best interest of both our clans."

"This was what our father requested, but I will discuss it again with Fearchar to see if some arrangement can be made."

Darach found it hard to be as diplomatic as Coll. "I'm sorry, Coll, I suppose I understand why Da wanted me to come home and stay while he still lived. I cannot see why he would insist I stay after his death."

"I know ye can't, but I suspect Da wanted to bring his sons together. We have seen little of each other over the last few years, and with him gone, he wants us to lead the clan together. Still we value the alliance with the MacLeods. I'm sure we can come to some agreement soon."

"I hope so," said Graham. "Darach will be missed."

Darach didn't believe Coll's answer. The three of them certainly were not going to lead the clan. Fearchar was going to do it alone. Coll would do his best to prevent financial ruin. Darach had no role at all.

After the MacLeods had ridden out of sight, Darach turned to Coll. "Why did ye tell him that?"

"Because I do hope we can convince Fearchar to let ye return briefly. I don't want MacLeod to see this as an insult. We need to maintain that alliance."

"That's not what I meant. Why did ye say Da wanted us to lead together? Fearchar has made it very clear who leads this clan."

"And do ye think Fearchar will be a good leader?"

"Nay, I don't, and neither do ye, but that doesn't change the fact that he is laird now."

"Darach, Da knew the skills Fearchar lacked too. He did want both of us to stay for that reason. He had seen enough of Fearchar's character to know he has the ability to ruin this clan. Da hoped we could become the tempering influence that he had been over the last few years."

"He was the laird and I believe that is the only reason he could exert any control over Fearchar. Da was daft if he thinks we'll be able to do anything now that Fearchar is laird."

"Not daft, brother, hopeful. And the only sure way to fail is not to try."

"Well then, I am going to try to convince Fearchar to let me go back."

Darach tried to raise the subject several times that day—unsuccessfully. He understood why Coll wanted him to stay, or at least to return soon, but he could see no good reason why Fearchar had dug in his heels.

During the evening meal, Darach tried a new argument. "But Fearchar, Andrew's wedding is just days away."

"How does that concern ye?"

"I want to go. It'll be a huge celebration. The feud is ending with the MacKays."

"Aye, because they kidnapped that poor wee thing." Somehow there was a light in Fearchar's eyes that belied the sympathy in his words.

Darach shook his head. "Ye needn't worry about her. She's quite a bold lass." He smiled. "She can hold her own with Andrew, and she's been very good for Mairi too."

"Why do ye care about that?" asked Fearchar, a note of suspicion in his tone.

"I like Mairi, she's my friend and it's good to see her happy." Darach wanted to add that she was like a sister, but feared it might cause the topic of Clair to come up.

"And Anna? Do ye like her too?"

Darach couldn't help but smile. "Aye. She's a nice lass. She'll be a good wife to Andrew."

"Is she pretty?"

"I suppose she is. I hadn't thought about her like that. Aye, she's very pretty."

As they talked Darach thought maybe Fearchar was softening. "I'd really like to go back, at least for the wedding." Once there Darach was certain he would be able to find a way to stay.

"I said nay, Darach. I don't want to hear anymore. Ye'll stay here."

Darach let the conversation drop, but Coll took it up the next day. Even though Coll wanted Darach to stay, clearly he hadn't missed Graham's veiled warning, because he also tried to make Fearchar heed it. "Fearchar, the sad truth is, the MacLeods don't need us as allies and never did. Da needed them, he needed to ensure that we had unfettered access to their ports."

"I'm laird now and I will not dance to MacLeod's tune. I'll manage this clan my way."

Sadly, Darach knew that was the truth.

Coll shook his head. "I'm not suggesting that ye have to lay down like a whipped dog, but simply yanking Darach home, with no explanation and no attempt to appease them will be seen as an insult. Insulting the MacLeods is not in our best interests."

"Then what do ye suggest, Coll?"

"Allow me to go with Darach to Curacridhe and discuss the alliance. Perhaps we can agree for Darach to stay with them a few more months before coming home."

"Go *with* Darach to Curacridhe? Now there's an idea we should consider."

Coll looked immensely relieved until Fearchar said, "But I believe I shall go. I need ye to stay here and collect the rents. After all, the feast of St. Mark is only a few days away."

"The feast of St. Mark is the day of Andrew's wedding to Anna MacKay. It would not be a good time to arrive, unexpected, in order to discuss an alliance," said Coll.

"We aren't unexpected. At least Darach isn't. He's gone on and on about the wedding and nagged me like an old woman. Ye do still want to attend the wedding don't ye, Darach?"

"Aye, Fearchar, but—"

"There is no 'but.' Laird MacLeod's esteemed representative, *his youngest son*, clearly said the MacLeods hope I'll send Darach back to Curacridhe to finish his training. They surely won't object if I join him on the journey. And since Andrew MacLeod is marrying *my* intended, it seems only right that I should be there."

Darach's brow furrowed. "Yer intended? I don't understand."

Coll explained, "In February Da sent a message to Eoin MacKay, seeking a betrothal between Fearchar and Anna."

"Aye, and the MacLeods captured her before the papers could be signed. She would have been my betrothed had they not interfered."

"Fearchar, ye don't know that," said Coll. "Laird MacKay never responded to Da's request."

"Only because Anna was kidnapped before he could. He would have agreed."

Coll shook his head in frustration. "Frankly, I doubt it. In early December, Laird Macaulay sought a betrothal for Bennett with Anna. Eoin declined that one because he didn't want to send Anna to Lewis."

"I'm not Bennett Macauley. Eoin wouldn't have refused me."

Fearchar's cockiness knew no bounds. Darach believed Coll was right that Laird MacKay would not have agreed to the betrothal Da had proposed, but Fearchar was too arrogant to accept that. Darach also worried that if Fearchar was at Curacridhe for the wedding, he might cause trouble. He and Coll tried to reason with him, but it became clear that this had been Fearchar's plan all along and there was no talking him out of it. The best Darach could hope to do was warn Laird MacLeod and hopefully limit the damage.

Fearchar chose a handful of his most loyal men—those who would do his bidding without question—and left with Darach the next day, only three days before the Feast of Saint Mark. "We don't want to miss the wedding. I want to see what treasure was stolen from me."

Chapter 20

Anna was walking beside Grizel along the edge of a forest.

"There are lots of blossoms on the blackberry bushes this year," Grizel observed. "Be sure ye take that lad picking blackberries come August."

Anna smiled. "Do ye think he and I will bring back more than ye and I did?"

Grizel chuckled. "Aye, ye were a great one for blackberries. I think there was always more on yer face and hands than in yer basket."

"Davy will like picking berries."

Grizel cocked her head and her eyes twinkled. "I daresay ye'll enjoy his da kissing the remnants from yer lips."

"Grizel!"

"Now, why are ye so shocked by that? Ye like his kisses don't ye?"

"Aye, but..."

Grizel chuckled. "There is no reason to be bashful with me. I've always known yer heart, lass, and there is nothing wrong with enjoying his kisses."

Anna smiled.

They walked a little farther, enjoying the peace of the afternoon. Eventually Grizel broke the silence. "I'm very proud of ye, lass. Ye did what I asked ye to and poured out yer love where it was needed."

"Ye said I had to pass it on, but Davy was already well loved by the clan. His father just needed a wee push."

"Aye, and I'm glad ye did that, but that isn't what I meant. Yer love was needed at Curacridhe. The MacLeods, *the entire clan, needed it. Feuds can end with a quill stroke, but hearts need much more. Yer love was needed for that. But more than anything else, ye needed to pull him from the ice."*

"Grizel, I had already done that."

"Ye pulled wee Davy from the loch, but 'twas Andrew whose heart was frozen."

"That's who ye meant?"

"Aye. Wasn't that clear?"

Anna gave a very unladylike snort. "Nay, not really."

Grizel winked at her. "Well ye know now. He was meant for ye. His heart beats with yers.

Never forget that. Ye will share lots of blackberry kisses. 'Tis a good year for blackberries."

Anna glanced back at the blossom-laden bushes. "Aye, it looks like it will be."

Grizel smiled, looking very satisfied. "Give me a hug now, sweetling, it's time to go."

Anna hugged her, absorbing her warmth and love. "Aye, I suppose I should go home."

"Ye are home, Anna. Look there."

Curacridhe's village lay just ahead, the castle not far beyond it.

"Aye, Grizel, I'm home."

~ * ~

Anna woke the next morning to a cold, damp April day, but the warmth of Grizel's love enveloped her, banishing the chill. She smiled to herself as she dressed quickly. Perhaps it wasn't just the warmth of Grizel's love. She was marrying Andrew MacLeod in three days. Representatives from clans all over the Highlands had already begun arriving at Curacridhe and her family would arrive today.

She could barely contain her excitement as she and Ena put the finishing touches on the dress she would be married in.

"Good heavens, Anna, ye're nearly worse than Mairi today." The grin on Ena's face belied the severity of her tone.

"I can't help it. It's been nearly five weeks since I've seen my brothers and over two months since I've seen Fiona or little Adam—I missed his first birthday."

Ena smiled indulgently. "I know ye're excited. I would be too."

"They'll be here before the midday meal. Ye'll adore Fiona."

"Anna, I know Fiona. Or at least we've met over the years. She was just a child at the time, but she was at my wedding."

"I didn't know that."

"That's understandable. While not allies precisely, the MacNicols and the MacLeods were friendly, but the MacNicols and the Chisholms have been allies for many years."

Anna sighed. "And the MacKays weren't allies with any of them."

"So, I'm wondering if ye've thought about how the first few minutes might go after yer family arrives."

"Nay. Should I have?"

"When ye last saw yer brothers, was everyone as happy as ye are today?"

Anna gave a very unladylike snort. "Not exactly. Eoin had been forced into something he didn't want, I had just sobbed all over him, begging him to take me home. I was so angry, given a weapon and the opportunity, I might have killed yer da."

Ena chuckled. "I can well imagine."

Anna blushed. "Things have changed a bit since then"

"I know they have. We've both gotten over being angry with Da and ye don't hate Andrew."

Anna's face split in a smile, "Nay, I don't."

"And he's come to his senses too. But, Anna, while things here have changed and ye've come to love us as much as we love ye, yer family probably hasn't changed. Things might be tense for a bit when they arrive. The last time yer brothers saw ye, ye were heartbroken and angry, and they were not happy with the MacLeods. I expect they'll be no happier when they arrive today."

Anna frowned. "I hadn't thought about that. What should I do?"

Ena laughed. "Ye don't have to do anything. Just be yourself. Everything will be resolved with time. I just didn't want ye to be upset or disappointed if things don't go perfectly smoothly at first."

Several hours later when her family arrived, Anna was extremely thankful for Ena's insight. She waited in the bailey flanked by Andrew and his father. Graham, Davy, Mairi, Ena and her family as well as the Sinclairs stood with them.

When her brothers rode into the bailey, all three of them looked grim. If possible, Marcus, the captain of Eoin's guard and the other guardsmen who rode with them looked even grimmer. The only person who didn't appear ready to do battle was Fiona, who held a very happy Adam on her lap.

There was a tense silence for a moment until Dougal said, "Laird MacKay, ye and yer family are most welcome to Curacridhe. Please allow my stable hands to tend to yer horses and join me in the great hall for a welcome feast in yer honor."

Eoin nodded. "Thank ye, Laird MacLeod." He dismounted, and as soon as his feet hit the ground, Anna ran to embrace him while Aidan and Tasgall dismounted.

"Ah, sweetling, we've missed ye so," said Eoin, adding, "Are ye all right?" in a softer voice.

"I've missed ye too and I'm more than all right. I'm very happy."

"I'm glad ye're happy, pet," said Tasgall as he gave her a hug.

When Tasgall released her, she hugged Aidan. "Are ye still sick of MacLeods telling ye what to do?"

"It's really more a case of her having us wrapped around her little finger," said Dougal, stepping forward and offering Eoin his hand.

Eoin took Dougal's hand but cast a skeptical glance at Anna.

She smiled and shrugged.

Dougal introduced the remainder of the family and visitors.

The only member of Anna's family who expressed genuine warmth was Fiona. She greeted the MacLeods and the Chisholms with hugs and kisses.

Otherwise, there was a palpable tension between the two families. That was until Dougal introduced Davy to Eoin.

"Laird MacKay, this is my grandson, David. Davy, this is Laird MacKay, Anna's brother."

"How do ye do, David," Eoin asked, smiling for the first time since entering Curacridhe. "Are ye the young man who my sister fished out of the frozen loch?"

Davy grinned. "Aye. I thought she was an angel."

Eoin stifled a smile, but both Tasgall and Aidan chuckled, Aidan adding, "I can assure ye, she's not an angel, lad."

"That's what my da said."

None of her brothers could keep from laughing at that.

At Davy's slightly confused expression, Fiona smiled and said, "They're just jealous because no one has ever mistaken any of them for angels.

That raised a few chuckles on both sides.

Davy smiled again, slipping his hand into Anna's. "But she is going to be my mama and that's better than an angel."

Eoin crouched down and smiled broadly at Davy. "Aye, lad, I think so too. And I expect Anna will be a very good mama."

Davy nodded. "Aye, she already is. But I was wondering something."

"What's that lad?"

"If Anna is going to be my mama, and ye're her

brother, does that make ye my uncle?"

Eoin smiled resignedly and looked up at Anna for a moment. "Aye, lad, I suppose it does. Ye can call me Uncle Eoin."

If that small interaction greatly eased the tension between the clans, the feast broke down the final barriers. Andrew was very clearly a man deeply in love, and Anna basked in the glow of that love.

It didn't take long for all of her brothers to notice and make small comments, but Eoin finally addressed it head-on. "Anna, the last time we saw ye, ye clung to me, crying and begging for me to take ye home and, if anything, ye were more furious with the MacLeods than I was. What happened?"

Anna shrugged. "The betrothals were signed, nothing would change that and going to Naomh-dùn was not an option. I had two choices. Stay here and be miserable or stay here and be happy. I decided to stay here and be happy. Everything just grew from there."

Laird MacLeod gave her a smile so filled with fatherly love it warmed her to her toes. "Aye, it did, because when Anna decides to be happy, she pulls everyone along with her."

Chapter 21

After tensions had relaxed the previous day, Anna was thrilled to see both of her families begin to forge tentative friendships. Five weeks ago she had never imagined this was possible. But then she never imagined falling so much in love with Andrew MacLeod. Now she was in the great hall trying to oversee final preparations for the midday meal, but she couldn't get her mind off the fact that she was going to marry him in two days and all she wanted to do was jump up and down, squealing like a wee lassie.

Janet interrupted her daydreams. "Excuse me, Lady Anna, my mother said she will have yer arisaidh finished today. She was hoping ye'd stop by in the afternoon so she can see it on ye."

Anna had to suppress another urge to squeal with glee. "That's wonderful, Janet, thank ye. I'll take a walk down after the midday meal."

"Can I come with ye?" askedasked Mairi.

Mairi was the one tiny problem that remained. She had been introduced to all of Anna's family, but upon meeting Tasgall, she scowled. As much as Anna had been determined to be happy, Mairi seemed to be determined to be unhappy.

It would be three years before Mairi would marry him and Anna knew there was plenty of time for her to get over her pique, but still, Anna wished the lass wasn't so dead set against even being friendly. Well, Laird MacLeod had said it the day before, when Anna was determined to be happy, she pulled everyone along, and she would drag Mairi kicking and screaming to happiness if she had to.

"Certainly ye can come, if ye don't mind Tasgall

coming too."

"That's blackmail."

Anna laughed. "Mairi, ye're hopeless. But I haven't spent time with my brothers in months, so if ye want to do anything with me while they're here, ye'll have to put up with one of them."

Eoin's wife, Fiona, tried to suppress her amusement. "Ye know, Mairi, my clan was feuding with the MacKays when I was…ah…a guest at Naomh-dùn." She grinned at Anna. "The MacKays grow on ye."

Mairi didn't look convinced. "Maybe." Her expression brightened. "Do ye want to come with us?"

Anna gave Fiona the slightest shake of the head. Having someone else along, someone with whom Mairi felt more comfortable, would give her someone other than Tasgall on whom to focus. She knew Andrew would insist on sending a MacLeod guard with them, so she even intended to ask for Barclay who was not particularly outgoing and always difficult to pull into conversation.

Fiona smiled at Mairi. "Thank ye ever so much for asking me along, but this wee lad," she bounced her son on her hip, "has been cutting a new tooth and kept me up last night. I think I shall take a rest when he does this afternoon."

~ * ~

Fearchar had arrived with Darach and his men in the wee hours of the morning. The rising smoke from fires told him visiting clans were encamped all around Curacridhe. It would be best to stay a bit farther afield until he had a plan.

"But Fearchar, we should tell them we're here."

"It's late. Tomorrow will be soon enough for that. Let's get some rest."

The next morning Darach had been even more insistent about riding up to the gates and announcing themselves.

Finally, a little before midday, Fearchar agreed. "I'm going for a walk for a bit and when I return we will ride to the castle." Privately, he gave his men orders to keep Darach away from Curacridhe, using any means necessary, until he had returned.

Fearchar needed to think and he needed to be alone to do that. He had to figure out a way to rescue Anna from Curacridhe. It was probably best if they announced their arrival. He and Darach would be given lodging within the castle, and that would give him access to his betrothed. Perhaps it would only be necessary to offer his assistance and the poor lass would be thrilled for the chance to escape. But he had to have another plan too—just in case.

As he walked, a faint whining drew his attention. He followed the sound and discovered a small dog, a puppy who had been caught in some dense undergrowth.

"Here now, lad, what've ye done?"

The puppy just whimpered. Fearchar chuckled. It looked as if the pup had managed to squeeze into a spot and didn't know how to back out of it. "Let's see if we can help ye."

He gently maneuvered the beastie's head backwards and pulled him free of his trap. Fearchar held him for a moment, scratching behind his ears. The exuberant puppy wiggled and licked him in the face.

"Well, ye're free now, lad. Do ye know which direction yer home is?"

Even as he said it, little voices drifted to him. "Shep. Sheeeh-ep."

He grinned. "Ye wouldn't happen to be Shep, would ye?" He rubbed the dog's head again. "I'm betting ye are. Let's see if we can find yer owners."

He walked towards the sound of their voices until two lassies came into view. "Is this the wee beastie ye're looking for?"

"There he is, Bridget," squealed the younger one.

The lassies ran to him. "Oh, aye, it is. That's our Shep. He wandered away," said Bridget, who looked to be about ten.

Fearchar continued to hold the puppy, cuddling and

petting him. "He's a lovely puppy. And where dodo ye fine lassies live?"

"In the village, at the edge of the forest. Ye just walk that way until ye come to a glade. It's not far beyond that," answered the little one, who he figured was six or seven at most.

"Does yer da know ye're out here? I don't think I'd want wee lassies of mine wandering off."

The little one's lower lip began to tremble. Her sister put her arm around her. "Wheest, Molly. Our da died a few years ago," Bridget offered by way of explanation.

"I'm sorry to hear that, lass. So ye live with yer mother?"

Bridget nodded. "Aye, and our older sister."

"She works at the keep," offered Molly proudly.

"Does she?" He had planned to walk them home, but this opened up new possibilities. "And does yer mama work at the keep too?"

"Nay, she's a weaver," said Bridget. "She wove the arasaidh Lady Anna will wear for the wedding," she added proudly.

Molly nodded. "And Lady Anna is coming to our house to get it this afternoon."

Oh, this was even better.

"And ye like Lady Anna?"

Both girls nodded.

"She's nice," said Molly.

"Hmm. I think I'd like to meet her."

"Just go up to the keep," said Molly. "There are lots of visitors right now."

"Aye, that there are. I think I would rather meet her alone. When she comes to yer house, would ye bring her here to meet me?"

Bridget frowned. "I think if ye want to meet her, ye should go up to the keep."

"But that isn't what I want to do."

"Can we have our puppy back now?"

Wee Bridget had clearly caught on. Bright lass.

"Now Bridget, I think a trade is in order. Ye bring me Lady Anna, and ye can have Shep back."

She nodded. "I will. Come on, Molly." She pulled Molly's hand, stumbling backwards.

Fearchar reached forward with his free hand, grabbing Molly's arm. "Nay, now that I think on it, Lady Anna for a puppy isn't a fair trade. I think, I'll keep Molly here with me. Ye can have them both back when ye bring me Lady Anna."

"Please, sir, ye can keep Shep. Please let my sister go."

"I said I will." His tone was sharper. "When ye bring me Lady Anna."

"What if she won't come with me?"

"A bright lass such as ye should be able to think of something. Tell her ye want her to see yer new puppy. I don't care what you tell her."

Bridget nodded. "And ye'll be here?"

"Did ye say there is a glade close by?"

Bridget nodded again.

"That sounds like a lovely place to meet Lady Anna. Bring her there. But lass, pay close attention, because this is very important. Ye must bring her alone and ye mustn't tell anyone I'm here. It's our secret. If ye tell anyone, I'll know and I'll kill Molly." He smiled at her. "Ye wouldn't want that, would ye?"

Tears welled in her eyes. "Nay. B-b-b-but she'll have a guard. Lady Anna always h-has a g-guard."

"I see." He considered her for a moment. "I suppose one guard will be fine. But if there is more than one, I'll know ye told someone our secret."

The tears slipped down Bridget's cheeks. She was terrified. That wouldn't do. How could he fix this?

"Now, Bridget lass, there's no need to cry. Ye aren't doing anything wrong. Do ye know why Lady Anna is marrying yer laird's son?"

"Sh-she saved D-davy."

"Aye, that's right. Ye're a smart one. That was very nice of her, and I'm glad she did that, but Lady Anna was supposed to marry me. It doesn't seem fair that she did something so nice, and now she can't marry me. Does it?"

"N-nay."

"So ye understand and ye'll bring Anna to the glade, with no more than one guard and then I'll give ye back Shep and Molly."

She nodded.

"Good lass. Run on now. I'll see ye later in the glade."

Bridget turned and ran away, stumbling occasionally in her haste.

He looked down at Mollie, who also had tears streaming down her face. "Wheesht, Molly. We'll just take a stroll and meet Bridget again very soon. Would ye like to hold yer puppy?"

Molly sniffed and nodded, taking Shep in her arms.

Not knowing exactly how much time he had, Fearchar had to work fast to set his trap. He returned to the clearing in which they had camped for the night. He didn't want Darach to see him so he stayed out of sight until he could catch the eye of one of his men. Kenneth finally saw him and sauntered over.

"Get three other men to come with me. Tell the rest to wait until after midday then saddle the horses and be ready to leave when we return."

Kenneth glanced down at the wee lass holding the puppy but made no comment. "Aye, Laird." He did as he was bid and within minutes they were following Fearchar towards the glade.

Fearchar explained as they went. "I figure, if we tie this lassie to a tree on this side of the glade when Lady Anna and her guard see her, they'll rush to save her."

"What if they suspect a trap, Fearchar?"

"That's why I brought all of ye. Several of us will

hide on the village side of the glade. If they turn around, we'll stop them there. If they don't, we'll close in behind them in the glade."

As they neared the glade, Molly started crying again. Fearchar had to gag her to avoid attracting attention.

Just as planned he secured her to a tree at the edge of the glade. He took the puppy from her. "I'll keep him safe. I promise. Ye can have him back when Lady Anna gets here."

"Laird, what if the other lass tells. What if she brings an army back?" asked Kenneth.

"We'll hear them coming. If there's more than a guard or two with her we'll cut this one's throat and disappear into the forest."

"Ye'll kill a bairn?" asked Iagan.

"I'd be forced to, Iagan. I told her sister if she didn't obey me I would kill Molly, and I'm a man of my word."

~ * ~

As soon as the midday meal was finished, Anna left the keep with Mairi, Tasgall and Barclay. She and Tasgall chatted while Mairi pouted. Ah, well at least she came with them. Anna supposed that was something.

When they reached the cottage, Maeve welcomed them. If she was shocked that Tasgall MacKay was in her home, she didn't show it. Things had certainly changed.

"Bridget, love, give the table a quick wipe so I can show Lady Anna the arisaidh I made for her," said Maeve to her middle daughter.

"Aye, mama," said Bridget before quickly wiping the table with a dry cloth.

Then Maeve carefully spread out the plaid on the table. It was woven in shades of red and green on a cream background.

"Maeve, it's beautiful."

"Thank ye my lady. It was an honor to make it for ye. Can I see it on ye?"

Anna grinned. "Of course."

Maeve helped her drape the garment and Anna turned

to Tasgall and Mairi. "Do ye like it?"

"Anna, it is perfect. It will look so pretty over the new dress," said Mairi, stroking the soft wool.

"It is lovely, Anna. It makes yer eyes sparkle," said Tasgall. "Of course, something has them sparkling quite a bit already. I can't imagine what that is."

Mairi huffed. "She's in love."

Maeve laughed and winked, "Aye, sir, anyone can see that."

"Well, thank ye for clearing that up for me, ladies," said Tasgall with mock seriousness. "I must pay better attention to these things."

Anna laughed. "Aye, Tasgall, understanding what makes a lass's eyes sparkle is a skill ye should work on." Turning to Maeve, she said, "I'll just take this off and we'll not take up any more of yer time today. Thank ye again for yer hard work."

"Ye're very welcome, my lady."

Maeve helped Anna take it off and folded it before giving it back to her.

"Lady Anna, before ye leave, do ye want to see our new puppy?" Bridget had been so quiet, Anna had forgotten she was there.

"Oh, Bridget, sweetling, I have so very much to do, can I meet yer puppy on another day?"

Bridget's eyes filled with tears. "Please, Lady Anna, ye have to come see Shep."

"Bridget!" scolded her mother, "Lady Anna said not today."

"I like puppies," said Mairi, "I'll come with ye. Anna, Barclay can stay with me and ye can go back to the keep with yer brother."

Barclay, shook his head at Anna. His message was clear; she could not return to the keep without him.

"Mairi, yer brother would not want us to do that."

Mairi pouted. "But I really want to see the puppy."

Bridget's lower lip wobbled.

Anna couldn't bring herself to say nay. "All right. We can take a couple of minutes to see the puppy."

Bridget gave her a watery smile. "Molly was playing with him. Come with me." She took Anna by the hand. Mairi, Tasgall and Barclay followed them.

When Bridget realized they were all coming, she said, "Ye don't have to come."

"I want to see the puppy," said Mairi.

"I meant them." Bridget gestured towards the men.

Barclay scowled. "We go where Lady Anna goes."

Perhaps it was his fearsome countenance, or maybe his low rumbling voice, but Bridget trembled and a tear slipped down her cheek. "We don't have to go see the puppy."

Anna put an arm around her shoulder. "Nonsense, Bridget. Take us to see yer pet and don't let Barclay scare ye. He loves puppies, don't ye Barclay?"

"Aye, my lady," he said in all seriousness.

Tasgall suppressed a grin. "So do I."

Bridget nodded and led them behind the cottage.

Seven-year-old Molly was nowhere to be seen.

"I thought ye said Molly was playing with him?"

"She is. She's in the glade with him. It's not far."

Anna frowned. "Bridget, does yer mother know ye left Molly in the forest alone?"

"We're allowed to play in the glade," answered Bridget.

"Aye, but Molly is very little. Perhaps ye shouldn't leave her alone in the future."

Bridget just nodded, still looking on the edge of tears.

They had walked for nearly ten minutes when they finally could see through the trees to the glen. As they drew closer, Anna glimpsed little Molly, gagged and tied to a tree. She gasped, dropped the arisaidh and took one step towards the child when Barclay pulled her back, motioning for her to stay quiet. At the same moment Tasgall grabbed Mairi, clamping a hand over her mouth just as she started to scream.

"It's a trap," hissed Barclay. He looked to Bridget, who stood silently, tears flowing down her cheeks. "What have ye done?" he whispered.

"He said he'd kill Molly if I didn't bring Lady Anna or if I told anyone or brought help."

"There's no time," whispered Tasgall. "Take these three back and bring more men. I'll give ye a moment's head start before I go to the wee lass."

"Ye'll be ambushed," whispered Anna.

"Better me than the two of ye. Go!"

Barclay silently drew his sword and scooped Bridget up with one arm. "Now, my lady." His whispered command brooked no argument.

Anna grabbed Mairi's hand, pulling her along with them.

It wasn't long until the sounds of a sword fight reached her ears. *Please God, keep Tasgall safe.* The silent prayer had no sooner entered her thoughts than Barclay stopped.

He thrust Bridget behind him. "My lady, stay back."

Anna understood why in an instant. Two men, swords drawn, stood in front of them. Hearing a noise, Anna spun, shoving Mairi and Bridget between her and Barclay just as a big bearded man moved into position behind them. They were surrounded.

"Mairi, Bridget, run!" yelled Anna, as Barclay engaged the men in front of him.

The girls did run, but the big bearded man grabbed Anna, jerked one arm up behind her back and held his dirk to her throat, its point drawing blood. "Don't take another step lassies, or I'll kill Lady Anna." As Barclay continued to battle the other two men, the bearded man yelled, "That goes for ye too, man. If ye value yer lady's life, drop yer sword."

Barclay spared the slightest glance towards her and failed to fend off a blow from one of his opponents in time. He parried at the last moment, but couldn't prevent the other man's sword from slicing into his right thigh. He stumbled forward and one of the men raised his sword with both hands, slamming the hilt into the back of Barclay's head. Barclay crumbled to the ground.

Mairi screamed and rushed towards him, only to be grabbed by one of the men, who clamped a hand over her mouth.

"Get the other one and follow me," said the bearded man holding Anna.

Bridget stood trembling, too terrified to move. A hulking man threw her over a shoulder and followed.

When they reached the glen, Tasgall had felled one opponent and continued to battle another, keeping him away from Molly, who was still bound to the tree.

The man holding her made the same threat he had to Barclay. "If ye value yer lady's life, drop yer sword."

Tasgall looked at her, his eyes full of anguish.

"Do it!" the man commanded, pushing the point of his knife a little deeper into her flesh.

"Don't hurt her," Tasgall said, stepping back and dropping his sword.

"Is Kenneth dead, Steenie?" The bearded man asked.

"Aye, Laird."

"Then run the MacLeod through."

"Nay!" Screeched Anna. "He's my brother, not a MacLeod. He'll bring a huge ransom."

"Hold. If he is one of Laird MacKay's brothers, he will bring a tidy sum. Besides, once he finds out what we're about, he may be pleased to help us. And it was just Kenneth, after all. Bind him." To the other men he said, "Tie the lassies to the tree with the other one. We don't need them slowing us down."

As Tasgall's opponent shoved him to his knees and bound his hands behind him, Tasgall tried to reason with them. "Let Anna go and I promise my brother will pay three times the ransom as thanks for yer mercy."

The man laughed. "I'm not ransoming her, lad. I'm marrying her." He laughed harder at their shocked expressions."

"Ye can't marry her, she's marrying my brother," said Mairi.

Anna cringed and Tasgall groaned. It had looked as if they were planning to leave Mairi behind until that moment.

"Marrying *yer brother* ye say? That must make ye Mairi MacLeod. Change of plans, lads, just leave the wee ones; we'll take her with us."

The bearded man holding Anna, bound and gagged her as well. Before they dragged their captives away he crouched down before the terrorized lassies bound to the tree. "Wheesht now, ye have no reason to cry. I promised I would give ye back yer sister and yer puppy if ye did as I asked. And ye were a good lass, Bridget. So, the puppy is tethered to a tree not far from here. He's a very nice dog. Be sure ye take good care of him. I gave him a bit of dried meat to chew on while he waits. When the MacLeods find ye, which I'm sure will be soon, ye can fetch him home."

Chapter 22

Darach was beside himself. First Fearchar had refused to announce their presence on MacLeod land, assuring him they would as soon as he returned from a walk, of all things. Then four of his brother's men disappeared. Darach decided to go on to Curacridhe on his own, but the men his brother'd left behind stopped him.

"Darach, the laird said to wait for him, and we will."

"The MacLeods are allies and this is my home, Athol. I don't feel right, hiding in the woods."

"We aren't hiding. We'll ride to Curacridhe as soon as Fearchar returns."

Some form of this argument continued off and on until well after midday. Finally, Darach simply walked over to where to the horses were tethered and began to saddle his mount.

"That's not a bad idea," said Wallace. "We'll saddle up the mounts and be ready to ride the moment Fearchar gets back."

Darach had no intention of waiting longer than it took to ready the horses. Fearchar could follow with his men when he returned. But just as he was about to swing up onto his horse, the sounds of men moving quickly through the trees reached them.

Moments later Fearchar and three of his men emerged from the forest with three captives—Lady Anna, Mairi and a man who Darach didn't know, but assumed to be one of Anna's brothers. He turned on his own brother, prepared to demand that he release them immediately, but the mad gleam in Fearchar's eyes stilled his protests. He might be able to get them out of this, but not by confronting Fearchar at this moment.

"Brother, we have my betrothed now. Mount up and we'll take her home."

"How did ye find her so quickly?" He glanced at Mairi; not only was she was bound, gagged and terrified, but she stared at him in shocked disbelief.

Fearchar grinned. "God is on my side. He put two wee lassies in my path who led Anna to me."

"But she doesn't look happy to be with ye."

"She doesn't know I'm rescuing her and I don't have time to explain. When we're away it will all be made clear."

"But if ye're rescuing Anna, ye don't need the others." Darach wasn't sure if his brother knew that the other lass he held was Mairi MacLeod. Maybe if he didn't, Darach could convince him to leave Mairi behind.

"Nay we do, brother. The MacLeods might attack when they find I've rescued Anna. Having Dougal's wee Mairi is leverage to prevent that. I'll give her to ye. Maybe if ye have a sweet plaything of yer own on Lewis ye'll be happy enough to come home where ye belong. Aye, that's just the thing."

Plaything? Darach could scarcely contain his shock and revulsion. Mairi was like a sister. But he had to keep his head about him. "And the man?"

"Tasgall MacKay. He killed Kenneth. But once he understands what I'm doing, he'll thank me. Enough talking. Mount up."

Fearchar put Tasgall on Kenneth's horse, giving the reins to his man Iagan, then handed Mairi up to Wallace before lifting Anna onto his own horse and mounting behind her.

Darach's mind spun. He had to save them but he wasn't certain how. Surely someone would miss them and follow. As long as his brother didn't suspect anything, when the rescuers caught up to the Morrisons, Darach might be able to ensure Mairi and Anna weren't harmed.

They traveled as fast as the horses could carry them

for perhaps half an hour. When it became clear no one was following them closely, Darach began to worry more. They needed to slow down, so the MacLeods would have a chance of catching them. "Fearchar, the horses are becoming winded. They'll drop if ye run them this hard for long."

"Aye. We don't want that." Fearchar slowed their pace significantly.

Before long, much to Darach's confusion, they turned westward. "This isn't the way to Durness."

"We aren't going to Durness."

"But that's the port we sailed into and where ye must return the hired the horses."

"I don't care about returning hired horses."

"Then what port are we going to?"

"We're not going to any port. We're going to a deep inlet on the west coast. Sandy has the ship anchored at the mouth of it. The MacLeod's will expect us to go to Durness. We'll be away before they realize their error."

Dear God. Fearchar'd this all planned before they left Lewis. How was Darach going to get them out of it?

In a little while, they stopped to rest and water the horses.

His brother seemed a bit calmer. Maybe Darach could try reasoning with him. "Fearchar, I don't think ye want to do this."

"Of course I want to do this, little brother. I'm saving my betrothed. "

"I know ye believe that, but Fearchar, she's bound and gagged. If she wants to be saved, surely ye could let her be free."

Fearchar seemed to consider. He pulled the gag from Anna's mouth but left her hands bound. Her eyes were wide with fear.

"Let me give her something to drink."

Fearchar nodded.

Darach helped her take a drink of water from his costrel. He wanted to tell her that he feared Fearchar was losing his mind, but his brother was too close.

"Can I give the others a drink too? There's no one to hear them now."

"Go ahead," said Fearchar absently.

Darach untied Mairi's gag, first whispering, "Please stay quiet." After giving her a drink, he did the same for Tasgall. When he turned to Fearchar, his brother stood in front of Anna, stroking her hair.

"When Da offered for ye, I didn't know ye had red hair. I've always been fond of women with red hair and fair skin."

Anna stood rigidly as if fearing to anger him by pulling away.

"That's a good lass," Fearchar said, taking her bound hands in his. He untied the ropes, rubbing her chafed wrists. "Now ye understand, don't ye? I'm rescuing ye. The MacLeods had no right to hold ye captive. Da offered for ye. Ye're mine."

"I-I know he did, Laird Morrison, b-but that betrothal was never signed," said Anna.

"That is an insignificant detail. It was just a matter of time."

"P-perhaps it might have been. But my brother did sign the betrothal agreements with Laird MacLeod. The MacLeods are yer allies."

"The MacLeods stopped being an ally the day they kidnapped my bride, forcing me to save her."

"If ye are truly saving me, allow me to return to my home with my brothers."

"Ye have one brother with ye. That'll have to be enough."

Darach tried again. "Fearchar, ye must know that Laird MacLeod will declare war on the Morrisons for this."

"He won't, because ye'll be married to his daughter."

"Fearchar, she's already betrothed to Tasgall."

"It was forced. Just like Anna's. The MacKays will thank us. Ye'll marry little Mairi and then ye'll be happy to stay on Lewis."

"Nay," gasped Mairi.

Darach shook his head. "Fearchar, I cannot marry Mairi. She's like a sister to me. I will not marry her."

"Ye will if I say ye will. I'm yer laird."

"Fearchar, please, let's try to stop a clan war. Da would never have wanted ye to do this. Ye and yer men can go on and meet Sandy. Let me take these three back to Curacridhe and smooth things over with Laird MacLeod."

As the conversation became more heated, one by one, the Morrison men began to stop what they were doing and gather around.

"Ye don't want that, do ye Anna? To go back to Curacridhe?"

"I-I do."

"What is this? Ye should be thanking me for saving ye."

"I know ye thought I needed to be saved, but I don't. I'm betrothed to Andrew MacLeod and I'm happy."

"*Ye're mine!*" roared Fearchar, raising his hand to strike her.

Darach grabbed Fearchar's arm holding him off her. He knew no one else would intervene. Fearchar ruled by fear and these men were loyal. They would stand by and watch, even if their Laird was beating Anna to death. In his short time on Lewis he had heard a few whispers of Fearchar's brutality.

Fearchar turned on him, a look of realization dawning in his eyes before they grew black with fury.

"Now I understand. It isn't MacLeod she wants. It's ye. That's why ye don't want the other one. Ye want my woman."

Without warning, Fearchar picked Darach up and threw him backwards to the ground, knocking the breath out of him. Fearchar was on top of him in an instant. Lifting him by the shoulders, Fearchar slammed Darach's head repeatedly on the ground. Darach heard screaming, then the blackness closed in.

~ * ~

Anna screamed and grabbed one of Fearchar's arms. He flung her off easily.

Tasgall lunged toward them, even with his wrists bound, but two of Fearchar's men grabbed him, holding him back.

Mairi screamed until Darach lost consciousness, then she began sobbing.

Fearchar dropped his brother's limp body to the ground. He stood and unsheathed his sword, looking from Anna to Darach. "I'll send ye both to the devil today."

"Nay!" Tasgall bellowed, trying to break free from the men who held him.

Fearchar raised the sword over Darach but one of his men, Iagan, drew his own and stepped between them. "Laird, stop. He's yer brother."

"He tried to steal my woman."

"Nay, he didn't," said Anna. "I am not yer woman and I'm not in love with yer brother. I am betrothed to Andrew MacLeod and I love him. Yer brother just wants to take me back home."

Fearchar turned to face her. "Ye dirty whore. Ye could have been Lady Morrison."

"Laird," Iagan touched his shoulder. "Let's be away. The tide's going out and in order to reach the mouth of the inlet tonight, we have to make it past the cliff face before the tide turns and comes back in and the sea cuts us off."

The rage that had come over Fearchar receded. "Aye. We have to make haste. Bind her and put her on your horse, Athol. I don't want to touch her filth."

The man called Athol bound Anna's hands again, and threw her up on his saddle. Mairi was lifted, still sobbing, onto Wallace's horse. Tasgall was forced onto Kenneth's horse again and one of the Morrisons threw Darach face down across his saddle.

"Iagan," Fearchar called, "come here."

"Aye, Laird."

"Iagan, I should probably thank ye for not letting me kill my brother."

"'Tisn't necessary, Laird."

"Ye're right. It isn't." Fearchar stabbed him with his dirk. "I won't tolerate interference."

Anna was too shocked to scream.

Iagan clutched at the wound in his side, falling to his knees.

Fearchar looked around at his men. "I won't tolerate it from any of ye. Do ye understand?"

"Aye, Laird," they all murmured.

"Darach would have had a nice, quick death if it weren't for Iagan's interference. Now he must suffer and it is all Iagan's fault."

With that, they rode off, leaving Iagan to die, his horse still tethered to a tree.

They made their way down to the inlet, and around the north side of it. Rocky cliffs dotted with caves rose from the narrow strip of sand. Fearchar grinned malevolently. "I don't think I want this MacKay garbage anymore, and I'm certain I don't want that MacLeod wench screeching the whole way. And as ye're already aware, I don't want a brother who betrays me. I think we'll leave them in these sea caves."

Practically paralyzed with fear, Anna couldn't believe he meant it until he had his men put Darach in the first one they passed.

"Tie him to something upright. As the tide comes in, maybe it will wake him from his stupor, so he'll know he's dying and who killed him. No one crosses me and lives. Not even my brother."

Not a single one of his men offered any argument. Anna supposed Darach might have a better chance of surviving and escaping if the cold water did wake him. At least that was her prayer.

They passed several more cave openings before

Fearchar instructed the men to put Tasgall and Mairi in one together. "She chose this worthless MacKay over my brother. We'll let her see what a mistake that was. Tie her so her head is on the ground and make sure he is tied where he can watch her drown."

"Nay, please, Laird Morrison. Please, I'll do whatever ye wish. Please don't do this. She's only a lass," Anna begged.

"*Shut up, whore!*" yelled Fearchar.

Mairi screamed and fought for all she was worth but it was to no avail.

Tasgall too fought, taking blow after blow, until they dragged him out of sight.

When his men emerged from the cave, Fearchar grinned at her. "Don't worry. We'll find a cozy place for ye too."

As they rode away, Anna fought despair. She couldn't bear the thought of Mairi and Tasgall dying. He was so strong, it had taken three men to subdue him. With that thought a glimmer of hope rose in her. Tasgall was strong. He would not give up. Anna knew with certainty that he would do whatever it took to save Mairi. That thought kept her calm.

They rode for perhaps another half hour before Fearchar stopped and stared at the rock face ahead. "Manus," he called.

"Aye, Laird." The man who answered was wiry and very small of stature.

"Do ye see that crack in the rock?"

"Aye, Laird."

"I know there is one other cave farther along that I could put the whore in but I'm wondering if that is a cave too. I know of others—on the islands—with openings like that. Go see."

"Aye, Laird." Manus dismounted and went to inspect the fissure, reaching his arm into it. "It does go deep into the rock. I'll try to squeeze in." Although he was a small man, and it took a good deal of maneuvering, eventually Manus disappeared into the cleft. A minute or so later he reemerged looking triumphant. "Aye, Laird, it is a cave—quite a large one."

Fearchar's mouth curved into an evil smile. "Perfect. Crawl back in there, then we'll shove her in after ye. Tie her well with her head as high up as ye can. If Andrew does manage to find her, they'll hear her screams. No normal-sized man will be able to get into the cave to save her. Imagine the torture that will be. It almost makes me want to stay and watch. This wee whore screaming on the inside as she is about to drown and her big strong husband screaming on the outside because he can't save her."

Anna vowed she would not break down. She had begged the madman on behalf of Mairi and Tasgall, but she wouldn't do it again. Athol lifted her off the horse and waited by the cave entrance while Manus worked his way in.

Even though he was a small man, he was still much larger than Anna. When Athol pushed her in, she slipped through the opening easily. The light from the entrance was enough to dimly illumine the inside of the cave. It was much bigger than the entrance would suggest, and it had a ceiling that she estimated to be more than ten feet high.

Manus followed Fearchar's instructions perfectly. He dragged her to the back of the cave and high up onto a pile of rocks. He tied her hands and feet before leaving. She remained stoic until he was well out of the cave. When she was sure they were gone and would be unable to hear her, she gave into tears. She saw no way out of this. The tide would come in, she would drown and she would never see Andrew again.

Chapter 23

Andrew had been on the lists when the alarm went up. The message he received was that Barclay had crawled from the forest, half dead. Someone had used Molly and Bridget to set a trap to capture Lady Anna and they had managed to capture Mairi and Tasgall as well.

Andrew felt as if the world shattered around him. He ran to Janet's cottage, where Barclay was being tended. His father, Fearghas Chisholm, Graham, Eoin and Aidan MacKay and Laird Sinclair, were not far behind him.

Bridget and Molly had been found tied to a tree but unharmed.

"Who did this to ye?" asked Laird MacLeod.

"I don't know," said Bridget. At his father's request, the little girl described the man, but no one seemed to know who he might be.

Then Molly said in almost a whisper, "One man called him Fearchar."

"Fearchar?" asked Laird Sinclair. "Fearchar Morrison?"

"It couldn't be," said Dougal. "The Morrisons are not here."

"But, Da," interrupted Graham, "the man Bridget described sounds exactly like Fearchar Morrison."

"If it is Morrison, he surely headed north," said Andrew.

"I would think so," agreed his father, "but we can't take a risk. We'll ride north with a large contingent of men, but I want men fanning out in all directions. Graham, ye coordinate with the other visiting clans."

Eoin MacKay turned to Aidan. "Ye go with him. I

want ye at the head of the men who ride south onto MacKay land. I don't want any of our men there to mistake ye for an invading army."

It wasn't long before a huge force, including Ranulf Sinclair, Fearghas Chisholm and assorted members of their guard, rode out of Curacridhe with Andrew, his father and a contingent of MacLeod guards and men-at-arms.

It seemed as if they had ridden for hours without seeing any sign of the Morrisons when, in the distance, they saw a lone rider approaching, slumped over his horse's neck, only just managing to hold on.

When they reached the man, he was barely conscious. "Laird Morrison…rode west…"

"Not to Durness?" asked Andrew.

"West…a ship waits…mouth…inlet. Darach didn't know. Hurry…tide."

"What happened to ye?"

"Stopped him…killing Darach."

"He did this to ye because ye stopped him from murdering his brother?"

The man nodded before losing consciousness. Laird MacLeod ordered several men to tend to the wounded man and get him back to Curacridhe.

"What does he mean by the rest of it?" asked Laird Sinclair.

"Just west of here, there is a long inlet jutting in from the sea. It sounds like Morrison has a ship waiting at the mouth of the inlet."

"What did he mean about the tide?" asked Fearghas Chisholm.

"Ye can only traverse the northern edge of the inlet, all the way to the mouth, when the tide is out," explained his father. "If we don't hurry, the sea will cut us off."

"Is there no other way?" asked Eoin.

"Aye, there is," said Dougal. "We can ride a little farther north, cut west to the sea and head south along the coast. It takes a little longer, but the mouth of the inlet can be reached with no obstacles."

"Then we should split up," said Laird Chisholm.

"Aye," agreed Dougal. "Andrew, ye and Fearghas take half the guardsmen and head to the inlet. Ranulf, ye and Laird MacKay will come with me and take the coastal route."

~ * ~

Darach slowly became aware of his surroundings. It felt as if every bone in his body was broken, but his wrists were on fire and his head ached unbearably. He was in a sitting position, his hands tied over his head. His ankles were also bound but were not tethered to anything. A chill dampness seeped through his clothing. *Where am I?* He opened his eyes cautiously. His vision was blurred, and he had to blink several times before things came into focus, but he appeared to be in a sea cave, his hands tethered to a rock. The light from the entrance suggested it was late afternoon.

He tried to stand up to relieve the pressure on his arms, but as he struggled he was overcome with nausea and retched. He sat back down until the queasiness passed, then tried again. This time he gripped the rope in his hands, pulled his knees up, pushing with his feet while pulling on the rope, and he was able to stand. His head swam and nausea threatened again. He took several deep breaths until it had lessened.

With the tension on the rope slackened, he began to work the knots of his binding with his teeth. The rope was damp and the knots had swelled. As he worked, he tried to remember what had happened. His head hurt. Why did his head hurt so terribly? An image of Fearchar's furious countenance loomed in his foggy memory. It had been Fearchar. He had attacked him, slamming his head against the ground. He remembered someone screaming. Women screaming. *Lady Anna and Mairi*. Then the memories came rushing back in a horrifying flood.

Fearchar had Lady Anna, Tasgall MacKay and Mairi.

Darach redoubled his efforts to free his hands, eventually succeeding. He was able to undo the bindings on his ankles much faster with the use of his hands.

Once free, he took several steps toward the mouth of the cave. The dizziness made him unsteady on his feet, but moving slowly and supporting himself against the wall he eventually reached the mouth of the cave. He was on the narrow bank of the inlet, but what now? Should he head west, following his brother or east to try and get help? He wanted to go after them, but he could barely stand, much less fight off his brother's men to rescue the others.

Nay, his best chance of helping them was to get help. His decision made, he headed east. He wasn't sure how long he had walked before he heard the sound of horses approaching. It couldn't be Fearchar, he would have continued on westward towards the mouth of the inlet. His relief was profound when he recognized Andrew MacLeod at the head of the riders.

~ * ~

Andrew was off his mount in an instant, grabbing Darach by the shoulders. They hadn't gotten much out of the Morrison guardsman other than where Fearchar was headed, and that the man had tried to stop Fearchar from killing Darach. Now here stood Darach, alive but with no sign of anyone else. *"Where are they?"* Andrew demanded.

"Heading to the mouth of the inlet. Apparently Fearchar has a ship waiting. How did ye know to come this way?"

"Fearchar stabbed one of his men and left him for dead after he stopped yer brother from killing ye."

"That could only have been Iagan. No one else would have stood up to him for me. Andrew, I swear I didn't know what my brother had planned. He said he was bringing me back to finish my training. I knew he believed ye had ruined his chances for a betrothal to Lady Anna but I had no idea he would do this."

"I know, the man—Iagan ye say?—told us that."

"Fearchar's lost his mind, Andrew. He beat me senseless. I awoke bound to a rock, in a sea cave. He was leaving me to drown as the tide came in."

"*Dear God.* Are ye sure he still has them?"

"I am not sure of anything. He had them when he knocked me out."

"But he wouldn't harm them," Andrew said, praying that was the truth. "Ye said he wanted to marry Anna and both Mairi and Tasgall would fetch large ransoms."

"I'm not sure of anything now. Andrew, he's not in his right mind. When I tried to get him to let them go, he accused me of wanting Lady Anna for myself. That's when he beat me senseless."

Andrew was torn. It made no sense for Fearchar to harm his captives, and if Andrew didn't get past the narrow strip of traversable land before the tide came in, he would lose his chance. But if he raced to reach the mouth of the inlet and Fearchar had left Anna, Mairi and Tasgall in a sea caves, as he had Darach, there would be no way to get back to them until the tide turned again. By then it would be too late.

Andrew looked at Fearghas Chisholm. "I can't risk their lives on the sensibilities of a madman. I know of at least seven caves between here and the mouth of the inlet and the tide is rising. We will have to leave men at each one to search. I'll keep going until I reach Fearchar."

~ * ~

Tasgall shook his head, trying to clear it. One of Fearchar's men had hit him with a rock as he had tried to fight them off. He hadn't completely lost consciousness, but had been too dazed to resist anymore. They had shoved his back against a thick pillar of rock, stretching his arms behind him. His hands didn't quite meet, so a short length of rope stretched between them.

Just as Fearchar had ordered, his men had laid Mairi flat on the floor of the cave, near its mouth, about ten feet from the place they had bound him. Her hands and feet were bound and she was tethered between two boulders, her arms stretched over her head. She couldn't move. She had stopped sobbing but trembled violently. She was terrified. He had to get them out.

"Mairi?"

She started at the sound of his voice. "Tasgall, we're going to drown."

"Nay, we aren't, sweetling. The way they have me tied, I think I can rub the rope against the rock and free myself." He had started to do just that.

"Do ye really think it will work?"

"Aye, it will just take a bit of time." He wasn't sure he believed that. The force required caused the rope to cut into his wrists and he feared the rock scraped more skin off his knuckles and the backs of his hands, than fibers off the rope, but he wanted to calm her fears.

"What if ye can't?" She looked to be on the edge of tears again. "I'll drown as soon as the tide floods in." She began struggling at her own bonds.

"Mairi." His tone was sharp. "Look at me, sweetling." She did.

"I need ye to do something for me."

"There's nothing I can do."

"Aye there is, lass. The rock is scraping my knuckles a little." That was an understatement; his hands were already slick with blood. "I need ye to distract me."

"Distract ye?" She sounded incredulous, and he suppressed the urge to chuckle.

"Aye. It's easier to push through a little pain if one is distracted." This was true, but his real goal was to distract *her*.

"How can I distract ye?"

"Tell me about ye and yer family."

"I don't know what to tell ye."

"Well, how about starting off by telling me five things ye like."

"Really?"

"Aye, pet. Five things ye like."

She frowned and thought for a moment. "Well...I like

peonies."

"Peonies? Tell me why ye like peonies."

"They are very pretty. And when they start blooming, summer's not far off. I love summer. There, that's number two."

She continued to ramble on, his little game doing exactly what he had intended it to—she remained calm. However, he found the distraction did help him as well.

When she reached number five, "Anna", he smiled at her admission. "I know she was really angry about the betrothals at first, but I was so happy she was staying at Curacridhe." She smiled for a moment as if thinking of Anna. "She'll be all right, won't she? We'll find her?"

"I'm certain she'll be all right." A lump rose in Tasgall's throat at the lie. He wasn't certain of anything, but he prayed fervently that they would all make it through this.

His words seemed to reassure Mairi. "Good." She was quiet for a moment before saying. "It's yer turn now. What are five things ye like?"

"Well, right about now, I have a serious affection for weak rope." Would that he had been tied with a piece of it.

Mairi giggled. "I'm serious. I told ye five things, now ye tell me."

Tasgall did his best to talk about his five things without revealing how much pain he was in, or how worried he was that this was not going to work. But before long, some fibers began to fray, making him redouble his efforts.

Mairi remained calm until the wind outside picked up and began blowing sprays of icy water into the cave. As close as she was to the entrance, she was quickly soaked and reminded that she had been left here to drown.

She began to tremble and cry again. "Tasgall, I'm afraid. I don't want to drown."

"Mairi, sweetling, stay strong for just a few more minutes. I almost have the rope split."

"But I'm so cold."

"I'll wrap ye in my plaid as soon as I'm free." He put

all his effort into breaking through the last fibers.

She saw his hands swing free. "Ye, did it!"

"I told ye I would." He rushed to her and began working to untie the ropes holding her hands. The backs of his hands were raw and bloody, and his fingers were clumsy. He shielded her with his body as the wind blew more icy spray on them while he worked, but he was able to free her.

She threw her arms around him. "Thank ye, Tasgall."

"Ye're welcome, lass. Now, let's get out of here." He wrapped her in his plaid and helped her out of the cave. He frowned. The tide was rising fast and the narrow strip of land between the cliff and the inlet was quickly disappearing. To make matters worse, a misty fog was rolling in.

He knew his sister was trapped in a cave farther west. But if he went that direction, they might not be able to make it back this way safely. If they pushed on to the mouth of the inlet, they might cross Fearchar's path again. Outnumbered, with no weapon and destroyed hands made that choice beyond foolhardy.

He couldn't risk Mairi's life to save Anna. Anna wouldn't want that. He put a hand on Mairi's shoulder, gently directing her eastward.

"But, Tasgall, they took Anna that way." She pointed to the west.

"I know that, Mairi, but we are on foot and the tide is rising. The only way I can be sure to get ye to safety is to go back the way we came."

"And leave Anna?"

"I'm certain I can save ye by going back. If we go west, I risk losing both of ye. We won't have time to make it back before high tide."

"Then we'll go on, past the cliffs to the mouth of the inlet."

"Where we risk running into Fearchar again, and I won't be able to protect ye."

"But Anna saved Davy."

"And that's why I know she would want me to save

ye. We have to go now."

"Nay, Tasgall, please…" She began to cry.

There was no point arguing with her. He scooped her into his arms. She buried her face in his léine and wept. Tasgall had to fight back tears himself at the choice he had just made.

They hadn't gone far when, to his great relief, he saw riders approaching, Andrew in front. He nudged Mairi. "I never thought these words would cross my lips, but thank God, MacLeod warriors are approaching on horseback."

As soon as Andrew reached them, he took his wee sister from Tasgall's arms. "Andrew, ye have to save my sister."

"What happened? Where is she?" Andrew demanded.

"It was Fearchar Morrison."

"We know that, lad," said Laird Chisholm, "but does he still have Anna?"

Tasgall shook his head. "I don't know for certain but she is probably in one of the caves west of here. He decided to leave us to drown. I managed to escape and freed Mairi." He held up his bloodied hands as testament. "I couldn't risk Mairi's life searching for Anna."

Andrew handed Mairi off to Cormag. "Thank ye, Tasgall. I'll find Anna."

"Darach is in a cave east of here, if ye give me some men, I think I can find it."

"We found him already," said Fearghas.

"Then with Mairi safe now, I'll come with ye to find my sister."

Andrew shook his head. "Nay, Tasgall. Ye're injured and ye'd be a liability."

Tasgall looked again at his hands. Andrew was right. He could only hinder them. "Please, find her. There is no telling what the cruel bastard did. He had Mairi tied down on the floor of the cave, but bound me upright so I would have to watch her drown as the water filled the cave."

Andrew blanched.

Fearghas swore. "I hope I can send his soul to hell today."

Andrew mounted his horse again, calling orders for a few men to accompany Mairi and Tasgall eastward.

~ * ~

Andrew's panic grew, the farther west they rode. After finding Tasgall and Mairi, there were still three caves left to check. As they came to a cave he sent men to search it and kept moving onward. If anyone found her, they would send a messenger to Andrew. Only four men and a squire remained with him as they approached the last cave. The opening was at least eight feet up the face of the cliff. With a boost up from Donald, Andrew was able to climb into the cave.

His heart fell. This cave wasn't deep and the opening was wide, letting in a lot of light. It was empty. He turned around and called down to the men with him, "She isn't here."

His despair must have been plainly evident. The Chisholm guard with them said, "Then one of the other groups must have found her and the messenger hasn't reached us yet. Perhaps we should go back."

"Or Fearchar still has her, in which case, we just go on," said Rory.

Andrew nodded. "Go on. I think that's our only choice." After he climbed down, he turned to Donald. "Did I miss something?

Donald frowned. "Ye've had all the known caves checked. But it seems to me…at least I have a vague memory of venturing into another cave once as a lad. But it had a very narrow entrance."

"Where is it?" Andrew demanded.

"I'm not certain, back a ways, I think. The entrance was little more than a crack."

"So onward, or back?" asked Chisholm.

"As much as I would like to squeeze the breath out of Fearchar Morrison with my bare hands, if there is the slightest chance that Anna is in the other cave, I cannot risk it. I'll leave Fearchar and his men to my father. We go back."

~ * ~

Anna had only given into tears for a moment. There was no point. She took a deep breath, trying to regain control. She tried to think of something pleasant. Her mind drifted to the wonderful dream she'd had of a visit with Grizel. Had she only just awakened from that yesterday morning? She closed her eyes and tried to recapture the warmth and happiness that had lingered after the dream. Her old nursemaid had told her Andrew was meant for her. What were her words? *His heart beats with yers. Never forget that. Ye will share lots of blackberry kisses. 'Tis a good year for blackberries."*

She sighed. It might be a good year for blackberries, but it seemed unlikely that she would share any blackberry kisses with him. It looked as if there wasn't anything but a watery grave in her future. However, the memories did calm her. She opened her eyes and glanced around, trying to figure out a way to escape. She could see the whole cave from her vantage point. Manus hadn't tethered her to anything. She wondered if she could slide down and work her way to the opening still bound?

She quickly ruled that out. With her hands tied behind her, she wouldn't be able to control her descent or brace herself if she fell. She could be seriously hurt and unable to save herself at all.

She thought perhaps she could find a sharp stone or something that she could use to cut the rope. She just couldn't see a likely prospect, but as she searched, she noticed a line that went all the way around the cave wall about five feet from the floor. The rock below was darker than the rock above. She stared at it for a moment before realization dawned. It was the water line. She almost laughed. Manus had followed Fearchar's instructions so well, he had secured her *above* the water line.

She wouldn't drown. She was damp and chilled but she had been colder—she smiled to herself—much colder.

She could live through this.

Ye can live through this if someone finds ye, which seems unlikely. No one knew who had taken them. If they did manage to figure it out, they would have assumed Fearchar had escaped to a port. But even in the unlikely event that someone knew the direction he had actually come, who would think to look in the sea caves for them?

By the time anyone knew that she, Mairi, Tasgall and Darach had been trapped in sea caves, they would likely have drowned and she would die of thirst or cold.

Nay. She must stop thinking this way. She believed if anyone could get out of this, Tasgall could and he would keep Mairi safe. She prayed fervently for them both. She thanked God for her brother's strength, honor and his keen mind. *Ye have given him all he needs, Dear God, please be with them.*

She was filled with peace and confidence that Mairi and Tasgall would not drown. Tasgall would free them. He had to. And if they got out, maybe they could save Darach. After all, they knew where he was.

'Tis a good year for blackberries

It would have been fun to take Davy blackberry picking. It would have been nice to pick blackberries with Andrew too. She smiled at the idea of blackberry kisses. The thought of never kissing Andrew again tore her heart. She loved Andrew's kisses. They were gentle but demanding; they quieted her mind while stirring her desire, and were both all-giving and all-consuming.

His heart beats with yers. Never forget that. Ye will share lots of blackberry kisses. 'Tis a good year for blackberries.

Grizel had been so sure, just as she had been in the first dream.

Ye can do all things in Him who strengthens ye.

But she had been right.

Then Anna realized what the blackberry dream had meant. Grizel was telling her not to give up. "Andrew will find me and, come August, we will share blackberry kisses," she said confidently to the empty cave.

She just had to have faith and wait.

And wait

And wait.

The light spilling through the crack in the wall faded into the gloom of evening. Water started flowing through the crack as well. It looked as if she would have to stay here until the tide turned again. Her arms ached from being tied behind her back and her wrists were chafed and raw. But she had faith. If not tonight, Andrew would find her tomorrow. There were blackberry kisses in her future.

~ * ~

As they road eastward, Andrew fought the dread that threatened to engulf him. The tide had risen until the narrow strip of land on which they rode was covered with water. It was still very shallow, but if they didn't find the fissure in the rock that Donald remembered... Andrew didn't know what he would do.

"I think that's it," shouted Donald.

Andrew's joy was only momentary as he dismounted to inspect the opening. "It can't be. No one could fit through there."

"I can, Laird," said Fearghas's squire.

Tadhg was tall for a lad of ten, but slender. Aye, if anyone could, he could.

"Go ahead, lad," said Fearghas. "We've no time to waste."

Tadhg slid off his horse and splashed through the water to the fissure. He had to crouch down and wiggle sideways, but in a moment he disappeared into the cave.

Andrew heard Tadhg call, "Lady Anna, are ye in here?"

"Aye, lad. Up here. I'm well, but my hands and feet are bound."

"I have a knife, my lady. I'll climb up and cut ye loose."

Relief flooded Andrew. "She's there," he called to the other men.

It took a minute or so for Tadhg to cut her loose, but the instant she was through the opening, Andrew gathered her in his arms. "Are ye truly all right?"

"Aye, Andrew, but there's no time, Mairi and Tasgall—"

"Are safe. Tasgall was able to free them before we found them. Darach is safe too."

"Oh, thank God."

"My precious angel, I feared I'd lost ye."

"Not until I've had a lifetime of blackberry kisses."

Andrew wasn't sure what that meant, but he didn't care.

Tadhg too squeezed back through the opening, and Fearghas said, "Declarations of love will have to wait. We have to ride hard now, or we won't make it back."

Andrew put Anna on his horse, mounted behind her and they rode eastward, trying to beat the rising tide. They were riding in water that was nearly two feet deep before the bank widened and they reached dry ground, where the men who had searched the other caves awaited them.

"Anna, we can find a place and rest for a while, if ye need to."

"Unless, ye and yer men need to rest, can we just go home?"

He smiled. "Aye, lass, we can go home."

Chapter 24

Eoin MacKay rode hard alongside the warrior who he had always considered an enemy. But today they had a common goal: stop Fearchar Morrison, the man who threatened both of their families. Laird Ranulf too was single minded. They stopped for nothing.

By evening, they were riding south on the coast, approaching the mouth of the inlet. A small ship lay at anchor just offshore, a longboat poised to be lowered over the side.

As they rounded the head, they saw Fearchar waiting with seven of his men. Eoin's heart fell when he saw no signs of Anna, Tasgall or Mairi.

Dougal too noticed their absence. He appeared calm and controlled, but the raw fury rolling off of the older man was palpable.

In that moment, Eoin was absolutely sure Fearchar was about to die.

They stopped a hundred paces or so from the Morrison party. Dougal called, "Laird Morrison, ye stole something precious to me. What have ye done with my daughter?"

"Ye stole something from me too. Anna was my bride."

"And yet, ye no longer seem to have her. Where are they?" Dougal asked, his calm tone belying his suppressed rage.

"Well, I offered yer lass to my foolish brother. He didn't want her. He calls her a sister. He's no brother of mine. I left her tied up in a sea cave with her betrothed." He glanced over his shoulder at the sea. "The tide's in far enough, I suspect she has drowned by now, although Tasgall might last a bit longer."

A sea cave? Andrew and Chisholm had been trying to reach Fearchar before being cut off by the tide. They wouldn't be searching caves. Eoin wanted nothing more than to run Fearchar through at that moment. But somehow the stoicism of the man next to him kept him from reacting. They needed to learn what they could before putting an end to this.

Dougal asked, "And, Anna? She's with them?"

"The whore who chose yer son over me? Nay, she's in a cave all by herself. She didn't want me, so she can die alone."

Eoin could barely believe his ears when Dougal said, "Ye're out-manned and out-matched. Ye can't escape, Fearchar. Save a few Morrison lives and lay down yer arms."

Both his sister and his brother were either dead or facing imminent death as a result of this man's actions, and MacLeod was giving him an option? He didn't care what choice Fearchar made, he would see him dead today, along with every man with him who'd stood by as he left bound captives to drown.

In disbelief, Eoin cast a sidelong glance at Dougal, relieved to see the old laird was tensed for battle. Clearly Dougal didn't expect Morrison to accept the offer. His gesture was noble, perhaps out of respect for Fearchar's young brother.

"I will never surrender." Fearchar spat. "MacKay, I'm surprised to see ye've become one of MacLeod's lapdogs. Ye should be standing with me."

"*Standing with ye?* Why would I stand with ye?"

"Yer sister was my betrothed. Andrew MacLeod doesn't deserve to marry her simply because he stole her from ye. Ye should be thanking me for getting her back."

"Getting her back? Leaving her bound in a sea cave to drown while ye try to escape is not getting her back, ye coward," roared Dougal.

Eoin seethed. "Ye're a fool, Morrison. Ye were not

betrothed to Anna, and I would have handed her over to MacLeod on a silver platter before I would have ever married her to ye."

Those words sent Fearchar into a rage.

"I'll send ye to hell for that," he screamed, charging forward.

The battle was on, but those would be Fearchar's last words.

Before either Eoin or Dougal reached him, Laird Sinclair had charged forward approaching from Fearchar's left and nearly cleaving him in two with one deadly swipe of his blade.

Fearchar's men charged forward to avenge their laird, but Laird MacLeod had the right of it; not only were there half as many Morrisons, Fearchar's men were woefully unskilled. All seven were dead within minutes and Eoin had barely lifted his blade.

He turned his eyes to the sea. If the captain of the vessel sought to reinforce Fearchar's numbers, their feet would never touch dry ground. Clearly the captain too had realized this. He had hoisted the longboat and set sail.

With no foe left standing, and the heat of battle waning, Eoin's attention shifted to his family. He rode past the battle scene and started down the north shore of the inlet. Perhaps there was still time to reach Anna or Tasgall and Mairi. But his hope died as he reached the point where the cliff met the water. It was already impassable. He roared in anger and frustration.

He turned at the sound of hoof beats behind him. Dougal and several of his men approached. "Laird MacLeod, is there any other way to reach them? Can any of the caves be accessed from cliff?"

Dougal's expression was grim. "Nay, lad. Some are little more than deep indentations in the rock. a few reach farther into the cliff, but the passages become impassable fairly quickly. If there are other access points, they haven't been discovered."

"They're lost to us?" Sorrow nearly overwhelmed him.

"I won't accept that yet. Andrew may have reached them in time."

"But he wasn't searching sea caves for them. He was trying to reach Fearchar."

"Aye, but he didn't. We came the longer way around. By all rights, Andrew and Fearghas should have arrived here before us, but they're not here. Let's not despair."

Eoin clung to that glimmer of hope. It was all he had.

When they returned to the site of the battle, the men who had remained behind had already begun to bury the dead.

Boyd Sutherland watched as Fearchar's mangled body was thrown into a hastily dug grave. Eoin couldn't quite read the emotion on the young man's face.

Laird MacLeod put a hand on his shoulder. "I know Darach is yer friend, lad, but we had no choice."

Boyd looked his laird directly in the eye. "I don't mourn Fearchar Morrison. Darach is my friend, but he is nothing like his brother. Fearchar chose this evil path and it ended in the only way it could. "

Laird MacLeod nodded, his admiration for the young man evident. "Aye, it did." To all of the men he said, "I need four of ye to finish burying the dead, return their hired horses to Durness and then see that a messenger is sent to Lewis for me. As we don't yet know what Andrew and Laird Chisholm encountered, the rest of us will leave immediately for Curacridhe."

Chapter 25

Once they reached the place where they had encountered the wounded Morrison guardsman, Andrew sent two men northward to find Laird MacLeod and inform him of all that had transpired. Then, he took his bride home. It was after midnight when they finally neared the castle.

Eventually Andrew learned that news had trickled into Curacridhe since early evening. The first bit was brought by the men who arrived with the wounded Morrison. Sadly, in spite of Isla's best efforts, he had succumbed to his injury a few hours earlier. It had been too much to hope he could survive a knife to his belly.

Once it was clear the Morrisons had fled northward, messengers were sent to the men who searched elsewhere and they had all returned over the course of the evening.

The next news came hours later when the contingent of men arrived with Mairi, Tasgall and Darach. The joy at having found the captives alive had been tempered by the horror of the tale they told and the knowledge that Anna MacKay had yet to be found. It seemed that all of Curacridhe and the assembled clans had waited, watching vigilantly, praying for her return.

It wasn't surprising then that cheers went up as they rode past the encamped clans. They were surrounded and could barely pass when they reached the site of the MacKay's camp.

"Andrew, let me down."

"Angel, it's very late and ye're exhausted."

"Please, Andrew. I'm not too tired to greet my brother's clan. I love them. It won't take long."

It took longer than he wanted it to, but she seemed

truly overjoyed, so he waited as patiently as possible to take her the rest of the way home.

When they finally rode through the castle gates, the greeting they received was even more exuberant. His heart swelled as Anna went from one embrace to the next. His clan loved her.

Fearghas had greeted his wife with a vigorous bear hug followed by a tender kiss. Afterward, Ena extracted herself from her husband's arms and worked her way towards Andrew. After embracing her brother, she turned with him to watch Anna.

He nudged his older sister his face splitting into a smile. "Do ye still think Da made a mistake forcing the betrothals?"

Ena shook her head. "Nay, she was meant for ye, Andrew.

~ * ~

Anna had never been so happy to be home. She wanted to put the horror of the day behind her, and the loving welcome they received helped. On the long ride home she and Andrew had exchanged stories. She knew what had happened to Darach and what Tasgall had done to save Mairi. She saw him standing near the hearth with Aidan and Graham. His hands were bandaged, but he looked well otherwise. When she finally made it through the throng, she threw her arms around both brothers. "I love ye both so very much. Thank ye for everything."

"We love ye too, sweetling," said Aidan as he kissed the top of her head.

When she stepped back from her brothers, Graham gave her a hug too and kissed her cheek. "We were terribly worried when Darach told us everything that happened. When I went to old Laird Morrison's funeral, I thought Fearchar was odd, but nothing made me think he would do this."

"His own brother didn't see how warped Fearchar had become. Ye couldn't be expected to," said Aidan.

Her lips curved in a sly smile. "Was that my brother defending a MacLeod?"

"Aye and ye needn't rub it in, Anna."

"And ye rode onto MacKay land at the head of a hoard of MacLeods," she teased. "I bet ye never dreamed ye'd do that either."

He grinned at her. "Little sister, where ye're concerned, I've learned to expect the unexpected. But I would have ridden to hell and back to find ye."

She gave Aidan another quick hug before turning to Tasgall. Tears welled in her eyes as they hugged each other again. "Tasgall, ye were so brave. Ye saved Mairi. I knew ye would."

"Anna—" his voice broke. "I had to choose."

"I know, and ye made the right choice."

"But if Andrew hadn't arrived in time…"

"He would have saved me tomorrow. I was above the waterline. I might have been hungry and cold by low tide, but I was in no danger of drowning."

"Thank God," he said. She could feel the tension leave him.

She let go and stepped back. "Speaking of Mairi, where is she?"

Andrew came up behind her, enfolding her in his arms. "Ena made her go to bed."

Tasgall laughed. "She made Fiona take Adam and go to bed too. Fiona was worrying herself sick and needed the rest. Mairi, on the other hand, wasn't happy about it at all and she made certain everyone knew it."

Aidan smiled. "She's like ye in that, little sister."

"She swore she would not sleep and she would come back down here as soon as ye arrived," added Tasgall.

Andrew looked toward the stairs. "Well, if she can sleep through this, I expect she'll sleep until morning." He kissed Anna's temple. "Ye need sleep too. Let me take ye upstairs."

~ * ~

Andrew should have expected an argument.

Anna frowned at him. "I want to wait for Eoin and yer da to return."

"I know ye do. But it could be hours and ye're exhausted. I'll see ye to yer chamber and come back down here. I swear I'll wake ye if there is any news."

"Aye, go on, Anna. Ye too Tasgall," said Aidan. "I'll wait with Andrew.

"Frankly Andrew, ye need rest just as much as she does," said Graham. "Ye look ready to drop too. Go on to bed and I'll keep this fractious MacKay company."

Andrew nodded. "Aye, I will then. Thank ye both."

Anna sighed. "Ye swear ye'll wake me if there is any news, Aidan?"

"Aye, Anna. Go to bed."

She nodded wearily. "Then I'll say good night."

Andrew put his hand in the small of her back and guided her toward the stairs. When they reached her chamber door, he cradled her face in his hand and kissed her deeply. The feel and taste of her and her ardent response fed his soul.

When he broke the kiss, he gathered her in his arms and she rested her head against his chest, seemingly content to stay there. The last twelve hours had been among the worst in his life. He had feared he would never hold his precious angel again. Now that she was in his arms, he didn't want to let her go, but she needed to rest. Even so, he simply couldn't bring himself to move.

"Andrew, I…well I…"

"What, angel?"

"Please don't think ill of me, but I don't want ye to leave me. I don't want to be alone."

"Oh Anna…"

"It is a scandalous thing to ask, I know, and I'm not asking ye to…well…to make love to me. I just want yer arms around me. I want to feel ye and know I'm safe."

He lifted her into his arms and pushed the chamber door open. "I want nothing more than to sleep with ye in my arms, and I will always keep ye safe, my love."

He carried her to the bed, and after laying her on it, he removed her plaid and shoes. Then he removed his own plaid and shoes, as well as his belt and weapons, before climbing into bed with her. He pulled her close, until her back was against his chest, before drawing the covers over them.

She sighed contentedly and was asleep in a matter of moments.

It was a measure of how exhausted he was that he too fell asleep almost immediately, even with the woman he loved snuggled intimately next to him.

Andrew was awakened by the sounds of horses in the bailey as dawn pinked the sky. Anna still lay in his arms exactly as she had been when they fell asleep, but she too was waking to the noise.

He rose from the bed. Kissing her cheek he said, "Go back to sleep, Anna. I'll go see what the commotion is, and I'll wake ye if there is any news." Then he reached for his shoes and pulled them on.

She sat up in bed, cocked her head to one side and said, "Ye're daft if ye think I'm going to sit up here and wait to find out what happened to my brother."

He chuckled, picked up her shoes and handing them to her. "Suit yerself. However, ye might wish to put on fresh garments first. If both of us arrive downstairs in the travel stained clothes we wore last night, we might raise a few eyebrows."

To his delight she blushed, but her lips curved into a smile. "Aye, well we wouldn't want raised eyebrows. I'll be down in a few minutes."

~ * ~

As she had stirred in Andrew's arms Anna felt more content than she ever remembered being. While she worried about what might have happened to Eoin and Laird MacLeod, she knew, with Andrew at her side, she could face anything.

After he left, she did take a moment to wash, change

her shift and léine and wrap a clean plaid around her shoulders.

As she entered the great hall, she sighed with relief. There didn't seem to be anyone missing. Laird MacLeod, Laird Sinclair, and Eoin had all returned. Fiona and the baby were already in Eoin's arms. Laird MacLeod sat in a chair by the hearth, Mairi cuddled in his lap like a wee lassie, Graham and Andrew nearby. News of their return was spreading fast, because clan and family members were flooding into the great hall.

"Anna," Eoin opened his arms to her, "I was so worried about ye."

She went to him, giving him a hug. "It seems I've worried ye a lot recently, and Fearchar Morrison was the problem both times."

"Well, he won't be a problem anymore," said Laird MacLeod."

"What happened?" asked Anna.

"The short story is that we caught up with him and his men before they could make it to the ship anchored just beyond the mouth of the inlet. They wouldn't surrender, so they were killed. However, there are so many different parts to this tale, I would like to hear all of the details from beginning to end. Make yerselves comfortable."

Comfortable? There was only one place to be comfortable. She crossed the room to Andrew's waiting arms.

Piece by piece the story came together, from Darach, to Mairi and Tasgall, to Andrew, to Anna and finally ending with Laird MacLeod. The morning meal had been served and cleared before the last detail was shared.

"Darach, son, I am sorry for yer loss. Yer brother gave me no choice."

"I understand, Laird. In truth, I don't consider it a loss. I barely knew him. Until Da fell ill, I hadn't spent more than a few days with him ever. He was a stranger to me. That's one reason I couldn't understand why he wanted me to stay on Lewis. Now it's fairly obvious it wasn't because he wanted me at home. He intended to use me for this. I'm sorry, Laird."

"None of this is yer fault. I've sent a message to yer brother Coll, explaining what happened and asking to meet with him in Durness on the first of May." Laird MacLeod considered him for a moment. "Darach, tell me, how do ye think yer brother and yer clan will take this?"

"When Coll hears what Fearchar did, how deranged he became, he won't seek vengeance. Frankly, Coll will be a much better leader than our brother. Apparently many in the clan disliked and mistrusted Fearchar. When Da was alive he could exercise some control, but when he died...well, it became clear very fast that Fearchar was cruel and ruled by intimidation. Neither Coll nor I had any power over him. I suspect that not only will most of the clan not shed a tear, there may be quite a few who raise a glass to ye."

"Were there none loyal to him?"

"Only a handful, and mostly limited to the men who died with him."

"Well then, we should be able to reestablish our alliance."

Darach smiled. "I'm glad to hear that, Laird."

Laird Macleod looked around the room his eyes resting briefly on Tasgall before turning his attention to Eoin. "Laird MacKay, I find that my debt to yer family simply keeps growing. Not only did Anna risk her life to save Davy, but Tasgall suffered pain and injury to save my daughter's life."

"I'm glad they were able to help."

Dougal smiled. "A better man than I would offer to release ye from the betrothals which I forced on ye."

Anna felt Andrew tense and Eoin looked shocked.

Dougal continued. "But I'm not a better man. I fear I am too selfish to do that. I love Anna. I want her to marry my son and help lead this clan as Lady MacLeod. The fact that they love each other is an added boon.

"I also love my daughter. I want a husband for her who is strong and kind and will always protect and care for her. At the tender age of two and twenty, Tasgall has shown himself to be that kind of man. So don't even bother asking. The betrothals stand."

Eoin laughed. "Well there's no point arguing then. Besides, Anna would make my life hell if I did anything to prevent her from marrying Andrew."

"Well then, by the grace of God, there will be a wedding tomorrow, and I suspect there is still much to do today that isn't getting done by sitting here."

There was indeed a lot to do and Anna was exhausted by the time she fell into bed that night. She had only slept in Andrew's arms one night, but she missed him and looked forward to marrying him tomorrow and spending many nights to come sleeping in his arms.

Chapter 26

The feast of Saint Mark dawned grey and misty, but Anna didn't care at all. She was perfectly happy. Jesse was there, almost before Anna was out of bed, with a tray of food for her breakfast and a parade of servants to prepare a bath.

It was delightful and Anna soaked in the rose scented water until it became chilly. Reluctantly she stepped out of the bath and dried herself before slipping on a new silk shift. She wrapped a blanket around her shoulders, and was sitting by the fire letting Jesse comb out her hair when Ena, Fiona and Mairi arrived. She spent the rest of the morning being fussed over and pampered by these three women each of whom she considered to be a sister.

By midday, they declared her ready. She wore a deep green léine that intensified the green in her eyes, and a jeweled gold belt at her waist. The arisaidh that Maeve had lovingly woven for her, and then retrieved from the forest, was held on by a beautiful jeweled gold brooch. Fiona had pinned it on her, explaining, "Tasgall and Aidan wanted ye to have this. It was yer mother's."

The last touches were a sheer lace veil held on by a wreath of heather and a bouquet of fresh herbs containing lavender for devotion, myrtle for everlasting love and marital bliss, sage for long life and domestic virtue and mint for warm thoughts.

Ena put her hands on her hips, looked at Anna intently and declared, "Ye're a perfectly beautiful bride. My brother won't be able to take his eyes off ye. Of course he's rarely able to take his eyes off ye as it is, so that might not be saying much, but ye are beautiful all the same."

Fiona laughed. "Aye I have to agree—with

everything she said." She hugged Anna. "I'm so glad ye've found love, Anna."

"I don't think I've ever seen a prettier bride," said Mairi.

"That's because she was just a bairn when I was married," teased Ena. All four women laughed.

"Well now," said Fiona, "I'll go tell Eoin, ye're ready." She kissed Anna's cheek before leaving.

"And I'm just going to make sure my lassies are ready. Heaven knows, they have the ability to destroy themselves in nothing flat." She too kissed Anna's cheek before leaving.

Anna smiled at Mairi. "Are ye ready?"

Mairi nodded. "Aye. Are ye?"

Anna laughed. "I think I was ready ages ago."

"Anna, I'm so glad ye're happy and that ye love Andrew."

"I am very happy, pet."

"Can I tell ye something?"

"Of course."

"I uh…I don't hate Tasgall."

"I knew ye wouldn't."

"Do ye know what he did?"

"To free the both of ye? Aye."

"Everyone knows that, but he did something else. I didn't realize it while it was happening, but I do now."

"What did he do?"

"When we were tied up in the cave…Anna, I was so scared."

"I know ye were."

"Well, Tasgall did too. He asked me to tell him five things I liked. And then he asked questions about the things I told him. He kept me talking and I wasn't so scared."

Anna smiled at her, tears welling in her eyes. "He's a good man. Ye are very lucky to be marrying him someday."

Mairi's face split in a smile from ear to ear. "I think so too."

~ * ~

Andrew waited on the steps of the chapel with Graham and Davy beside him. His father had pulled Father Ninian aside and was speaking with him quietly. Ena and her family, as well as Tasgall, Aiden and Fiona MacKay were nearby too. The bailey was filled with MacLeods, MacKays and the members of all the visiting clans. Perhaps it was the heavy mist, but everything seemed hushed. Then the door to the keep opened. His little sister stepped through first, positively beaming, followed a moment later by the light of his life.

Davy made an audible gasp. "She really does look like an angel, Da."

Andrew took his son's hand. "Aye, she really does."

She descended the stairs, on Laird MacKay's arm. Mairi parted the crowd as Andrew's lovely bride drew ever closer.

Finally, Father Ninian asked who gave her to be married and Eoin kissed her cheek before placing her hand in Andrew's.

Father led them through their vows of marriage, but Andrew could scarce focus on anything but the beautiful woman at his side. When Anna said, "And thereto I plight thee my troth," Andrew's only thought was, *thank ye, God.*

Then Father Ninian blessed the gold ring that would symbolize their union and gave it to Andrew. Andrew took Anna's left hand in his, slipping the ring on the third finger. "With this ring, I thee wed, in the name of the Father and the Son and the Holy Spirit."

Father blessed the couple and led them into the chapel, followed by their families and the leaders of the visiting clans. Andrew knelt before the altar, beside Anna while the priest prayed again. *Please, God, keep her by my side until the end of my days*, was Andrew's prayer.

As Father Ninian proceeded with the nuptial Mass, the sound of Anna's voice, responding to the ancient liturgy, wrapped around him like a gentle caress and filled him with warmth. At last, the Mass was over and Father gave them a final blessing before saying, "Ye may kiss yer bride." Perhaps Andrew should have only brushed his lips over hers, but when he took her in his arms and their lips met he knew that would not be enough. It would never be enough. Anna's lips parted and he longed to be lost in this kiss forever.

Andrew became vaguely aware of appreciative chuckles around the chapel just as Davy tugged on his plaid. "Da, can I kiss my new mama now?"

The chuckles became laughter and Anna, her face wreathed in smiles, knelt down, hugged Davy close and kissed him until he giggled.

~ * ~

The wedding feast was magnificent. Course after course of delicacies were presented to their guests. Anna tasted it all, but it could have been bread and porridge and she still would have been delighted. She was surrounded by the people she loved most in the world and at her side was the man she adored. It was hard to believe that there had ever been a time when she fought with him, refused to dine in this hall and wanted nothing more than to leave Curacridhe forever. This was her home now and she loved it.

The sumptuous dinner was followed by music and dancing. She laughed and danced and simply relished being near her new husband.

Finally, late in the evening, Andrew maneuvered her close to the stairway entrance. Then he wrapped his arms around her and whispered, "It's time to go." Before she could react, he scooped her, laughing, into his arms and announced, "Lairds, Ladies, beloved family and friends, I fear Lady MacLeod and I must say good night. Please continue to enjoy the celebration in our absence." He ducked into the stairway with her and practically ran up the steps.

He carried her to his chamber, entered and closed the door behind them.

She had never been in his chamber before, but she didn't spare it a glance. Her world became him alone. His caresses, his lips, his heated gaze. The circle of his arms was her universe. This man who she had fought with, and then for, was her everything. His kisses, his touch, inflamed her. As he joined with her, she became pure sensation, formless bliss. She existed only with him, her heart beating with his, their very souls entwining.

When she finally floated down from ecstasy it was to find herself wrapped in his arms. Protected. Cherished. Adored.

~ * ~

After their exquisite joining, Andrew simply held his beloved Anna in his arms, close to his heart. This strong, brave, resilient, passionate, beautiful woman was his, forever.

Ye've been greatly blessed, Andrew.

Indeed he had been.

He brushed her temple with a kiss. "I love ye, angel."

"I love ye more."

"That simply isn't possible."

"Why not?"

"If I have learned nothing else, it's that love is not measurable, it is infinite."

She smiled at him. "Ye've learned that, have ye? Well it's about time."

He chuckled and nipped her earlobe, causing her to giggle. "Ye're too cheeky by half, Lady MacLeod."

"But ye like that about me."

He chuckled. "Aye, I do."

They lay in the peaceful cocoon of each other's arms for several minutes. He caressed her face, trailing his finger down her cheek and across her soft lips. He loved kissing those sweet lips. It was then that he remembered the odd thing she had said to him when she emerged from the cave.

"Anna, my love, what are blackberry kisses?"

She had begun to doze. "Hmm?"

"When we found ye in the cave, you said something about blackberry kisses."

She smiled and snuggled closer. "I had a dream a few

nights ago about my old nursemaid Grizel. We were walking near the forest past blooming blackberry bushes. She teased me about picking blackberries as a child and going home with more on my face and hands than in my basket. She also said that ye'd enjoy kissing the remnants from my lips."

"I'm fairly certain I will."

Anna laughed. "I don't doubt it. But when I was in the cave, I remembered something else Grizel said that made me absolutely certain ye would find me."

"What was that?"

"She said that it is a good year for blackberries and that we'd share a lot of blackberry kisses. The only way could is if ye take me blackberry picking in August, and I knew that would only be possible if ye found me. So, I was confident ye would."

"Blackberry kisses. Aye, my wee angel, we need a lifetime of those."

~ * ~

Paradise, beyond the limits of time

"Are ye satisfied now, Joan?"

"Aye, Michael, I am. I couldn't be happier."

He contemplated her for a moment before saying, "You are a remarkable woman. There are many who don't want those left behind to find love again, even if it means years of pain and loneliness. Perhaps it is jealousy or selfishness, or perhaps they fear they will be forgotten."

"Aye, I have heard talk, but I don't understand it. How could I wish that loneliness and pain on my beloved? How could I want my sweet child to grow up without a mother to love him? I know they don't love me less because she is in their lives. It's only that the pain of their loss that's been lessened."

"That is very true, but, Joan, there were easier paths to achieve that objective. Paths that didn't involve the MacKays. You know, I thought you were daft when you asked me to send her to save Davy."

"I know ye did." Her musical laughter filled the air.

"But ye see now, it had to be her."

"You had another plan all along," he said, giving her a knowing smile.

"I only hoped, Michael. When Sulwin and Grizel told me about her, I knew she was perfect. She is spirited, fiercely loyal and she positively overflows with love. I was certain she could capture the MacLeods' hearts and make room for them in hers. There was just that one wee problem we had to get around."

"You think it was a 'wee problem?' She was a MacKay and in spite of your great plan, they nearly killed her first."

"Aye, that was a bit unexpected. But Michael, I wasn't worried for a moment. Ye're a great Archangel, I knew ye could protect her long enough for them to come to their senses, and then ye could keep her there long enough for Dougal to see the way forward. After that it was simply a matter of time."

Epilogue

Anna walked hand in hand with Andrew, the late afternoon sun warm on their backs. The basket she carried was nearly full of blackberries. She couldn't say the same thing for their young daughters' baskets. They walked well ahead of Andrew and Anna, squabbling about who picked more.

"Wheesht," called Andrew. "The answer to who picked more is mama—and it always will be until ye put more in yer baskets than in yer bellies."

Eight-year-old Lissa frowned. "Ye and mama eat berries too."

"At least we're taking *some* back," said twelve-year-old Ella. "When David and Callum and Kent used to pick berries with us all the baskets were nearly empty."

A sad smile crossed Anna's face. She missed her sons. David of course had returned to Curacridhe after completing his training several years ago. At twenty five he was Andrew's right-hand, just as Andrew had been Dougal's until the old laird passed away.

"Mam, I am *not* going berry picking with my wee sisters today," her ever so grown son had informed her when she suggested it after the midday meal."

Andrew noticed her wistful look. "Angel, ye know David would have come if ye really wanted him to."

"I know, but it isn't quite the same as when at the merest suggestion of berry picking they tumbled out of the keep—making us practically run to keep up with them. They grow up so fast and I miss my wee sons. I hate that we send them away."

"Anna, our sons weren't so very 'wee' when they went to train. All three were fourteen—or very nearly. Davy was already home again before Callum left and Kent only left a year ago—plus he's just at Sutherland's. We see him often."

"It all sounds very logical and reasonable when ye put it that way, but reasonable or not, I miss them."

He lifted her hand, kissing the back of it. "It sounds like Mairi likes it no better."

Mairi and Tasgall had just gone back to Naomh-dùn with their two youngest children after attending the Lammas Feast at Curacridhe. And just over a month ago they had travelled to Brathanead castle, in the southern Highlands, so their oldest son, Dougal, could begin training as Laird MacLennan's squire.

Andrew smiled. "Tasgall said she cried the whole way home."

Anna rolled her eyes. "Mairi said Tasgall exaggerates." At Andrew's arched eyebrow she added, "But I expect she did cry a bit. The MacLennan holding is so far away."

"It's nearer to Naomh-dùn than it is to us, and it's fairly close to the Chisholm holding as well. Plus Ena's youngest has gone there too."

That was true. Shaw was two years older than Dougal and a year older than Kent. As they grew, whenever the cousins were together, those three were inseparable.

Anna nodded. "Aye, Dougal will like that."

"It was wonderful to hear the Matheson's good news."

Anna smiled broadly. "Aye, it was. Even though I watched him grow up, it is hard to believe the gangly lad who freed me from that cave is a married man with a child of his own on the way."

Andrew squeezed her hand a little tighter as he often

did whenever that horrible day was mentioned. It was as if he still feared she might slip away from him. "That was another case of the right person being in the right place at the right time. If Fearghas had ridden with Da that day, instead of me, I don't know if anyone would have been small enough to get into the cave and free ye. By the saints, the fact that Tadhg was with us at all was a miracle."

"Why? Ye've never told me that before."

"Nay, I guess I didn't, but I only found out when Fearghas told me at Tadhg's wedding."

"What did he tell ye?"

"Apparently, Fearghas had no intention of bringing Tadhg that day. The lad was still quite young and had only just started training. But in the uproar that ensued after we learned ye'd been captured, Tadhg simply mounted up and went with us. We were well on our way before Fearghas realized it, and by then he figured there was no point making a fuss over it."

"That's...well...amazing."

"I thought so. Although it is a bit less amazing than ye being near the strait when David needed ye."

"Why do ye say that?"

Andrew winked at her. "Fearghas hadn't specifically told Tadhg that he couldn't go but I believe a certain wee MacKay had been forbidden to walk north on the bluff."

Anna laughed and supplied the words that usually followed that statement, "But ye'll be forever grateful that I did."

"Aye, I will."

They walked a bit in silence, before Andrew asked, "Speaking of that day, have ye had anymore dreams of Grizel?"

Anna had loved those dreams. "Not in years. I think the last one was the one when Lissa was about three. Grizel said that year was a good year for blackberries too." Anna sighed and smiled. "Now that I think about it, it was a very good year. David had just returned from training and Callum hadn't left yet. All seven of us went blackberry picking several times that summer."

Andrew laughed. "I remember. Lissa wanted to pick her own but she couldn't quite manage to avoid the thorns catching her clothes. Each time she got stuck, she squealed and one of the lads would pluck her loose. Finally David swung her up on his shoulders and handed berries up to her to eat as he picked."

Anna laughed heartily. "That's right. She had blackberry juice all over her little hands and Davy had purple stains all over his face from where she held on. Aye, that was a very good year for blackberries."

"Every year that I get blackberry kisses is a good year. In fact, ye have a bit of blackberry on yer lips that needs kissed off."

She grinned, "I do not have blackberries on my lips."

"Oh, I beg to differ." He reached into her basket, smashed a berry between his fingers and smeared the purple pulp on her lips. Then he cupped her cheek in his other hand, lowering his lips to hers.

Even after nineteen years of marriage, his kisses still thrilled her, transporting her to a place where nothing existed but the two of them and nothing mattered but the feel of his lips on hers. Before she was quite ready, giggles from the two lassies pulled her back to the here and now.

Andrew broke the kiss, gave her a roguish wink and turned to their daughters. "Yer mama had blackberry juice on her lips. And ye know how I love blackberries."

Author's Note

I hope you enjoyed reading about Anna and Andrew's story. It might surprise you to learn that while Highland Angels is my seventh published work, Anna was the second heroine I created. Just like Katherine (Highland Solution), she existed in my imagination before I ever wrote the first word of my first novel. In fact, I started writing Highland Angels while I was still writing Highland Solution. When I ran into a block on one, I shifted to the other.

However I had to keep postponing Anna's story because others needed to come first. When I finally could focus on her, she had evolved. The initial plot centered largely on Andrew trying to win her love. But as her character became even more fully formed, I realized that Anna gives her love freely, at least when she isn't afraid. As Andrew tells her at one point, it is part of who she is and why she didn't think twice about saving Davy. It was Andrew and not Anna who needed saving and who needed to open his heart again.

Finally, I would like to share a story about the source material for Anna's dreams about Grizel. When I was six, my grandfather, a coal miner most of his life, died from Black Lung Disease (coal workers' pneumoconiosis). When I was a young adult I started having recurring dreams about him which were very similar to Anna's dream. I would be with him. We would talk for a bit until he said it was time to go. He hugged me and I didn't want to let go; I didn't want him to leave. But he always said, "I have to go, it's the rules." Like Anna, each time I awoke from one of these dreams, I felt as if I had actually been with my grandfather. Also, like Anna, I felt the loss, but more importantly the sense of being profoundly loved. Anna had been so terribly disappointed when she wasn't allowed to go home. I thought she needed a brief visit from Grizel to realize how much she was loved as well as to help redirect her anger and disappointment into purpose. Then it seemed only fitting that Grizel share her joy at being in love and offer her the promise of blackberry kisses.

With love,
Ceci

About the Author

Ceci started her career as an oncology nurse at a leading research hospital, and eventually became a successful medical writer. In 1991 she married a young Irish carpenter who she met at a friend's wedding. They raised their family in central New Jersey but now live with their dogs and birds in paradise, also known as southwest Florida. While she loves spending time writing "happily ever afters" she still works fulltime in the pharmaceutical industry.

Her bestselling, Duncurra series, Highland Solution, Highland Courage, and Highland Intrigue are available as e-books, audiobooks, and paperbacks. There are also inspirational versions of each of these which close the bedroom door. Ceci will be continuing this series in the near future.

Highland Angels is part of the Fated Hearts series and includes Highland Revenge, Ceci's novella from the Highland Winds collection, and Highland Echoes. These are all standalone books which can be read in any order.

Ceci started a new time-travel series called The Pocket Watch Chronicles, with novella, The Pocket Watch. The next book in this series, The Midwife, will be released in March 2016.

"Few authors touch hearts so deeply."
-Sue-Ellen Welfonder,
USA Today Bestselling Author

Highland Revenge - Excerpt

Meet a younger Anna MacKay in Highland Revenge (available as e-book, audio book, and paperback) the first book in the Fated Heart series—Eoin and Fiona's story.

MacKay Territory, May 1340

Eoin MacKay hadn't gone terribly far when he caught a glimpse of white halfway up a massive oak. She was well hidden. Her plaid was dark green; he wouldn't have noticed her among the leaves if he hadn't been specifically looking for her. He strode closer to the tree, stopping once so he could look up through the branches. There, perched in the crotch of two thick limbs was a woman so perfectly beautiful she might have been part faery. He was left momentarily speechless. Her skin was fair, with a faint pink blush to her cheek. He couldn't see the color of her eyes, but they were ringed with sooty lashes. Something told him that, regardless of their hue, they would sparkle. Her rosy lips were full and soft—lips that were made to be kissed. The late afternoon breeze ruffled the mass of black curls around her shoulders. Her léine was torn, but otherwise she appeared none the worse for wear. *She is not a faery, she is a MacNicol*, he reminded himself.

She looked down at him silently with her head cocked to one side, as if she was trying to solve some puzzle. She didn't seem remotely frightened. That would have to change if he was to exact his revenge. "Have ye had a lovely day perched in yer tree, watching us search for ye?"

"I suspect my day was better than yers."

Her impertinent answer irritated him. "Well ye've had yer bit of fun, but it's over. Climb down."

She ignored him. "Who are ye?"

"Yer captor, and I ordered ye to climb down. Do it now."

"Nay, I asked ye a perfectly reasonable question, and ye aren't my captor if ye can't reach me. Until I know who ye are, I think I'd just as soon stay free, even if I am up a tree."

"Free? Nay lass, ye're as good as locked in my dungeon, and I promise ye will regret yer impertinence."

He called to one of his men. "Donald, it fair breaks my heart, but the MacNicol lass doesn't wish to join our company."

"An arrow would bring her down quick enough."

"Aye it would, but ye heard her guardsman. This is Fiona MacNicol, Bhaltair's niece. I wouldn't want to harm a hair on her wee head."

Donald snorted. "Ye have no love for the MacNicols, and neither do I. Have ye forgotten? One of my older brothers rode with ye that night."

"Ye're right, Donald. I have no love for the MacNicols, but the ransom this one will fetch will hurt Bhaltair's greedy, black heart nearly as much as a steel blade thrust into it. Mark my words, we'll have our revenge. We are leaving. Climb up, drag her down and bind her. She managed to evade us once and I won't have it happen again. We have already wasted too much time on her." He didn't spare her another glance but called over his shoulder, "By the way, lass, I am Laird Eoin MacKay, and ye're most assuredly my prisoner."

Highland Echoes - Excerpt

Sutherland Castle, Early June 1340

Soaked by the late spring rain and chilled to the bone, Bram Sutherland thought the gates of home had never looked so inviting. It had been a long, wet ride from Castle MacKay. The skies had only cleared in the last hour. They would have been welcome to stay another night waiting out the storm at Naomh-dùn, the MacKay stronghold, but thankfully his father had declined. Bram couldn't stand the thought of spending another minute there. His betrothed had married Eoin MacKay. Bram hadn't wanted to linger and be reminded of his loss.

Letting Fiona MacNicol go had been the right thing to do but that didn't make it less disappointing. Until yesterday he hadn't even met her. But once he had, he found her not only beautiful, but strong, loyal, and possessed of a loving heart—a heart that was, unfortunately, deeply in love with Eoin MacKay. Even though Bram had been tempted to force the terms of their betrothal contract, her heart would never belong to him and he couldn't bear to see her unhappy.

They slogged into the courtyard. His father gave his mount to the care of a stable hand. "Son, I expect supper is nigh on the table. Leave yer beast to one of the lads. We'll fill our bellies with good food and ale and try to put this mess behind us."

Bram generally preferred to care for his own horse and while he had been looking forward to the warmth of hearth and home for hours, arriving at the start of the evening meal had disadvantages. He was less than anxious to face the onslaught of questions about what had happened and why they didn't have Fiona MacNicol with them. "I'll see to Goliath myself but I won't be long."

"Bram, ye could have had her. The law was on our side."

"Nay, Da, we have been through this. It would have been wrong. Fiona and Eoin love each other."

"Bah. Love. Kentigern MacKay would never have stood for this." His father's tone of voice clearly conveyed how unimportant that detail was.

"Perhaps not, but he is dead. Eoin is laird and in spite of being solid allies for years, if we had forced the issue, he would have become a mortal enemy to the Sutherlands until either I lay dead or he did. Not to mention the fact that I would be married to a woman who would have hated me forever. This was the right course."

"Whether it was or wasn't, it's done now and we'll need to find another way to ally with the MacNicols. I think I must consider Bhaltair's daughter for Boyd, and the sooner the better. We need to get that sorted while they are young—before either of them gets any foolish notions about love in their heads."

Bram just shook his head at his father's utter dismissal of the emotion. Bram had understood from an early age that he would marry a woman of his father's choosing, a woman who strengthened clan ties. He hadn't thought much about love and perhaps had discounted its importance as thoroughly as his father had. That was until he saw Fiona and Eoin together. He didn't want to admit it, but he envied them.

His father must have taken his silence for agreement, because he continued, "Aye, the more I think about it, the more I'm convinced. I will take care of it as soon as Laird MacNicol has recovered. And we will find a bonny bride for ye too, Bram. That young Anna MacKay is quite a pretty thing, even if she is a bit too bold for her own good."

"*A bit too bold?* That is an understatement. Whoever marries her will have his hands full. I'm not sure I'm up to the task. Besides, she is very young."

"Seventeen is not that young. But there is also Annice..."

"Nay, Da, please, can't this wait? I don't wish to discuss another betrothal at the moment and I need to see to Goliath."

"Fine, we won't discuss it now. It can wait…a few days. Don't dwell on this, Bram."

"Aye, Da."

His father turned toward the keep, calling as he went, "Don't be all night. Yer mother will want to hear every detail of what happened and I don't have the patience."

By all the saints, Bram loved his mother but he didn't have the patience for an inquisition tonight either. Bram led Goliath into the stable, removed his tack, rubbed him down, and fed him an extra portion of oats. When he had finished, he was still not anxious to face the crowd certain to have formed in the great hall. He could avoid it by going straight to the kitchen. Innes would give him food and ale and he could slip up the backstairs, avoiding the great hall altogether tonight. He actually might be able to get through this day without having to rehash everything yet again.

Bram walked from the stables through the outer bailey heading to the rear entrance to the inner bailey, near the kitchens. As he passed one of the small dwellings located within the outer bailey, a woman's voice, perhaps the most beautiful voice he had ever heard, drifted toward him on the breeze. He stopped to listen. The tune was unfamiliar and he couldn't quite catch the words, but it was delightful.

He followed the enchanting melody, drawing close enough to the source to understand the lyrics.

> *Hush my sweetling, hushaby,*
> *The sun sets slowly in the sky,*
> *Tis time to sleep for evening's nigh,*
> *Hush my sweetling, hushaby.*
>
> *Hush my sweetling, little dove,*
> *Mama's heart is filled with love,*
> *Papa watches from above,*

Hush my sweetling, little dove.

They were the nonsense words mothers crooned to bairns, but he was entranced by the soft, sweet voice of what could only be an angel. He stopped in front of the tiny cottage to listen.

Hush my sweetling, little sprite,
Too soon ye'll wake to morning bright,
So sleep now through the still dark night,
Hush my sweetling, little sprite.

The woman stopped singing words but continued to hum her lullaby until finally her voice faded away altogether. Bram was so captivated by the music it took him a moment to realize it had emanated from Innes' cottage. However, it certainly was not Innes singing. She would be in the kitchen or the keep now, overseeing the evening meal. Who was it then?

As if in answer to his unspoken question, a young woman he had never seen before stepped out of the cottage. She was perfectly lovely. Her face was delicately beautiful; as angelic as her voice. Rich auburn hair spilled from under a white kertch in soft curls that reached well past the middle of her back. Tall for a woman, she had full breasts and her belt cinched a narrow waist. She stretched and rolled her shoulders, her movements graceful and oddly enticing. Bram felt a twinge of disappointment when his brain registered the kertch. She was married. Of course she was—she had been crooning a lullaby to a child.

When she cast a glance his direction, she gasped and stumbled backwards, feeling blindly for the door latch. "I didn't see ye there. Ye startled me."

"I'm sorry, I didn't intend to." Why was he apologizing to her? He had committed no offense. He took a step toward her.

She went from frightened to ferocious in a matter of seconds. "Stay back. What are ye doin' here anyway? Who are ye?" she demanded.

Who did she think she was? She was certainly in no position to demand anything from him. "I think, lass, it is ye who needs to start explaining. *Who are ye* and why were ye in Innes' cottage?"

"Innes is my grandmother, she asked us to stay with her."

"Yer grandmother? Innes has no children. I won't tolerate liars, no matter how lovely they are. Who are ye? I want the truth and I won't ask again."

She scowled, affronted. "I am not a liar. I told ye, Innes is my grandmother and she did have a child, a son named Tristan. I am his daughter, Grace Breive."

Tristan, aye, he had a vague memory of that. "I stand corrected. She had a son. But Tristan died years ago."

"Nay, Tristan *disappeared* years ago. He didn't die."

"And ye are his daughter, Innes' long-lost granddaughter. How sweet. And unlikely. What game is this? Innes is important to Clan Sutherland. I don't want anyone taking advantage of her, playing on her feelings."

"I am not playing on her feelings. I am her granddaughter and have proven that to her. But it's a long story and I don't see how any of this concerns ye."

"It concerns me, Grace, because everything at Sutherland concerns me. I am Bram Sutherland, Laird Sutherland's heir."

Grace became immediately contrite. "I'm sorry, sir. I meant no offense. But, I have told ye the truth."

"The babe ye were singing to is yers?"

"Aye, I have a young daughter. I should go back inside. I just stepped out for a bit of air. The rain kept us indoors all day." Again, her hand groped behind her, searching for the door latch.

"This isn't over, Grace Breive. If ye and yer husband want to live at Sutherland, ye will need permission from the laird, whether ye are Innes' granddaughter or no. And I hope ye do have proof of who ye are. I won't allow ye to hurt Innes in any way and giving her false hope about a long lost son would kill her." He took a step towards her, reaching past to lift the latch, which so far had eluded her hand. "Goodnight, Mistress Breive."

He was surprised by the expression on her face. It wasn't anger or fear of discovery. The green depths of her eyes were guileless and she appeared…was it grateful?

"Goodnight laird—I mean Bram—I mean sir. Goodnight." She backed through the door and closed it.

He stood there for a moment, trying to sort out his thoughts about this newest addition to the clan. It all seemed odd. He would speak with Da about this…but not tonight. He resumed his walk, entering into the inner bailey. He had almost reached the kitchens when his brother Ian called to him. "Bram, there ye are. Da sent someone to fetch ye from the stables, but I figured ye were avoiding dinner in the hall and I'd find ye in the kitchens."

Ian was two years younger than Bram. For brothers, they looked nothing alike. Both were tall, but Bram had fair hair and blue eyes like their mother and Ian had dark hair and brown eyes like their father. Their temperaments were vastly different as well. Although Bram smiled easily, he tended to be quiet and often serious. Like Laird Sutherland, he revealed very little of what he was thinking, sometimes appearing aloof. Even so, most of their clansmen considered him level-headed and fair. They believed he would make a good leader when his time came. Ian, too, was quick with a smile but that was where the similarities ended. He enjoyed a good time, and seemingly took very little seriously. However, Ian was acutely observant and absolutely forthright. Most people knew exactly where he stood on any issue. As different as they were, Ian was truly his best friend. "Aye Ian, ye know me well. Do me a kindness and tell Da ye didn't find me."

"Ah, well now brother, I could tell Da ye weren't in the kitchens, because ye weren't. But Mother is anxious to see ye too and ye and she can see right through any guile."

Bram sighed heavily. "I suppose it was vain hope to think I could avoid this." Bran fell in step by his brother as they walked to the keep.

"Aye, it was. Ye know how excited mother was to finally have a daughter, or at least a daughter-to-be. Da would only say that ye were the one who chose to release the MacNicol lass from the betrothal. When Mam kept asking questions he roared for someone to fetch ye from the stable and then he stomped off to his solar with a jug of whiskey under one arm."

"Damn, I wanted to talk to him about Innes."

"Ye heard about her long-lost granddaughter?"

"I just met her. Ye knew about her?"

"Aye, she arrived the day ye and Da left for Naomh-dùn. She seems nice enough. Innes adores her."

"I wish we knew more about her. It is hard to believe their story and yet I don't see what they have to gain by lying."

"Innes is certain the lass is her granddaughter. She had a brooch that belonged to Tristan."

"What about her husband? Have ye met him? What is he like?"

"She has no husband. She's a widow. She arrived with just her daughter, a few days ago. It was the day ye and Da left."

"A widow? She is an awfully young widow."

"Bram, let this go for now. Innes is thrilled. Tomorrow will be soon enough to sort out Innes' granddaughter. Besides, it will likely take ye all evening to answer to mother's questions."

"I suppose ye are right. Well then, let the interrogation begin," said Bram as they entered the keep.

~ * ~

Grace leaned against the door, listening for Bram Sutherland's retreating footsteps. For much too long a moment, she heard nothing. Then, finally, the crunch of the gravel told her he was leaving.

So that was Bram Sutherland. How could ye have been so rude and stupid, Grace? Her initial shock at finding a man standing outside the cottage had quickly shifted to fear. She supposed that feeling threatened, her protective instincts had kicked in and she had gone on the offensive to keep Kristen safe. Perhaps that is also why she didn't correct him when he assumed her husband was with her. Still, he would find out soon enough.

She had to admire how he wished to protect her grandmother though. But the idea that he thought he would have to protect Innes from Grace was worrisome. Now Grace feared she had only made it worse. She sat down and put her head in her hands as she realized she had just stirred the ire of another laird's son.

The Duncurra Series

All titles in the Duncurra Series are available as e-books, audiobooks and paperbacks.

Highland Solution

Laird Niall MacIan needs Lady Katherine Ruthven's dowry to relieve his clan's crushing debt but he has no intention of giving her his heart in the bargain.

Niall MacIan, a Highland laird, desperately needs funds to save his impoverished clan. Lady Katherine Ruthven, a lowland heiress, is rumored to be "unmarriageable" and her uncle hopes to be granted her title and lands when the king sends her to a convent.

King David II anxious to strengthen his alliances sees a solution that will give Ruthven the title he wants, and MacIan the money he needs. Laird MacIan will receive Lady Katherine's hand along with her substantial dowry and her uncle will receive her lands and title.

Lady Katherine must forfeit everything in exchange for a husband who does not want to be married and believes all women to be self-centered and deceitful. Can the lovely and gentle Katherine mend his heart and build a life with him or will he allow the treachery of others to destroy them?

Highland Courage

Her parents want a betrothal, but Mairead MacKenzie can't get married without revealing her secret and no man will wed her once he knows.

Plain in comparison to her siblings and extremely reserved, Mairead has been called "MacKenzie's Mouse" since she was a child. No one knows the reason for her timidity and she would just as soon keep it that way. When her parents arrange a betrothal to Laird Tadhg Matheson she is horrified. She only sees one way to prevent an old secret from becoming a new scandal.

Tadhg Matheson admires and respects the MacKenzies. While an alliance with them through marriage to Mairead would be in his clan's best interest, he knows Laird MacKenzie seeks a closer alliance with another clan. When Tadhg learns of her terrible shyness and her youngest brother's fears about her, Tadhg offers for her anyway.

Secrets always have a way of revealing themselves. With Tadhg's unconditional love, can Mairead find the strength and courage she needs to handle the consequences when they do?

Highland Intrigue

Lady Gillian MacLennan's clan needs a leader, but the last person on earth she wants as their laird is Fingal MacIan.

She can neither forgive nor forget that his mother killed her father, and, by doing so, created Clan MacLennan's current desperate circumstances.

King David knows a weak clan, without a laird, can change quickly from a simple annoyance to a dangerous liability, and he cannot ignore the turmoil. The MacIan's owe him a great debt, so when he makes Fingal MacIan laird of clan MacLennan and requires that he marry Lady Gillian, Fingal is in no position to refuse.

In spite of the challenge, Fingal is confident he can rebuild her clan, ease her heartache and win her affection. However, just as love awakens, the power struggle takes a deadly turn. Can he protect her from the unknown long enough to uncover the plot against them? Or will all be lost, destroying the happiness they seek in each other's arms?